Totally Bound Publishing books by C. Tyler

Single Books
Unbounded

Collections
Naughty or Nice: Hard as Stone

I0524368

UNBOUNDED

C. TYLER

Unbounded
ISBN # 978-1-80250-512-2
©Copyright C. Tyler 2023
Cover Art by Kelly Martin ©Copyright January 2023
Interior text design by Claire Siemaszkiewicz
Totally Bound Publishing

UNBOUNDED

Chapter One

Whenever I found myself in London, one place called to me, chanted my name over and over, enticing me to its belly.

Labyrinth was an establishment where membership was exclusive, and patrons had to fully trust one another. It catered to a specific clientele, to the people who enjoyed another side to eroticism, many of whom chose to remain anonymous.

Dress code consisted of whatever cocktail attire one owned and a mask. Whether made of lace, metal, cloth, or resin, a mask had remained mandatory since the beginning of Labyrinth's reign.

I was not a member in the official sense. I couldn't afford the fees, but the owner allowed me a free visit whenever I was in town, so long as I sang for my supper. And sing I would.

Music had been a passion of mine since childhood. The genre changed often, but my love for it never would. Music had the power to alter people's moods, be it uplifting or heartbreaking. It could trigger memories or help create new ones. It meant the world to me, and singing in Labyrinth was the closest I'd ever get to being a part of that world.

When I'd finished my short set to a room filled with mysterious men and women, I left the small stage, met an instant later by a man in a suit with a black resin mask. Intense eyes stared at me, so dark that they blended effortlessly with the rest of his attire.

He offered me his hand, which I accepted and used to descend the rest of the stairs. My leather dress, fitted enough to have been painted on, creaked and groaned with each step. It clung so tightly to my legs that I welcomed his help.

The stranger brought me to him, our chests together. We each remained silent, even as he hooked his index finger beneath the lime-green bracelet I wore. Raising it high enough for us both to see, there'd been a hint of green peeking out from beneath the cuff of his suit jacket as well. We were a match, something that made my heart race.

Labyrinth had a system in which members could wear a paper bracelet, not unlike those at concerts, of varying colors. Different colors meant the wearer was into different things and cut out needless chit-chat.

"Interested?" he asked.

Hmm-mm, European, but not English. What is that?

His deep, alluring accent tickled something within me, a desire I hadn't realized I'd had. I liked it and wanted more.

"Lead the way."

He smiled at me, his full lips curling at the corner and begging to be nibbled on.

The stranger took my hand and together we retreated down a long hall of doors. Some were open, revealing their scintillating secrets to the world.

In one room stood a man with a hand braced against a piece of furniture, the other entwined in a woman's hair while she bobbed up and down the length of his cock. The joy on his face told me all I needed to know.

In another room, a large, burly and hirsute gentleman donning a pair of impressive heels stood over a young man much thinner in frame, who placed multiple happy kisses to the toes of the stilettos.

Other doors had been shut, closing everyone out so that those inside could have the privacy they desired.

After a few moments, we came to an unoccupied room. He stood aside and motioned for me to enter before him, which I did.

Deep-colored walls surrounded me, lit by dim sconces. Each wall had been lined with racks of toys tastefully displayed and illuminated by beams of light as though they were modern pieces of art.

To the left rested a bed with cuffs in each corner to hold the player down, and not far from that sat a chaise lounge, a prime place for someone to sit while another individual groveled. But the suspension rack near the center of the room held my attention.

Cuffs and chains hung from each corner, but I had become more interested in the pair that dangled from the center beam, the wrist restraints that would bind one's hands together above the head.

When I was situated far enough from the wall that nothing would impede whatever hung from it, I stood within the frame and turned to the stranger. He remained near the door, hands in his pockets while he sported a wicked grin. With my gaze locked to his, I gripped the restraints and lifted myself off the ground. They were *very* sturdy.

His smile broadened and, with the unspoken understanding that I'd found what I wanted, he closed the door to give us much-needed privacy. Hearing the latch engage caused my skin to prickle with excitement.

The stranger removed his jacket and laid it across the chaise. His cufflinks were next, which allowed him to roll the sleeves of his white button-up shirt, revealing thick, strong forearms beneath. Tattoos dotted his caramel-colored skin, though I didn't bother identifying what they were.

As he prepared himself, I turned my attention to the walls of toys. One rack held whips, some with tips so thin they would break skin. Another held floggers like cat-o'-nine-tails. One held paddles, another slappers and from the last hung multiple riding crops.

Labyrinth catered to many preferences and, had I known the stranger better, I might have gone for something more adventurous. Seeing as I didn't, I went with a selection that would be fun, but safer.

I returned to the stranger with a riding crop in one hand and a three-strip slapper in the other. One would offer a more concentrated snap while the second created a slightly duller thud. His eyes sparkled as he looked them over.

"Hmm."

After a moment of consideration, he chose the slapper. My eagerness intensified. I quite liked slappers.

My stranger set the instrument aside and stepped behind me. Slowly but surely, he tugged the dress's zipper down, loosening it around my body. When it reached the end, he slid his hands beneath the garment and proceeded to peel it away.

He dug his fingers into my body, along the curve of my waist and the slope of my hips while he pushed the dress down.

Within seconds, it rested in a pool of fabric at my feet, leaving me in nothing more than my lacy lingerie and four-inch heels.

He took my hand and guided me to the rack where he promptly secured my wrists, staring deep into my eyes as he did. My heart raced, lodging itself in my throat. The anticipation coursed through every inch of me, priming my nerves for what was to come.

In spite of how it appeared, I didn't feel in danger. There was plenty of slack in the chains that would've allowed me to uncuff my wrists myself, and Labyrinth had a rigorous vetting process for their clientele. Regardless of how it may have appeared to someone on the outside, I was safe with the stranger.

"*Bellisima*," he said.

Oh. So this sexy bastard is Italian. Even better.

My core ached.

Smirking, he draped my dress over the chaise with his jacket, took hold of the slapper and stepped behind me.

The first moment it touched my skin, I flinched. The cool leather and shock of it caused me to gasp. He chuckled.

He teased me for a while, running the slapper over the curve of my ass, along my spine and even down the backs of my thighs. He'd been tender, delicate, allowing each passing second to heighten the tension, and just before I could speak, before I had the chance to urge the stranger along, it happened.

A loud crack echoed through the room, shortly followed by my lustful gasp. He left the slapper in place for a breath, as though allowing the welt beneath it to form on my ass. The pain radiated through the whole of my body, infecting the smallest atom and causing me to vibrate.

It was just the beginning.

For what had to be nearly an hour, the stranger played with me. He would lull me into a sense of calm before bringing the slapper hard against my ass or the backs of my thighs. He knew what to do, how to tease every iota of pleasure out of me.

At one point, he stepped in front of me, looming tall. His eyes had turned black, any hint of brown choked out of existence with growing lust. I dared a glance down. His erection strained against his slacks. Their dark color helped hide it, but I wasn't blind, more than able to see the line of his cock struggle to break free of the fabric. He was impressively sized, and images of me on my knees taking him into my mouth or him bending me over something and thrusting coursed through my head on an endless loop.

Sweeping my tongue across my upper lip, I stared at him through my lashes. He arched a thick brow. I doubted my intent had been unclear.

By that time in our play, my nipples had become painfully hard, rubbing against my bra and more wanting than before, while my clit throbbed and ached. I had no doubt that, if he chose to remove my panties, my excitement would've been visible. I couldn't remember the last time anyone had turned me on like that from nothing more than some paddling.

My stranger stared down at me. His jaw tightened, the muscles rolling beneath his olive skin. His chest heaved with each breath, and I knew I looked the same. Fire burned in my cheeks and between my legs. I wanted so badly for him to take me.

The image of him wrapping my legs around his waist and fucking me while I hung from the beam filled my mind. There was no hiding the shiver or the gasp that parted my lips. Sex wasn't part of the deal with a green bracelet, but God save me, I wanted it.

He looked me over, and while I was desperate to come through my skin, he reached forward. My stranger ran the back of his curled index finger over my nipple. Pleasure tore through me, intensified when he pinched the sensitive bud. He groaned, running his full bottom lip through his teeth while he massaged my breast.

"If only we had more time." He turned his attention to my other breast and gave it the same adoration. "I am certain we could have a lot of fun."

I have no doubt.

He shifted his grip, running his hands up my arms and massaging my biceps. He met my gaze, his eyes burning black.

"This would be perfect for it, yes?" His hands trailed back down, over my breasts, along the curve of my waist and my hips.

"Yes." The word had been little more than a whisper.

He bent forward, encompassing my ass with his hands. The softness of them did nothing to soothe the pain of his whipping.

My stranger lifted me with ease, guiding my legs around his hips and holding me close. I'd gasped at the suddenness of it, gripping my cuffs as best I could for better support.

He ground against my clit, keeping me at the perfect angle to feel the bulge of his cock millimeters from where I wanted it most. I chewed on my bottom lip, struggling to steady my breathing while my heart raced. He was giving me my fantasy, giving me what I'd begun to long for without me having to ask.

Jesus, was he made just for me?

"If given the chance," he said, breath gliding across my lips while the spicy scent of his cologne filled my nose, "I could spend the night inside you."

My pussy clenched on reflex, seemingly desperate to be given the opportunity, but I kept my exterior as calm as possible.

"You shouldn't tease. It's not very nice."

A dark, wicked smirk curled his lips. In it, I sensed he'd made a promise, not an empty offer. Delightful thought, to be sure.

Digging his fingers into my ass harder than before, he began the slow, deliberate action of guiding me up the length of his shaft. I held my chains, desperate for the aid of them while he continued.

"I could spend the night making you shake." His voice had grown as dark as the color of his eyes, a fathomless void that caressed me, called to me.

What'd begun slow and deliberate, as a teasing gesture meant to heighten the sex-filled atmosphere of our private room, had quickly devolved into something more. Within seconds, he worked harder, faster, eliciting sparks of joy each time my clit scraped along his shaft. It pushed me toward an end I hadn't expected that night, an end that I had become desperate for.

"Yes," I said on a breath.

My stranger leaned in, our bodies tight. The muscles in my arms burned. I'd been struggling to reach out for him, to wrap them around his thick shoulders, but the cuffs kept me in place. It remained my favorite part of being bound, the inability to touch my partner when I wanted to most.

He continued to bounce me in place, relentlessly rolling my hips into his unyielding cock. Dipping into the crook of my neck allowed his sweltering growls to glide across my exposed flesh, adding yet another layer to the moment.

The coil in my gut twisted more and more with each passing second. It wouldn't be long.

"I would worship you," he rasped, "just to hear your screams."

His words were fading, drowned out by the thundering pulse in my ears.

"Don't stop." The mewling words had somehow managed to escape me.

My stranger drew back. I struggled to keep his gaze, to stare into his beautiful face, but he'd become determined in his action, fucking me like a wild man without penetration, and it was more than enough.

A string of Italian words left his lips, their encouraging tone the only thing that I could discern.

His gaze never left mine, tempting me further into the abyss. In spite of the mask that concealed so much of his face, he was the most beautiful thing I'd ever seen.

"Come for me, *bella*," he said in a deep, rough voice. "I want to hear it."

I nodded and his efforts increased. I was swallowed up a second later.

When the coil sprang, I didn't hold back. I cried out, filling our chamber with the sounds of my elation, allowing it to wash over me and release all the glorious tension he'd spent an hour building.

From somewhere in the back of my mind, I might have heard a similar sound leave him, though I was too lost to notice.

My stranger held my ass in one hand while his free arm encircled me. I quivered and shook against him, struggling to draw air into my lungs. He kept me secured to him, engulfing me with little effort and helping to pull my shattered body back together.

I had finally given out, my muscles jellied from the orgasm.

Letting out a stiff breath, my stranger loosened his grip and allowed my legs to slide from his hips until I could stand on my own once more. It'd been difficult to manage, but the cuffs weren't suspended so high that they took me off my feet. Instead, they allowed me a bit of support.

His eyelids were heavy while a flash of pink swathed his cheeks. His full lips, perfect for biting, were parted with each huffing breath.

"I'm afraid this is the end of our play, my dear." Genuine disappointment saturated his voice. He reached up to unlatch my wrists, standing so close that the heat of him infected me further. "Truly regrettable."

I found his accent delicious, the way it affected each syllable and curled the consonants. He had the sort of rich voice that I could listen to for hours.

"Pity," I said. Regardless of what'd transpired, how exhausted I'd become, I wanted more.

He smiled.

When my wrists had been freed, he retrieved my dress and offered it to me. I put it on while he righted himself, and soon it appeared as though nothing had happened.

My welts brought me back to reality, however. Each scrape of my dress across the raw skin helped remind me that it'd been real, which only served to breathe new life into those smoldering embers.

Out of curiosity, I peered at his groin. A slick sheen had overtaken the dark fabric and I knew not all the dampness had been mine.

"Will there be another performance tomorrow?" he asked.

"I'm afraid not," I replied, stomach fluttering at the prospect of spending more time with him. "I actually have to leave Lon—"

My gaze drifted to the clock hanging near the door and my heart dropped. I'd been so invested in our play that I hadn't been paying attention to the time. At nearly one in the morning, I'd stayed much longer than I'd intended.

"Oh, shit," I said in shock. "I-I have to go." I raced for the door and threw it open. "I had fun!" I shouted over my shoulder while I ran down the hall as best as my tight dress and shoes would allow.

* * * *

I'd been lucky to find a taxi unoccupied by a drunk and leaped into it. Within a half-hour, the cabby pulled up to the docks, I paid, and with shoes in one hand, mask in the other, I ran toward the boat.

Shit, shit, shit!

My bare feet clapped against the wooden slats. I prayed there were no splinters waiting to wedge themselves into an unsuspecting passerby.

The Aurora came into view, and I quickened my pace. I had no doubt I looked like an idiot, a woman in a leather tube dress down to her knees, stilettos hanging from her fingertips, a mask and hair waving in the breeze. God only knew what the cabby must have thought.

Before the crew could see me, I jumped onto the yacht as best I could and charged into the belly of the vessel.

I am so late!

Down winding halls, I found my room and ducked inside, but no sooner than I had tossed my shoes onto my bed, I was discovered.

"Well, well, well..."

My heart stopped and my stomach sank. Kennia Freeman, my roommate and best friend, slid into my line of sight, emerging from the tiny bathroom as though she'd been waiting for my arrival. She plopped herself down on my bunk, smirking at me.

"Cuttin' it a bit close, yeah?" she teased, her Australian accent filling my ears. "Now, either that means you had an encore, or..."

She let her sentence dangle, waiting for me to fill in the blanks, but I said nothing. The moment I removed my dress, she had her answer.

"Oh, wow!" Kennia slid off the bed and disappeared behind me. "Guess ya did find someone. This hurt?"

She poked one of the welts on my ass hard enough to send a shock of pain down my spine. I spun and slapped her hand. She erupted into a fit of laughter.

"You exchange numbers with this one?" She fell onto my bed once again, toying lazily with my heels.

I gave her a look, twisting my features in a way that told her *of course not*. She sighed and rolled her eyes.

"One o' these days, you might wanna see someone more than once."

"What for?" I threaded my arms through a work shirt and pulled it on. "That's not what these clubs are about."

"Maybe, but don't ya ever just wanna have somebody there? Not even a boyfriend, just someone you got things in common with that you can spend time around."

I smiled softly while I pulled my hair into a tight bun at the top of my head, ignoring the hairspray I hadn't bothered to brush out.

"There's no point. We're always working, and we don't spend enough time docked for it to matter." I shrugged at her and tried to ignore the sad look in her eyes. "It is what it is."

Kennia seemed resigned to the fact that she wouldn't convince me otherwise.

With a pair of scissors, I snipped off my paper bracelet. It held a surprising number of memories, all centralized around the Italian. In all honesty, if I had a normal life, I might have gone to see him again. He'd managed to touch on so many buttons, so many things I liked without my telling him. That was a *very* rare person.

I set the bracelet in the spine of a book and left my bunk.

Kennia meant well. She always meant well, but I genuinely believed there was no point in forming a long-term relationship with anyone. As a steward on a yacht, I couldn't offer anyone enough personal time to be a girlfriend, and I'd hit my limit for boyfriends. Perhaps it'd been a bit cynical, but when everyone I'd ever dated had left after learning what I like, I stopped telling them. I stopped dating.

What was the point? My perfect package didn't exist. Besides, I was far from the kind of person people wanted to be with. Too much baggage.

Chapter Two

Six years later

The phone call had been unexpected, but what could one do when a friend needed help? One flies to Italy, of course.

Kennia had become a deckhand on the super-yacht known as *The Silver Wind*. She'd been with that particular vessel for just over a year when a member of the crew had been hurt on duty.

Janice, a stewardess, had fallen on some slick stairs. There'd been a pop when she'd hit the deck. A doctor's visit later and they'd learned that she'd dislocated her shoulder. Surgery hadn't been required, but she would be down for the count for some time.

While in the off season, the injury wouldn't have been a problem. She'd have the chance to recuperate and heal, given minimal duties in the meantime. The trouble was *The Silver Wind* had a charter less than a week after she'd been injured. Janice wouldn't have time to recover on the ship, and the crew would be lacking.

Down a stewardess, my name had crossed Kennia's mind. I'd filled the position for a few years, but it'd been a while since then. Some skills tended to fade upon return to the civilian world. For example, I no longer vacuumed the walls of my apartment or crawled on my hands and knees to wipe away any and every fingerprint.

Since singing in bars didn't pay all my bills, I'd been more than willing to give it a chance. I had the skills, even if I was a bit anemic, and was available on short notice. With Kennia to vouch for me, the opportunity had been presented and accepted.

I flew into Genoa, Italy, and took a cab to the docks to meet her. It'd been a long time since I'd traveled, and though I could've done without the multi-hour plane trip, I couldn't deny the end result was worth it.

The sea glittered, sparkling when the waves rolled toward the shore. Mountains were decorated with buildings, both residential and commercial, but all old and unique. Genoa was a beautiful place, a glimpse into the past and without words.

When the taxi arrived, I paid, took my bag and headed for the water with Kennia's directions rattling around in my head. In the end, it didn't much matter. She met me near the street. I assumed she'd done so to avoid me getting lost.

Kennia's face ignited with a thousand-watt smile, and she raced for me. She'd changed since the last time I'd seen her in person little more than a year ago.

Her dark skin played against her white uniform shirt and was just as perfect as it had always been. Being out at sea, even for a short charter, my skin tended to break out. It always had for some reason, but not Kennia's. She could be on the water for months and no one would ever know. The woman had a complexion most anyone would kill for.

In fact, there were many times I guessed that the ocean air somehow made her skin glow even more than normal. *Lucky*.

"Oh, I'm so glad y'made it!" She looped her arms around me and squeezed.

"Oh God, Kennia." I groaned when she held me tighter. "You trying to crush me?"

The woman might've been small in stature, but, Jesus, she was stronger than most grown men.

"Sorry." She giggled and released her death-grip.

"Hair looks nice. What's left of it, at least."

She glared playfully, and while she knew I was kidding, she still ran her hand over her shorn locks.

Kennia used to have curls for days. Straightened, it fell to her shoulders, but because of the humidity at sea, seeing her let the curls run free had been more common. But regardless of the once-untamed mane, Kennia looked just as striking with her hair buzzed short.

"Yeah." A crooked smile curled her lips. "I's gettin' bit tired of the hassle. Cut it 'bout a year ago, actually."

"How would I know?"

"Get a bloody Insta and you can follow me, hmm?" she said with a mocking edge. "Come on." She hooked her elbow to mine. "Let's get you situated, yeah?"

Arm in arm, we headed for the massive security gate that separated the street from the docks. She typed in the code and, once we entered, guided me down the path, filling my ears with the basic rundown of the situation.

We walked for what felt like miles, passing slip after slip after slip. We had gone so far that I began to wonder whether or not there even *was* a boat, until we reached the end of the line. The reason for the trek had become clear.

"An' there she is," Kennia said. "*The Silver Wind.*"

The yacht in question was enormous, beautiful and shining in the afternoon sun, but if I were being honest, it looked like every other over-priced vessel. The only real difference from the outside had been the color scheme. Instead of being so pristine and white that it could blind an onlooker from the right angle, *The Silver Wind* was, well, silver. A silver body with black, white and chrome accents did make it easier to spot in a crowd of floating money.

I let out a long, low whistle. "Two-hundred?"

"Close. Two-hundred and thirty-six feet."

Who needs a boat that big?

"Layout's a bit wonky," she said as we boarded. "But all in all, you'll get it."

Kennia took me to the cabin we'd be sharing. She'd claimed the top bunk, as always, so I tossed my bag onto the bottom, and we left for the tour.

Two staples would be and always had been my anchors. The bridge was the highest point, so the captain could see everything. And the lowest point, the 'below deck', always had engineering, toys, sea deck and the entire living quarters for the staff, including the galley and the laundry room.

The two decks in between were a bit different and would take some time to memorize, but I was certain I could do it. I was less certain about the hidden stairwells and doors, however. Those would take a while.

Kennia led me to the bridge to meet the man in charge, Captain Gus Reeves. We found him standing at the computers checking an unknown number of important things. A tall man, slender in frame with stark-white hair, he looked like someone who could be the captain of a yacht.

"Gus," Kennia said, alerting him to our presence. The captain glanced up, his pale-colored eyes sparkling through the lenses of his glasses. "This is my friend I's tellin' you 'bout."

"Ah." He set his pen and reading glasses down. Flashing a smile, he rose to his feet and offered his hand. "Gus Reeves. Pleasure to meet you."

He was American like me, which had been more surprising than people might assume. In my experience, most of the staff on a yacht tended to be Australian, from New Zealand or British. Maybe it was true of all yachts, maybe not, but I had worked with a very small percentage of people from the States.

"You too, sir." I gave him a firm handshake.

"May I ask you a question?" Judging by his tone, I suspected what he planned to ask, so I chose to speak first.

"Yes, it's my real name," I replied. His thick brows rose in surprise.

"*Really*?"

"Yes, sir. My name really is Basil."

From somewhere behind me, Kennia snickered. While I wanted to jerk back and smack her in the gut for it, I didn't. It'd been a common response to my name.

Most people had an issue with it for the simple fact that it was strange. In England, Basil was a man's name and, while not incredibly common, it was used. Perhaps the pronunciation also offered a bit of leeway. In America, though, and assigned to a woman, Basil remained weird. Many people had told me so.

"And I have a sister named Sage, and another named Rosemary. We're waiting on the twins, Tarragon and Coriander."

Captain Gus' mouth fell slack and hung there for a moment. He seemed to struggle to say something, or at the very least *think* of something to say, but nothing emerged.

"She's kiddin'," Kennia told him. Gus relaxed a bit. "About the twins at least."

I nodded. "There really is a Sage and a Rosemary. And I go by Bay."

"Unique names."

"Mom's a hippie."

He cleared his throat, nodded briskly and said, "Fair enough. Now, all your paperwork's been filled out?"

"Yes, sir." I'd been more than willing to move on, too.

"And the NDA?"

"Yes, sir."

Working on a yacht meant hearing people's secrets or witnessing them doing things they probably wouldn't want someone on the outside to see. With usual clients ranging from celebrities, to politicians, to CEOs, an NDA was standard practice. Oh, the stories I could tell if I were allowed.

"Good. The clients will be here in the morning. It's an eleven-day charter, and we'll dock in Venice. Sound good?"

I smiled. "Sounds good, sir."

"All right." He gave a deep nod then turned his attention to Kennia. "Give her a nametag, the tour, introduce her to everyone and make sure she's got some uniforms."

Kennia stood up straight, clicking her heels together when she did, and saluted him.

"Aye, aye, Cap'n!"

He chuckled and shook his head while he returned to his work. Like before, Kennia hooked her elbow with mine and guided me out of the bridge. The tour commenced in more detail than before.

There were multiple sundecks, elegant dining rooms, an incredible kitchen and a few bars, living rooms, bedrooms, lavish bathrooms and a movie theater. I think I spotted a small gym as well. There was a pool, a sauna and a hot tub, too.

Who needs so much shit?

The Silver Wind was, in essence, a hotel on the water.

It would have been a lot to maintain, but I soon found out that, in a crew of fifteen, I would be one of five stewards, which had been a relief, but still meant I'd be working my ass off.

A fair bit of the crew had congregated in the galley during the few minutes I'd been gone, and the second she spotted them, Kennia began to introduce me. I had never been great with names, but the tags everyone had to wear would help.

"And that's Chris." Kennia pointed to a young man who looked barely out of high school sitting at a table. If his bearing hadn't alluded to him being older, it might have freaked me out a bit.

"Pleasure, darlin'."

His British accent was lovely, and while I could have been weirded out by his choice of pet names, it didn't bother me. It held no undertone of any kind, instead sounding no different than an American 'man' or 'dude' tacked onto the end of a casual greeting.

I liked him, and being a fellow steward meant we would be spending a lot of time with each other.

Another stewardess had been Mandy, a Kiwi who had playful fights with Kennia on a regular basis about which country had better sporting teams. There was Tommy, a deckhand, and Ryan the chef, who offered a passing hello on his way to the kitchen to give the inventory one last check.

No sooner than he'd scampered off did Kennia spot me glancing him over. She whispered that he was currently taken, and I had been far from his type. With a coy smile, she jutted her chin in Chris' direction. It seemed the two of them had been together for nearly ten months. That was a commendable time frame, considering working in close quarters with a partner could destroy a relationship as easily as build it.

Beyond those few, everyone else had either been asleep or tending to their duties.

I became certain in that moment that I would enjoy working on *The Silver Wind*.

* * * *

The following morning, mine and Kennia's alarms began their horrendous chorus at seven a.m. We both tumbled out of bed and pulled on our uniforms that consisted of a polo shirt and dark slacks, shorts or a skirt. Kennia and I chose shorts.

While Kennia did her makeup, I tied my dark hair into a braid and secured it to the back of my head in a bun. As I painted my face in makeup, Kennia finished up in the bathroom then we switched again. I'd been glad that we fell into the routine we'd developed years prior—otherwise, we'd have spent the morning running into each other. Crew bunks were only a few feet by a few feet.

At eight sharp, the entire crew lined up along the deck overlooking the docks while the most-senior members stood on the dock itself.

Back straight, bright smile, be polite.

"Oi," Kennia mumbled.

When I looked at her, she motioned in the direction of land. I adjusted my gaze and noticed the purpose. Down the convoluted dock, men in dark clothes approached. The group consisted of two older gentlemen, two middle-aged men and two younger than the rest, followed by burly gentlemen hauling luggage. I couldn't help wondering at the symmetry of it.

"Don't know who a couple o'v'em are," Kennia whispered. "But the short one there's been here before."

"How is he?" I asked, my attention still on the group. When Kennia didn't offer an answer, I glanced down at her. Her expression didn't encourage me. "What?"

"Grabby."

That'd been all she had to say to make my shoulders slump. While uncommon, grabby men weren't unheard of, either. I could never tell if it came from being wealthy enough that no one told them no, or if there was something about open water that gave them the courage, but I hated grabby, regardless of the reason.

Make no mistake, the majority of the people who chartered yachts were wonderful to work for, even if they ignored the crew. Things still moved smoothly. But every once in a while, there was a group who'd make their sexist comments, inappropriate offers and think their jokes were the funniest in the world. In that situation, it remained best to smile and move on.

Then there were those who thought it acceptable to slap a passing female's ass, pinch it or brush across her chest when 'the boat rocked' and they couldn't catch their balance. That continued to be a lecher's favorite string of excuses.

And as a stewardess, I would be in close proximity to them, even serve them drinks and meals.

"Shit."

"They tip well."

Kennia laced her voice with a tone that let me know it'd been meant as a consolation. I glared but didn't reply.

Captain Gus, the First Officer and Second Officer greeted the guests and motioned toward the ship after a few kind words. One after another, they boarded. Each of us smiled warmly, though the younger men had been the only clients to bother acknowledging our existence.

The first had been a handsome young man who knew it and the one Kennia had referenced. A smirk played at the corner of his lips while he ogled the female crew up and down, even me.

He was slender, with dark hair, pale eyes, dimples and perfect bronzed skin, and I had no doubt that he made girls go weak in the knees. I would like to think that grown women weren't as easily fooled by the bravado, but I'd fallen for my fair share of pretty assholes before.

The second younger man appeared to be a little older than the first, possibly older than me, and wore no smile. His full lips were together, his jaw tight. He didn't appear to be in the mood for the trip.

His black button-up shirt and black slacks draped a fit frame, and his olive-toned skin hinted at an outdoor lifestyle. The stranger had been the definition of 'tall dark and handsome', and when his gaze fell to me, I physically gasped.

He eyed me before proceeding on. My cheeks burned, turning a bright shade of pink. Never, not once in my life, had I ever gasped when I met someone, and I had worked for some pretty famous people on a yacht before. I didn't care how attractive they were, who the hell gasped when they met someone?

The fuck is wrong with you?

I became angry with myself for the slip. It'd been unprofessional and childish, things a twenty-nine-year-old woman shouldn't be.

The moment the clients had gone, the crew broke apart. Some of the deckhands and stewards descended to the docks to retrieve the bags left by the burly men while Mrs. Thorne, the head stewardess, and I retired to the interior to prepare the drinks.

Chapter Three

I didn't know what to make of Mrs. Thorne. She seemed a militaristic woman, concerned only with the professionalism of her staff and their ability. So long as her expectations were reasonable, I wouldn't imagine we'd have a problem with each other.

Mrs. Thorne finished pouring the champagne while I gave the silver tray one last rubdown with a soft cloth. Together, we loaded the flutes.

"Are you *sure* you can do this?" she asked for the third time.

I understood her worry. I'd been thrown onto the crew without her prior approval, a stranger intruding on her and her people. For all she knew, I could have been a complete disaster. However, my understanding of her reservations didn't make it any easier to hear her constant second-guessing. I knew my job, and I could do it well.

"Yes, ma'am," I told her again.

Mrs. Thorne watched me lift the tray of drinks with a surprising level of apprehension. Rolling my eyes to myself, I exited the bar and joined the clients, who sat at one of the large tables on the aft deck.

Hidden in the partial shade of an upper floor, they seemed deep in conversation when I arrived. I understood absolutely nothing they said to one another. I spoke fair Spanish, grade-school-level French and sometimes decent English, but Italian had been a tongue I'd never learned, though I didn't need to speak it to know they were agitated about something.

I made my rounds, handing off the champagne to each gentleman, and I'd been mostly ignored until I reached the arrogant young man. The moment I set his drink down, his hand molded around my ass. My back tightened, and when I looked, he smiled up at me, flashing his dimples in the process. The wink made me want to slap him.

He spoke soothingly to me, seductively, but again I had no idea what he'd said. Whatever it'd been made the older men chuckle and the other young man glower. When the other young man spoke up, his voice had been sharp and pointed, disciplinary. He scolded the arrogant one, whose smile had promptly faded.

The two had a short argument until Arrogant Boy finally removed his hand. I stepped away so he wouldn't have the chance to replace it and set the last champagne flute on the table beside the nicer of the two men.

He'd been relaxing in his seat, an elbow propped on the arm of the chair and his index finger tracing his bottom lip while he scolded Arrogant Boy, and it hadn't changed when he addressed me. His dark eyes landed on me and, as before, the urge to gasp came strong. Fortunately, I'd managed to keep from repeating my previous mistake.

"*Grazie*," he said in that beautiful deep voice.

"*Prego*," I replied, surprising us both.

I left shortly after and returned to the salon bar, wondering why I'd said anything at all. Aside from food, I suppose I did know a couple of words in Italian, but not enough to ask a question or order something in a restaurant. I could speak what the average populace did, and the only reason I knew 'you're welcome' had been because of manners.

The spaghetti sauce by the same name made me laugh, though. It was as though the sauce told people 'you're welcome' for buying it. Stupid, but funny to me all the same. I knew somewhere deep down that I had the sense of humor of a middle-aged dad.

Not long after the first round of drinks was handed out, the luggage had all been brought on board. Chris and I were responsible for dividing it up among the rooms while the deckhands untied us from the dock and weighed anchor.

Within minutes, we were coasting out of the harbor.

* * * *

During the first day, the stewards had little to do. We would serve the clients, clean up here and there and that was the extent of it. The ship hadn't been 'lived in' enough for us to do much, but that would change by day two.

Typical shifts were meant to consist of eight hours on, four hours off, another four hours on then another eight hours off before it started all over again. The strange arrangement ensured overlap, that people worked both day and night shifts, and that we still had plenty of sleep. But that could change, too. Stewards' lives revolved around the clients, which meant if they stayed up late, most that were on shift had to stay up late, too.

Ever wonder why yachts always appeared to be ultra-shiny and unnaturally clean? It was because a small team of people followed the passengers, wiping away fingerprints. Despite the yacht being full of people, it was my job to help make it appear as though the vessel had never been touched.

That night, my alarm went off about a quarter to midnight, waking me from a shallow sleep. Kennia's arm and leg hung over the edge of her bunk, forcing me to go full *Mission Impossible* to avoid hitting them.

Using the light from my cell phone, I grabbed my uniform, slid it on and exited our room as quietly as I could. Out in the galley, I put on my shoes, grabbed an apple and headed upstairs. Mrs. Thorne had been sure to remind me of my duties *many* times.

The hum of the ship's distant engine greeted me, along with the waves crashing against the hull, but while I ascended to the second floor, I heard nothing of the guests. Cleaning remained easier without a crowd.

After finishing my apple and lobbing the core into the ocean for a sea monster to chomp on, I retrieved the vacuum, picked a proper playlist from my iPod and began to work.

Content in my own world, I must have gone through a small handful of songs, singing most of them to myself. Singing was the best way to help pass the time.

I'd been grooving for a while when a shadow caught my attention. I spun on my heels and shrieked.

"Jesus, Mary and George!"

Heart in my throat, I did my best to steady myself. When my brain cleared and the room came into focus once again, I realized who'd been the cause for my near-heart attack.

Nice Guy, the only name I had for him, stood in the doorway that led to the aft deck, the massive space on the back of the ship. With minimal light, I had only seen his shifting silhouette, which had terrified me. Hell, the calm way he stood with his hands in his pockets had been a bit unsettling, too.

Popping out my headphones, I turned off the vacuum with my toe and gave him my attention.

"Um, sorry about that," I said. Then it dawned on me that he might not speak English. "Um...*mi scusi, signore.*"

That was the end of my conversational skills, and while I struggled to think of something to explain why I was there or ask if he needed anything, he approached me.

"Do you speak Italian?" he asked with a thick accent.

My brows rose in surprise. I hadn't expected him to speak English, let alone as well as he did. We'd picked him and the others up *in* Italy. It would have been logical that they only spoke their native tongue.

But the sound of his voice, of his accent, reminded me of someone I'd met years ago. I wished I could recall more of him, but our interlude had happened six, nearly seven years prior. Small details had long since vanished from memory, except the way he made me feel. That was something I could never forget, because it'd never been duplicated.

"Uh, no." I shook my head. "Not more than that, at least."

"You should learn," he said as he continued his advance. "It is a beautiful language."

"Um, sure." I wasn't certain what he expected me to say to that.

A strange silence passed between us until he spoke once again. "You have a lovely voice."

Heat bloomed in my cheeks. "Thank you."

"Do you sing for others?"

"Um, sometimes, but not very often anymore."

"Pity," he said. "I can see you singing in front of a crowd, perhaps in a lounge."

My blush intensified and my stomach fluttered. He spoke so leadingly, as though he'd seen me perform, but the odds against it were astronomical.

"I would like to apologize for my cousin's behavior this afternoon." He continued on as though we'd been in the middle of a normal conversation. "Dominic is…an ass."

The snicker left me before I could pull it back. It'd been the suddenness of the insult that had caused it. He smiled at my reaction, which eased my tension. At least I hadn't offended him.

But with that smile, I had been forced to remember his handsomeness. It annoyed me, far beyond what I could put into words, that my brain traveled back to how attractive he was when it had even the slightest lull.

I needed to be better than that.

I *was* better than that.

"You don't have to apologize, sir, but thank you."

He offered a slight head bow in acknowledgment before offering his hand. "Michele Sacchi."

The way his name rolled off his tongue had been beautiful, lyrical even, and I found I quite liked it.

"Basil Hurst," I replied while I shook his hand. My name mixed with my American accent sounded much blunter, less pretty.

He arched a thick brow. "Your name is Basil?"

Bay-zeel. It sounds so much nicer when he says it.

"Yeah, it is," I said with a nod. "So, is there anything I can get you, sir?"

"No, nothing."

"Okay, well, is it all right if I get back to the vacuuming?"

"Please." He motioned toward the room. "Do not let me keep you from your duties."

My actions became unsure. I'd thought Michele would have returned to his room or maybe to the aft deck, but instead he remained. He stood there, hands in his pockets, watching me place my earbuds back in and start up the Hoover.

While I did my best to concentrate on the task at hand, Michele lingered in my peripheral vision. He seemed to be examining me, looking me over from head to toe before granting me a reprieve and walking away.

Without a word, he went back to the aft deck and regained his seat. I could breathe easier the moment he was gone. For whatever reason, Mr. Sacchi seemed to rob me of my faculties, and I didn't appreciate it. Aside from a celebrity-who-shall-not-be-named who'd spent a week on a yacht during my former stewarding days, I had never, *ever* lost my control...until Michele Sacchi.

Somewhere deep down, I knew our meeting would end badly.

* * * *

Exhaustion hit when my alarm went off telling me that four a.m. had come. It'd been years since I'd worked the wonky shifts of a yacht, and it would take the length of the charter, at least, to get into the swing of things.

I made my way back toward the belly of the ship, running a cloth along the interior railing as I did. It gave off a satisfying squeak, telling anyone within earshot that it had been a damn-clean railing.

When I returned to the living area, the salon, I made sure to give it another once-over, grabbing my supplies and straightening a pillow here and there.

"Hey." Candace smiled as she joined me, still half asleep but ready for work.

"Hey,"

"You already do in here?"

"Yeah." I proceeded to tell her about the chores I'd completed so she wouldn't mistakenly do them herself. "And Mr. Sacchi was around here somewhere, but I think he finally went to bed."

"Which one is he?"

"The tall one," I said. "The one with the dark eyes."

It was a tightrope act trying to describe him without being too detailed, but my attempts to remain professional were in vain.

"Oh my God, he's hot." She giggled, not bothering to hide it. I smiled but didn't offer my opinion. She noticed. "Oh, come on. You don't think so?"

"That's not the point," I replied while I gathered my things, but I couldn't remove my smile.

"Uh-huh, that's what I thought." She continued to grin. "Like you wouldn't if you had the chance."

Oh, I definitely would.

And that was the problem. Not only would sleeping with one of the passengers be incredibly unprofessional, but my preferences tended to frustrate my partners, or they weren't willing to commit. BDSM wasn't for everyone.

Although, in reality, the categories and sub-categories covered such a wide array of things that I wouldn't doubt ninety percent of the world's population fell into one of them.

As a switch, I found it a bit difficult to find a partner willing to be dominated, as well as ticking all my boxes when I played a sub. That kind of energy, that connection, was hard to come by, and while fantasizing about Mr. Sacchi could definitely pass a few hours during the charter, they could only be fantasies.

I said goodnight and told her I'd see her for my next shift. Candace offered me a wave while I headed for the stairs.

I *hated* the stairs. They were steep, narrow and spiral, which made seeing around a corner almost impossible. Unlike other yachts, for whatever reason, the people who built *The Silver Wind* didn't think it prudent to add floor-length mirrors in the 'corners' to help people see if anyone was coming. They would have been helpful, and if I hadn't been as tired as I was, they might have helped me notice Michele before I ran into him.

"Oh my God!"

I nearly caused the pair of us to tumble down the spiral staircase in a heap of twisted limbs, but he somehow managed to catch me. Instead of plummeting to the depths of the ship, he fell back a step or two, then pinned me to the curved wall to steady us.

My body vibrated with fear, the small hairs on the back of my neck stood on end and my heart raced so fast that I swore it would burst through my ribs. White-knuckling the back of his shirt, Michele held me to his chest, his heavy breathing in my ear.

We stayed close to each other until we calmed — or I had calmed, at least. My grip loosened and I drew back as well as I could in such tight quarters. He did the same, staring at me with those stunning dark eyes that, had I not nearly died, I'd have lost myself in for a few minutes.

"I am *so sorry*, Mr. Sacchi." My voice trembled. "Are you all right?"

He nodded. "I'm fine, Miss Hurst. And you?"

I nodded repeatedly while I took a step down the stairs, putting some much-needed distance between me and him. A strange sensation trickled through me as his grip disappeared from my hips. I didn't like it.

"Yeah, I'm fine. Are you?"

Michele smiled, a kind expression that caused me to pause. His smile was incredible, changing the whole of his face from sultry and stoic to endearing and welcoming.

"I'm fine, Miss Hurst," he repeated, forcing me to realize I'd asked my question twice. My cheeks flushed with embarrassment. "Are you retiring for the day?"

"Mm-hmm, until next shift. Are you..." My brows furrowed. "Why are you still awake?"

The question came out more judgingly than I'd meant it to, but he didn't seem offended.

"I don't require much sleep," he said. "Never have, I'm afraid."

"Oh." I nodded, unsure of what else to do. "Um, well, goodnight, Mr. Sacchi."

To my surprise, he took my hand into his and raised it to his lips. "*Buona notte*, Miss Hurst." He kissed my knuckles, sending fire racing through my veins. "Watch your step."

The heat in my cheeks became unbearable. I was sure I'd graduated from a pink blush to crimson by the time I set off downstairs again. In Europe it was considered a polite action to kiss someone's knuckles or cheeks, but being American, I couldn't help but read further into it than I should have.

"Holy *shit*, that guy's sexy." I exhaled through my teeth, doing my best to regain control over myself so I could fall asleep before my shift. *He reminds me so much of that other guy.*

Chapter Four

Four days into the charter and I'd managed to find my rhythm. I was glad to have slipped into the crew with relative ease. I didn't get along with everyone, which didn't surprise me, given the size of the staff, but it'd been nothing that would dampen my experience or interfere with work.

I had learned a bit about our guests, as well. The two eldest gentlemen were named Paulo and Vincent. The middle-aged men were Patritzio and Antony, and of course Michele and Dominic rounded out the group. While I would continue to call them each 'Sir' for the remainder of the trip, having a name with each face helped.

From what I could tell, the clients were related, and the majority of their conversations were so intense that I assumed it had to do with money. Very few things angered people to that degree. In my experience, money and work were at the top of that list in one way or another, so perhaps they had a business together? I couldn't say, but one's mind tended to wander when one spent time around strangers.

Anchored off the coast of Malta, the ship had been left to drift in the serene, unmoving waters. I stood behind the outside bar mixing drinks for the guests while Kennia took a short break with me. She did her best to enjoy the sun for as long as she could. Starting Friday, she would be working overnight rotations. I didn't envy her.

People on the outside liked to think that deckhands were the bottom rung when it came to the hierarchy on a yacht, but they weren't. Stewards like me were. Deckhands sat above us because they dealt with so many of the technical and mechanical issues. And, unfortunately for Kennia, the deckhands working overnight, among other things, had to clean the exterior windows. Having cleaned the interior of those same windows, I pitied her.

"Never been a fan of vermouth," Kennia said while I poured the soda water over the back of a spoon and into the waiting glass.

"Me neither," I replied, watching carefully to ensure the liquids didn't mix too much. "But to each his own, I guess."

"Mm-hmm." She nodded and went back to her phone while I set the soda water aside and stabbed some olives with a rather attractive silver skewer.

The men in question, the ones who'd requested the vermouth and sodas, sat on the sundeck basking in the rays, talking very seriously to one another. A couple of them lounged at the table, their big bellies exposed by unbuttoned shirts and glistening with tanning oil. It reminded me of my granddad, especially the white chest hair.

A couple of the clients lingered in the pool, which made me laugh. It always made me laugh that there were pools and hot tubs on boats. On a very rational level, I understood their purpose. Not everyone wanted to swim in salt water. But in the most basic sense, a pool on a ship in the ocean made me giggle because I had a stupid sense of humor.

And what was the deal with the saltwater fish tanks? That seemed cruel, as though taunting the fish with the ocean just beyond their tank.

But amid the group of men, one remained missing. Michele had taken to swimming in the sea, and as childish as it was, I found myself grateful for the reprieve. I still didn't know what to make of him or my attraction toward him.

Throughout the last few days, my imagination had begun to run away with me. More than once I could have sworn I'd caught Michele staring. It seemed to happen all the time, and the only reason I noticed, or had begun to suspect, had been because I was trying to stare at him.

Every time I wanted to catch a peek of him reading, carrying conversations, on his cell phone or laptop, or even when he was just sitting in the sun, he was looking back. The guy must have had a sixth sense, because he somehow managed to catch me every single time.

Fully aware of how unprofessional it was, I argued with myself often about whether or not ogling a client was a good idea. It wasn't. Of course it wasn't. I wasn't stupid enough to think otherwise, and yet I couldn't help myself. Michele had some kind of exotic mystery about him. He was 'the handsome Italian stranger on the yacht'. How could I resist?

After four days, I decided to give up. Better to do so while I still had some of my dignity intact, so I was glad he seemed to spend the day in the water away from those I had to serve.

But then, because God hated me, the man himself returned from his swim. A familiar rush pulsed through me, and I loathed that I loved it.

Michele appeared over the edge of the deck, ascending the stairs that led up from the sea deck below. Water dripped from his body, highlighting the work he'd put into his physique.

Sculpted muscle shifted beneath perfectly bronzed skin. A spatter of dark hair spread across his broad chest, adding a level of primal attraction to the moment.

He had tattoos as well, none of which I'd noticed before. When done right, be it placement or quality, they proved to be a weakness of mine. His were both. A simple word in beautiful script had been inked above his heart. He had another on his shoulder, a crest of some sort, and a few on his fingers and the backs of his hands that I'd somehow missed. I didn't know what they were, but every hint of dark ink on his body had been a delightful addition.

Michele removed the towel he'd draped over the railing when he'd gone for his swim and dabbed at his body. I froze in the middle of pouring another drink, focused too much on the stranger for someone meant to be in the background.

Then his gaze fell to me. Standing yards away, drenched in sunlight as he dried himself by the pool, Michele somehow found me. In fact, he didn't even search. His gaze managed to land on me without hesitation, as though he knew where I'd been all along.

How he could see me within the depths of the ship cast in shadow, I would never know. It must have been the sixth sense.

He parted his full lips and water dripped from his chin while he continued to stare. So many things raced through me, from indecent thoughts to my internal voice commanding me to just look away. In the end, my respite came when one of the others spoke to him.

Michele diverted his attention and said something to whoever had spoken, which gave me the chance to get back to work. As quickly as I could, I finished pouring the drink.

Heart jackhammering away inside my chest, heat spreading throughout my limbs and a pulse thundering between my thighs, I'd been overtaken. I was almost thirty years old, a fucking adult, and I was losing drops of sanity whenever he looked at me, whenever he stood within twenty feet of me.

You're pathetic.

Before I had the chance to set the finished drinks on a tray, a shadow darkened my periphery. I didn't want to look up, unsure I was brave enough to manage.

"May I have some water?"

Michele's voice slid easily into my ears. It caressed me, stroked my growing desires.

Pathetic!

"Of course." I forced the words out, praying he hadn't heard the tremble in the back of my throat.

Without looking up, I dipped behind the bar and took a bottle from the mini-fridge. In those few seconds, I did my best to steady myself, but it helped little in the end.

The sight of his dark eyes had been no less enchanting than they were previously, but I forced my smile and offered him the bottle. How the hell could they affect me like they did? Certain people were attracted to certain things, i.e. legs, breasts, smiles, hair, eyes, mouths, etc. I had been no different, but one would have thought I'd lost my mind every time I met his gaze.

Why does it make me go so weak in the knees? There has to be a reason.

"Here you go, sir."

"*Grazie*, Miss Hurst," he said as he took the water, brushing his index finger along mine when he had.

As he walked away, revealing a back just as impeccable as the front, Kennia rose to her feet. She appeared at my side the instant he'd left us.

"So." She seemed rather happy with herself. "How's he know your name, then, huh?"

Her smile spread with each passing second.

"He introduced himself the first night, so I told him my name, too. That's all."

"Uh-huh."

I couldn't say whether or not she had attempted to hide the giggle, but it'd been there regardless.

"It was nothing, okay?" I didn't know what made me want to defend myself, yet I couldn't help it. "He apologized for his cousin grabbing my ass."

"*Oh.*" She sucked on her teeth in displeasure. "Couple o' the girls said that one's gotten a bit friendly with 'em, too. He's a bit of a prick."

I had to agree with her. Michele did, too, as it turned out. Unfortunately, there was little that could be done about it. Complaints might be filed and noted, stipulations put in place when the charter was over, but nothing else. We could only hope Michele reined him in in the end.

Kennia continued. "But, uh, are we just not gonna talk 'bout this lad eyin' you like a steak?"

I pursed my lips while I glared at her, something she found absolutely hilarious. Kennia laughed before she scampered off to finish her shift. Sometimes I couldn't specify why I liked her as much as I did.

Still, minutes after she'd left and even after I'd served the drinks, Kennia's words coursed through my mind. I couldn't help but glance up often, and multiple times I found Michele looking at me, too.

* * * *

A little after four in the morning, I ended my shift, as per usual. My internal checklist had been completed, and I could take a nap before noon. I still couldn't sleep very well for some reason. Naps seemed to be the best I could muster.

On my way downstairs, I took each step with care. Memories of my literal run-in with Michele flashed in my mind, and if he did have night owl tendencies, I didn't wish for it to happen again. There was no promise that we'd survive a second time.

Five sets of stairs ran from top to bottom of the ship, and I'd made it to the second from the last when I was met with another soul. I paused mid-step and stared down at Michele. It shocked me, not only because we were once again caught in the confined space together, but because he'd come from the below deck, the place where the crew stayed.

"Mr. Sacchi, um… What are you…?"

It felt rude to ask his intentions, given he was one of the clients, but it didn't make sense for him to be there, either.

Without a word, he lifted his hand. Clasped within his fingers had been a pint of gelato and a spoon resting on the lid. Everything made sense. Along with our bunks, the below deck housed the galley. He'd gone in search of food, nothing more. But with the understanding came guilt.

"I could've gotten that for you," I said.

"You were busy." He took a step closer.

"But it's my job."

His full lips curled at the corner forming a little smile. "I am capable of getting myself dessert."

"Yes, sir." I didn't know what else to say. "Well, um…"

"Are you going to sleep?"

"Yes, sir."

"Then let me move."

Michele continued up the stairs and together we tried to adjust our bodies to allow the other room. It never crossed my mind to backtrack to the previous floor so that we could each use the stairwell freely. I was an idiot.

While he slid by me, Michele took my waist in his hand. Our chests brushed when we moved. We shifted around each other carefully. The truth had been that the two of us could've passed one another in seconds, but we lingered. *We* lingered…not just me.

The scent of his cologne filled my nose, sparking desire while the heat of his body against mine helped inflame it. His breath on my cheek nearly ended me in that moment.

That man had power over me.

Just before we broke apart, while we still shared a step, Michele whispered, "Have you forgotten me, Miss Hurst?"

The strangeness of the statement caused me to look up. He'd become decorated with shadows, each accentuating his cheekbones and strong jaw. They darkened his features, made him appear sinister and wicked.

As we stared at one another, his gaze danced across my face. He swallowed hard and, to my surprise, he climbed his hand up my side. My heart raced yet again. It'd become a common thing whenever he was around. So common, in fact, that one would assume I had no control. Maybe I didn't.

Thoughts of him grabbing me, of pinning me to the wall and taking advantage coursed through my mind. They caused my nerves to tingle and my core to throb with need. If I didn't remove myself from the situation soon, I would overstep multiple boundaries.

"Because I remember you," he said.

His words barely made it through my clouding brain, caught in the cobwebs of my lust toward him, but one thing broke through it all.

"Perhaps a mask would have made it easier, hmm?"

My stomach sank. He took a deep breath. His hand stopped its climb just beneath my breast, and while my mind screamed for him to move it a few inches more, he didn't. Michele stepped away, putting a sparse distance between us that I helped by descending the stairs.

What did he just say?

"*Bouna notte*, Miss Hurst."

The moment he was gone, I exhaled a trembling breath.

No fucking *way!*

Chapter Five

For hours after the fact, I couldn't stop thinking about what Michele had said in the stairwell. Until that moment, I'd thought the similarities I'd noticed between him and the mystery man in London were my brain's way of connecting dots that didn't exist. But after that bombshell was dropped, I could see nothing *but* similarities.

How could he recognize me when we were both wearing masks that night? And besides that, how could he recognize me at all? It's been over six years.

Kennia slammed her hand down on the pile of cards so hard that the table shook. The shock of it snapped me back into reality.

"Ah-ha!"

A chorus of groans filled the galley as she gathered up the mass of playing cards, still beaming.

"Mwa-ha-ha." She mocked a villain's smile and the twirling of a nonexistent mustache. "No one, and I mean *no one*, can top me in Slaps."

"You cheat," I said when I tossed down the single card I had left. "You have X-ray vision or something."

"Oh, come on, Bay. No need to be a sore loser, yeah?"

It became harder to take her seriously when she cradled nearly two decks worth of cards in her tiny hands. She arched a brow at me, still smirking while she lazily shuffled her prize.

"It's all just fun an' games."

Like a mature adult, I stuck out my tongue.

"It doesn't matter, anyway. I'm out," I said.

"Aw, come on. You can still slap in," Chris said.

"Nah, I need to get back to work."

When I stood and slid out of the booth, Chris grabbed my wrist. He stared at me, his eyes wide and filled with mock terror.

"Please, *please* don't leave us with her." Then he added a shiver to his words. "She's ruthless."

"Bloody righ' I am," Kennia declared.

The rest of the group laughed and smiled, even Chris. As I walked away, I made sure to bump Kennia with my hip when I passed. She responded with a sharp slap to my ass in retaliation, a slap that echoed in the galley.

I jogged upstairs to start cleaning the guests' rooms, but I couldn't keep from smiling. While there were downsides to any job, including ones so exotic, I loved working with friends. I'd forgotten how much fun it could be, how much I'd missed Kennia.

The bedrooms were divided up among the stewards, which made it easier for us to devote the most attention to them and for a client to blame someone when they didn't like the end result or chose to accuse someone of theft.

Within a few hours, I'd finished my chores and even took the laundry down. It ordinarily wouldn't take someone nearly three hours to clean a pair of rooms, but when the beds had to be made a specific way and I had to clean every fingerprint and droplet of water, three hours was good time.

I walked briskly through the hall and rounded a corner, only to be brought to a halt by a tall, solid figure. When I gathered myself, I realized that I'd run into Michele, again.

You'd think this boat was a dinghy.

But he seemed unaffected. As he had many times before, Michele smiled at me, and it caused my body to act the same way it always did, further fueled by his earlier declaration.

In that moment, I remembered every little glance, every touch when we passed, every fantasy that had grown in my head and everything that'd happened in Labyrinth. I needed to walk away, to remove myself from the situation before I sank into it, but something kept me from moving.

"Was that really you?" I blurted out, thinking the direct approach might have been best.

He arched a thick brow. "In London, you mean."

My stomach twisted. "How?"

"The singing," he said. "I recognized your singing."

"Wha— No." I shook my head. "No, I mean…really?"

He nodded and said something that would forever make a little part of me swoon. "I will always recognize your voice."

Heat bloomed in my cheeks, and I dropped my gaze. The warmth of my blush spread throughout my limbs, through my chest and found focus in the apex of my thighs. I clenched my legs together, hoping he wouldn't notice and that it would save me from the ache. It didn't, not when confronted with the fact that my stranger from London stood inches from me, and I was exposed. There were no masks or illusions to blanket myself in. He could see me.

"How the hell did this happen?" I asked, forcing myself to meet his eye once more.

"I don't understand." He'd begun to look at me as though I'd lost my mind. Perhaps I had.

"The only reason I'm here is because someone got hurt and a friend of mine works on this boat," I said. "How the hell did I end up on a yacht with a guy I played with years ago?"

Michele said nothing. I didn't expect him to speak. I likely sounded like a crazy person, but with my mind fraying, how else could I sound? It had trouble calculating the odds of me ending up on a boat with the last man who had made me feel anything.

I had been stuck in my own mind for long enough that Michele spoke up again.

"Do I make you uncomfortable, Miss Hurst?"

I lied outright. "No. No, of course not."

"Are you certain?"

My response was slower to come. I had to find the proper words, the right way to phrase how he made me feel without exposing myself further.

"It's not discomfort, Mr. Sacchi."

"Is it fear, then?"

"What?"

"Do I frighten you?"

His accent sent shivers down my spine. His voice remained soft, calm, and it caused me to breathe deep. I found that the longer I stared into his eyes, the longer

I stood near him, the harder it became for me to keep the truth to myself.

I wish I knew what his power was. At least then I could combat it.

"Yeah, but I—"

Michele watched me, waiting patiently for me to continue.

"I don't know if it's good or bad yet."

You're an idiot, I thought to myself. *You should've just let him leave.*

"Good or bad." He slid his hands into his pockets and squared himself on me as best he could in the narrow hall. "How do you mean?"

"I—"

Shut up, shut up! He's a passenger. Just walk away.

But I didn't. I kept talking.

"I can't tell if I'm afraid of you because I should be, or—"

Don't say it!

"Because I want to be."

Stupid, stupid, stupid!

"Hmm,"

The regret came in an instant. I'd already admitted something I wished I'd kept internalized. Why not make a complete fool of myself and go for broke?

As the seconds ticked by, my nerves continued to unravel, and I had no choice but to remove myself from the situation entirely.

"Excuse me," I muttered as I attempted to go around him.

To my surprise, he stepped into my path. Even though I could sense him looking at me, I couldn't bring myself to meet his gaze. I froze.

There's a moment that sometimes passes between two people, a moment in which their energies and desires align. It's an unspoken sensation, an understanding that words could never fully express, and it happened in that corridor.

"Do you like to be afraid?"

A trickle of ice sputtered across the back of my neck and, in spite of everything, the truth began to bubble once more.

Almost too softly to hear, I mumbled, "Sometimes."

Michele shifted his stance, forcing me to do the same. My back touched the wall, and my breathing became shallow. The scent of his cologne filled me once again, sweet and somehow spicy at the same time. It transported me to that night in Labyrinth, to the sensations he created in me and the commanding lust that had threatened to consume me in that dark little room, shackled and bare.

My heart raced. Blood rushed in my ears and my clit pulsed with desire. He knew what he was doing and, worse yet, he seemed to know what effect he had on me.

"And now?" He pressed his chest to mine while keeping his voice soothing. "Are you afraid now?"

I forced my gaze to meet his. The intensity of his stare was something I hadn't seen since London, an incredible mixture of dark yet needing. It was the sort of thing I'd searched for, but never found afterward.

"Almost," I whispered, more than willing to see how far the moment would go.

Michele knew *exactly* what to do.

He reached for my throat and held it just firmly enough to ignite my body. I gasped and a breathy whimper fell from my lips.

He stood so close that I couldn't tell where he ended and I began. Each breath entered me, each heartbeat thrummed for him, and when he tensed his fingertips, I thought I would come through my skin.

"Are you afraid now?" His voice had become deep and rough.

My eyes drifted shut and my knees turned to jelly, but I did my best to continue speaking.

Fear had been far from my first emotion. In fact, unbelievable longing consumed me more than I could express, but I knew what he wanted to hear and what I wanted to say to keep it going.

"Yes."

He leaned forward, his forehead coming to rest on mine. His breath glided across my skin and his short beard pricked when our lips brushed.

He glided his strong hand farther up my neck until he wedged it beneath my jaw, forcing my head back. It became difficult for me not to reach out, a battle I lost when he nipped at my chin and continued to tease a kiss.

I grabbed his hand, cradling it to my throat. I didn't want him to remove it or dare to loosen his grasp.

"You like that, huh?" He pressed his body even harder into mine, grinding his erection into my stomach as he did.

His words from six years ago trickled into my head. *"I could spend the night inside you."*

"Yes."

When Michele clenched his fingers, a soft moan echoed in my throat. I was being overrun, overtaken by an unquenchable desire for the Italian man I barely knew.

My pussy throbbed with want, desperate and empty, almost begging for him to fulfill his distant promise.

"How much, I wonder."

Too enthralled to care about what would happen beyond that moment, I took his free hand and guided it to where I wanted it, *needed* it, most. Michele cupped my sex, wedging his hand between my thighs and applying just a hint of pressure, but little else.

"Tell me," he said with a growl.

Defiance roiled inside me, the little spark that would never truly fade.

"Find out."

A dark chuckle met my ears. He didn't hesitate to comply, unbuttoning my shorts with what seemed to be a flick of his fingers before shoving his hand into my panties, bypassing anything that might've separated us.

There was no hiding my mewling cry of pleasure the moment his sweltering skin touched mine. It'd been a relief, albeit a small one.

Shoving his body against mine, Michele's dexterous fingers went to work, parting my pussy lips and tracing my entrance with a single digit.

"Quite a lot," he said, his voice twisted into something borderline inhuman. He pressed his digits into my clit, sending a biting spark of pleasure tearing through me. He groaned deep within his chest. "I want to be inside you."

There'd been no hesitation on my part to comply. Michele seemed to be asking permission and so, lost to the sensation of him again, I was more than willing to give in.

"Yes," I said.

The finger that'd been teasing me slid effortlessly inside my core, which immediately clamped down around it. So desperate for the man, it didn't want to let him go.

He whispered beautiful Italian into my ears, a guttural scrape twisting each word. I wished I'd known what he was saying, but something about the mystery only added to my enjoyment.

"You like to feel me choke you?"

He sucked in a sharp breath when he tightened his grip briefly once more and sighed in satisfaction when I began to tremble. He knew how to do it, how to tense then release, tense then release, never obstructing air or blood flow, just reminding me of the power he possessed.

He slid a second finger inside, pumping them in and out with slow, measured actions.

A moan laced my words when I said, "I like a lot of things."

He seemed to sense my meaning without me uttering it aloud, and I couldn't tell if I was horrified or glad. I should have been completely horrified. Him knowing my buttons meant he had the potential to press them whenever he wanted, and that could have been dangerous.

He whispered in my ear, "You like to be dominated."

His speed increased while he continued to grind his palm against my clit. I clung to him for balance, clung to the one thing that had become the reason I was slipping.

"Sometimes." I choked on the word.

Every nerve in my body had become electrified, sparking with life after years of dormancy.

"And other times?" He bit my earlobe, sending another wave of pain-induced pleasure through me.

"I like…" My voice was stolen when he began to curl his fingers, touching that spot most men didn't know existed.

"Yes?" he cooed, delivering another sharp nip to my earlobe.

"I…like to dominate."

He let out an amused breath, as though he wanted to chuckle at the comment, but the situation had wound us both too tight for anything beyond strained speech.

My breathing became ragged when Michele drew back. Somehow, I gathered the strength to open my heavy lids and found myself staring into eyes so black that they refused to reflect the dim light of the hall.

Mere inches separated us, and it was too much.

"I have missed you, *bella*," he said. "Missed your cries and the way your face twists with pleasure."

As though to prove his point, Michele shoved his fingers so deep that he'd lifted me onto the tips of my toes, then slowly but surely lowered me once again. I panted through parted lips, my face feverish with want. He wasn't human, not with how he'd overtaken me with such minimal ease. He was something created just for me.

"I want it again. Want you."

His words enveloped me, and in that moment, I had been more than prepared to let him do anything he deemed fit, when something chirped in my ear. It startled me, but not as much as Mrs. Thorne's voice telling me to come to the kitchen to help Ryan, the chef.

Michele must have heard the same. While my ear piece hadn't been turned up very loud, he'd been so close that it was possible he'd overheard my orders. His disappointed expression said as much.

His body became rigid as he stepped back and stood against the wall across from me. We stared at one another, unanswered emotions coursing through us both with equal intensity.

With my gaze still locked to his, I touched my collar where the microphone and call button sat and told her I'd be right there.

Michele continued to stare at me, his full lips parted with heavy breaths, his eyes black with need and his dick straining angrily against his trousers.

I wanted to reach out and grab him, to stroke his chiseled face, to bite his bottom lip. I wanted to drop to my knees and show him how much I enjoyed his touch.

Still locked in our silent staring contest, Michele lifted his hand to his mouth and captured his middle and ring fingers. A satisfied groan echoed in his throat while he withdrew them, tasting every inch of me.

It was a sight I would commit to memory.

You have to go. Make your feet work.

"Goodbye, Mr. Sacchi." My voice had been foreign to me, still tainted by unquenched desire.

His response had been a grunt of acknowledgment. Doubtful I would get anything more, I turned and left. The ache between my thighs would accompany me for the following hour or more, begging to be slated, and I loved it.

* * * *

Late in the evening, I'd served the cocktails and was close to ending my shift, but there were a few things in need of being swept up or cleaned before I clocked out.

With dinner to be served in the next couple of hours, the responsibility of prepping the dining room fell on my shoulders.

The chamois cloth left a beautiful surface in its wake as I ran it over the table. I may have made faces at myself once or twice, but it was the best way to know that the surface had been polished appropriately.

"Good evening, Miss Hurst."

A phantom hand enclosed around my throat at the sound of his delicious voice, reminding me of the things I'd spent hours trying to ignore but never forgot.

Michele entered the living room adjacent to me. The entire space was open, which meant he could see me clearly when he fell into one of the chairs.

"Good evening, Mr. Sacchi. Is there anything I can get for you?"

He shook his head. "No, thank you."

I offered a smile in return and went back to my work, desperate to keep moving, to keep pretending I wasn't shaking at his proximity.

While I straightened the placemats, dusted off the dining room chairs and wiped the nearby knick-knacks, Michele continued to stare. I did my best to ignore him, but he seemed unwilling to *be* ignored.

"Tell me your rules."

I spun to face him, my brow furrowed. At first, I hadn't been certain I'd heard him correctly, but there was no way to *mis-hear* something so simple. When that realization sank in, I began to blush for the hundredth time.

I had no doubt that my cheeks were crimson. We were no longer hidden within the halls, late at night and away from the world. We were in a room bathed in sunlight, where anyone could walk in on the conversation, and I seemed to be the only one who cared.

"I don't think we should talk about this, sir," I said, returning to busy work.

"Why not?"

He tilted his head to the side, still staring at me while I did anything to avoid looking at him. With a clear head, I was able to see the foolishness of what'd happened earlier. London had been six years prior. The setting had been completely different.

On *The Silver Wind*, I was at work, on duty at all times, and he was a passenger.

Minutes ticked by and still I refused to acknowledge him further, and Michele seemed to have reached his limit—or perhaps he simply knew how to make me comply.

In the deepest, sternest voice I'd ever heard him use, he spoke. "Look at me, *now*."

My insides lurched, shocked by the suddenness of the shift. I immediately did as I'd been told.

Michele leaned forward in his seat, resting his elbows on his knees and lacing his fingers together. He stared at me from beneath his brows, equal parts intimidating and alluring.

"Tell me your rules." His voice remained hard but laced with curiosity.

"Why?"

I didn't understand why he would care. It wasn't as though we could start anything. Sleeping with a passenger or fooling around in any way was forbidden. I could've been fired, and that needed to be enough for me to suppress all my inclinations, all the feelings I had growing for the handsome Italian. Hell, I'd already fucked up once. I couldn't risk doing it again.

Until he said something I never thought I'd hear from another person.

"I wish to know if they're similar to mine."

I raised a curious brow, staring at the man who'd just hinted at more than I could have expected.

Seconds became minutes and I hadn't answered him. I had trouble comprehending our conversation. While I would absolutely assume to discuss such things in a club or some other establishment that catered to my particular preferences, the dining room was not the place.

And yet...

"I believe I already know what you like." He rose to his feet and approached me, gliding across the room. When he stood within arm's reach, he stopped. "Unless there is more."

Defiance rose within me, defiance and sarcasm, and for whatever reason, I allowed it to surface. I had to pretend to have more of a backbone than I'd shown him previously. I had to pretend to be strong around him.

"There's always more."

His eyes sparkled with excitement. "Tell me."

I said nothing. He bristled, and I found myself wondering if he'd react how I wanted.

"Tell me," he said, more firmly than before.

I remained silent.

Without warning, Michele snatched me by the throat. He spun me, pinning my back to his chest and enveloping me with ease.

My breathing became shallow, and my pulse raced. The shock of the action vibrated through me, and I knew in an instant that I was in the best kind of trouble.

I clutched at his arm, holding it tight, but in no rush to pull it away. Michele nuzzled the crook of my neck, his short beard scratching at my skin.

"Tell me." He cooed the words. "Do you like this?"

"Yes."

While his hand remained around my throat, the other glided into my hair where he tenderly fisted my locks. I struggled to catch my breath, swimming in anticipation.

"Do you like pain?"

"Yes."

No sooner than I'd uttered the word did he react. Michele pulled my hair, snapping my head back and causing me to bite down on a cry of pleasure. He growled in my ear before raking his teeth along the slope of my neck.

I reached up and cradled him to me, unable to keep the longing sigh to myself. While I kept him close, the hand on my throat descended to my chest. Michele groaned as he engulfed my breast. A whimper escaped me at the pleasure of being touched. Meanwhile, his cock pressed against the small of my back. There had been comfort in knowing that I wasn't alone in the moment.

My thin cotton bra put up no protection against his demanding touch. While he rolled my breasts in his hand, kneaded and massaged them, my nipples beaded. The moment they pressed against my shirt, Michele found a new focus. Each pinch, each brush of a finger over them, caused my hips to roll and grind against his cock.

"Tell me your rules, *bella*," he whispered, "so that I may play your game."

My refusal until that point had been for multiple reasons, but the longer Michele touched me, the more he plucked at the strings of my sanity and played into everything I had always craved, the harder it became for me to say nothing. A human being could only deny their wants for so long.

The words bubbled within my throat, ready to come to the surface when a commotion reminded us both of the real world. With his back to the doors leading out, Michele protected what we were doing from sight for the few seconds it took for me to slip out of his hands. I could have sworn I heard him growl in displeasure.

Someone spoke to him, but I didn't bother turning around to see who. Instead, I retreated to the shadows of the yacht to collect myself.

Chapter Six

On a charter, there were no days off. The staff was at the mercy of the clients, so instead of days off, there were staggered shifts. But every once in a while, the passengers wanted to dock for a day or two, which was the closest thing the crew got to a weekend.

When that happened, we tended to barter. We would trade hours among ourselves like cigarettes in prison.

I'll take two hours of overnight if you give me two hours midday.

If done right, a person could get a nice chunk of free time at prime hours to experience the world outside the yacht, to set foot on dry land. And Ryan might have been an amazing chef, but sometimes you just had to experience the local cuisine.

There was no substituting real life.

"C'mon, c'mon, c'mon!"

Kennia raced through our bunk like a whirlwind, a mini tornado of energy that threatened to sweep everything away.

"Calm down. Just give me a second." I couldn't help but giggle at her.

Kennia spun on her heel and stared me down in spite of having to look up.

"I've only got four hours, alrigh'. I'm not wastin' 'em."

"Really?" Rather smugly, I added, "I've got all day." *If looks could kill.*

Kennia stared at me, narrowing her eyes. The usually kind, soft-brown color of them had noticeably darkened.

"How the hell'd you manage that?"

My smugness faltered a bit. "I *may* have to work twelve hours straight."

"*Pft*, ha!"

I didn't think it was possible for a person to laugh as hard as she did in that moment. Her sides should have split open, but it didn't bother me. I got to spend all day in Hvar, Croatia, a place I'd never been and without that job would never go to.

And I would be away from Michele.

After our interlude in the dining room, it'd become more and more clear that nothing good would happen when we were alone. The rules I lived by, the ones that kept me from being fired and blacklisted in the stewarding world, were morphing into guidelines, and if I kept too close to the man, they'd become nothing more than faint remnants, thoughts that were easily dismissed.

I had to put distance between the Italian Adonis and myself. Jesus Christ, one might've mistaken me for a simpering little girl whenever he was around and, honestly, it didn't feel like that was far from the truth.

So I negotiated my ass off. I would worry about the exhaustion and consequences later.

* * * *

There were no words to describe Hvar. The moment I set foot on shore, I understood why so many wealthy people and celebrities visited.

Kennia's schedule made me laugh, but I understood it, too. She had a few hours to experience the island during the day, and she intended to do so to the fullest.

The beaches were first on the itinerary.

When she sported a white bathing suit that glowed against her dark skin, there hadn't been a pair of eyes Kennia didn't draw in. But she couldn't have cared less, more than content to lie in the sun on the warm sand.

In the years since I'd worked on a yacht, I'd lost the tan I once had. As a result, I bathed myself in sunscreen before joining her on a towel of my own. I remembered hearing as a kid that there was a scientific reason for why sunlight felt so good to lie in, but I couldn't remember what it had been. Perhaps a vitamin of some sort.

For a couple of hours, we played in the sand, the sun and the sea, until the time allotted had come to an end. Next came town. The moment she found out where we would be docking, Kennia had researched the perfect place to eat then shop.

After a delicious lunch and watching Kennia attempt to politely reject a young man who didn't speak English, we went shopping.

A dozen small shops lined the streets. Some sold dinnerware and fancy champagne flutes. Some sold outrageously colored clothing, some artwork and jewelry. There appeared to be something for everyone and the perfect place for souvenirs.

Kennia and I spent her last hour picking up things for family and friends. I did my best to get something for my sisters and mother when I traveled, a little trinket to let them know I was thinking about them. I found something for myself, too. An abstract painting of a woman's face had been too pretty for me to pass up.

Back on the ship, I did my best to stow my things while Kennia got dressed for her shift. She looked so disappointed. I would have traded some of my hours, but I had no idea how to do her job. She could've slid into mine easily, I had no doubt, but what did I know about working on the technical side of a yacht? *Jack shit.* There were cranks and release valves and gauges, things that could cost hundreds of thousands of dollars to fix if done wrong. I didn't feel like sinking the boat or making something explode.

Wearing a dress of the non-leather variety, I gave myself a final once-over in the mirror to make sure my makeup hadn't shifted and that my dark hair remained wavy. Curls were impossible. 'Braid waves' were the best I could manage.

"Right, then," Kennia muttered. I turned to see her staring at me despondently. "Well." She clicked her heels together, standing straight-backed and saluting me. "Godspeed, soldier. Have a drink for me."

I snorted a laugh and pulled her into a hug. "It's okay," I said in a mocking voice. "I won't do anything you wouldn't do."

She scoffed as we parted and gave me a look that said *that's a lie*. I winked at her and left.

* * * *

The nightlife in Hvar had surprised me more than it should have. Logically, of course they had clubs and a thriving entertainment district. Given the high-profile people who vacationed there, why wouldn't they? I had no idea why it shocked me.

A few of the crew members who'd bargained that night off and I danced to our hearts' content. There'd even been some alcohol, but we weren't stupid. No one could call in sick the following day, so we didn't go overboard.

Sweat trickled down the side of my neck, tickling the baby hairs. I'd been dancing for so long that I needed a break. I was hot, flushed and my feet had begun to hurt an hour prior. I made sure the others knew I was walking away before I stepped outside so no one would worry, assuming they noticed I'd left at all.

The ocean breeze hit me right in the face the second I was outside. The coolness of it brought immediate relief. Taking hold of the railing, I closed my eyes and relished it.

But I couldn't have been standing there for ten minutes before the air shifted. Opening my eyes, I spotted a stranger. He approached me, a smile on his lips. When he spoke, I couldn't understand a single word of it.

"Oh, I'm sorry. I don't speak..." My words fell away. I didn't know what the official language of Croatia was, but it didn't seem to matter.

"American, eh?" he asked in a very, *very* thick accent. I nodded. "Eh!" He happily held his arms out to the side, as though excited about the prospect. "How do you find Hvar?" he asked as he stepped closer.

"It's beautiful."

"Very romantic city, yes." He stood beside me, shifting to look out at the sea. He was closer than I would have liked, but I tended to give people the benefit of the doubt, especially when our cultures varied. "The sea is lovely, yes?"

He motioned toward the water. My gaze drifted. A decent amount of the bay had been visible from the club. The city lights glittered across the water and not far from the shore had been the dock where *The Silver Wind* was anchored, though there were far too many yachts for me to pick it out of the group at night.

As we stood, me content in the silence, something touched me. His hand. It began at the base of my back then slowly, but surely, descended farther. I became rigid and turned my attention to him. He stared at me, a wide smile across his lips, which he promptly licked. I arched a brow, my brain struggling to comprehend the blatant groping.

"Romantic, eh?" he asked again, his voice lower than before. To my horror, he proceeded to squeeze my ass.

"Okay," I sighed as I righted myself. I slapped his hand away and stepped back. "I'm going back inside."

I hadn't taken two steps before he grabbed my wrist. When I looked at him again, the kind exterior had vanished. Cold, angry eyes stared at me. They didn't appear human anymore.

In the background, movement caught my attention. Two other men who hadn't been there before appeared from the shadows. Their dark clothing helped them blend in, and they shared an expression similar to the handsy guy.

This is bad. This is bad. This is so fucking bad.

"You come with me, yes?"

"Um, no."

Before he had the chance to react or I could think better of it, I reared back and swung. My fist made contact with his face, a sharp *crack* echoing in our immediate area.

It stunned him into letting me go and seemed to have a similar effect on the henchmen. I immediately dashed back inside, running as best I could with my heels on.

The crowd engulfed me, but I hardly felt safer for it. There would be no way for me to know whether or not the trio were human traffickers, but I had no intentions of finding out.

I found Kyle at the bar and told him that I was returning to the ship. I also warned him of the guys, telling him to not let anyone out of his sight, because there were creepers about. When I knew he understood the gravity of the situation, I left.

He might've called out for me to stay with the group, but over the music and my own nerves, I hadn't heard it.

Removing myself from the club would have been the best bet. I didn't want the creepers to see me with my friends. It might have been presumptuous, but I felt like them seeing me with the other crew would give them ideas, that they might try to use me to get to them — or them to get to me.

Brains concocted worst-case scenarios with a body full of adrenaline and weren't known for thinking clearly.

The moment I was out of the club, I slipped my heels off and clutched them tight. I wanted to be able to run or stab a bitch if I had to.

The streets weren't empty, for which I'd been grateful, though they didn't offer me any true comfort, either. Ten people spread out over two blocks wasn't much cover. But I kept my eyes peeled while my brisk walk continued down the path I'd taken to the club.

A few blocks away from the port, I began to relax. I let myself slip into a calm that I shouldn't have.

A shuffling came from behind and I dared a glance back. My blood ran cold. The three men from the club had been following me for who-knew-how-long. They'd gone still when I'd spotted them.

A tense moment passed between us then, as though someone had fired the starting gun at a race, we sprang into action.

I charged down the street, small pebbles and uneven cobblestones biting into the balls of my feet. The bones in each foot throbbed as they smacked against the ground, but I kept running.

Their grunting breaths grew louder and louder, their footsteps closer. Terror swept through me. At any moment I would be snatched up and taken somewhere, never to see my family or friends again.

Rounding a corner so quickly that I stumbled, I spotted something that made my heart leap. Perhaps fifty yards away were Michele and Dominic with one of the older men. I didn't know if he was Paulo or Vincent, and I didn't care.

I didn't have time to register the confusion across Michele's face while I ran for him, the wind stinging my eyes. His brows furrowed and his head cocked to the side as I raced toward them. Not a second later, his entire demeanor had changed. I could only assume he saw my pursuers.

The next few seconds happened faster than most.

When I reached Michele, I'd gained so much momentum going downhill that I couldn't stop. He held out an arm, catching me by my midsection. I might have taken him to the ground with me if he hadn't spun, defusing some of the energy in the process. He held me close while he faced the attackers again, a gun suddenly emerging from within his grasp. I didn't know where it'd come from, and if my nerves weren't tattered beyond repair, I might have been horrified that he had one, but in that moment, I couldn't have been happier.

The three creepers skidded to a stop and made sure to keep distance between them and the matte-black weapon Michele had leveled on them.

"Eh," the main creeper chuckled, panting from the run. "No worries, man. She is my girl. I need to take her home."

"No," Michele said firmly.

The creeper's expression hardened. While I clung to Michele, fisting his expensive silk shirt and trembling against him, Dominic spoke to his cousin. The Italian flowed between the three. I had no idea what they'd said, but their attitude toward the pursuers changed drastically. A second gun emerged, held by Mr. Grabby himself, Dominic.

"You should leave," he said. It'd been the first time I'd ever heard Dominic speak English. I didn't know he could.

The three grumbled to one another in their native tongue until realizing they didn't stand a chance and left. The tension lessened with each foot they put between us and them. When they disappeared, Michele and Dominic both lowered their weapons. Michele turned his attention to me.

"Are you all right?"

I nodded repeatedly, far more than what would've been acceptable, but I'd lost control over small actions.

"Yeah, no, fine," I said, still nodding like a bobble head. "I just, I need to um, I wanna..." I couldn't form a coherent sentence.

Michele stowed his gun in his waistband and covered it with his shirt. He spoke to the others and a reluctant agreement seemed to be reached.

"Come," he said, unlatching me from his side and taking my arm. "I will take you back to the ship."

"Yeah, sure, okay."

We walked in silence for some time. Michele didn't press me for details. He didn't berate me with questions. Instead, he held my arm in his and guided me back to the yacht.

I hadn't spoken until we were on the dock and a large gate separated me from the streets of Hvar.

"I'm sorry," I said.

He glanced down at me with his brows creased in confusion. "For what?"

"I didn't mean to interrupt whatever you guys were doing." My voice quivered. A lump had formed at some point, and it scratched while I spoke. Tears were close at hand as the gravity of the situation began to sink in, but I wanted to get everything out first. "I know I surprised you, but I was running and running, then I saw you and I was so glad because maybe they'd stop chasing me, but you were there with your family, and I didn't want to interrupt, but I didn't know what to do, so I ran for you and —"

During my rambling, the tears had come, and I began to cry. Reality had descended and I'd been forced to see how close I'd come to being hurt or worse. I only stopped speaking when Michele threw his arms around me, engulfing me in a tight embrace.

"Shh, shh, shh," he whispered while he hugged me.

I clung to him, shaking like a frightened rabbit and clutching his shirt once more. I struggled to breathe while I buried my face in his chest.

Michele threaded his fingers through my hair and cradled my head to him while he ran his other hand up and down the length of my back, doing his best to soothe me.

Minutes ticked by and my grip on his shirt lessened. Soon, I held him as tenderly as he did me. My breathing had calmed, too, and I was no longer shaking like I had been.

He rested his cheek on the top of my head, still caressing me when he spoke. "Do you feel better?"

I nodded and relaxed. He let me step out of his arms. Before I looked up, I was sure to wipe away the tears I knew I'd spilled.

Forcing a smile, I met his eye. "I'm fine."

Concern twisted his features. He didn't seem to believe me outright, which made me wonder what I must have looked like. Perhaps I hadn't removed as much of the fear as I thought I had.

Michele reached forward and swept his fingers down my cheeks, wiping away the tears I must have missed. His brow remained furrowed, and his eyes darkened with worry when he met my stare.

"Are you certain?"

I lied once more, "Of course."

"Hmm."

He didn't seem to believe me any more the second time, but he didn't press, either. Offering me his arm, I took it and together we finished our trek to the ship.

"Will you be all right on your own now?"

I smiled internally. He'd walked me to the ship. I stood less than six feet from the deck, and he remained concerned for my well-being.

"I'll be fine, yeah," I said. "Um, thank you, though. I really appreciate you walking me back."

A very sweet and kind smile formed across his lips. Michele took my hands in his and kissed my knuckles.

"*Buona notte*, Miss Hurst."

"Goodnight, Mr. Sacchi."

I turned and climbed onto the yacht. Glancing over my shoulder when I had, I'd expected to see Michele already making his way to land, but he hadn't moved. He remained where he was, his hands clasped behind his back as he watched me. He had waited to make sure I was all right.

Heat took my cheeks. I offered him a smile, a nod of the head, then disappeared through the door to the staff hallway. It passed a window as it descended. Through the small porthole, I saw Michele finally begin to walk away.

A wider smile than before touched my lips. Mr. Sacchi seemed a very sweet person, and there were no words to describe how grateful I'd been for him walking those streets. The reality of what might have happened otherwise didn't bear thinking about. I owed him a lot.

Chapter Seven

Coming home early the previous night had given me the chance for a few extra hours of sleep. Or, at least it would have had I been able to fall asleep. The truth was I couldn't, no matter how I'd tried. I'd remained pent-up and anxious over the *what-ifs* when it came to my run-in with the creepers.

By the time my shift came around at eleven o'clock that morning, I could have fallen asleep standing up. It didn't bode well for me.

But I did my job to the best of my ability. I smiled when the moment called for it, served the food and drinks without spillage and made sure that no one on the outside could see how utterly exhausted I'd become by three in the afternoon.

When given the chance for my first break, I ducked into an alcove where I was out of the way, set my alarm and dared to close my eyes. I didn't know I'd fallen asleep until someone woke me up.

My arms flailed and terror shot through me. As my vision cleared, I saw Chris standing a few feet back, his hands up and eyes wide in shock.

"Jesus," I sighed as I slumped in my seat. "You scared the shit out of me."

He chuckled. "Yeah, well, your alarm's been going off for a bit. Helped me find you."

"Shit, what time is it?" It'd been rhetorical so he hadn't replied. I found my phone and looked at the time. My heart sank. I'd been asleep for half an hour. My alarm must have been going off for nearly fifteen minutes, and I hadn't heard it. "Damn it."

I shot to my feet and raced by Chris, thanking him in passing for waking me up. His laughter followed me.

By the time I made it to the galley, the other stewards were already lined up. Mrs. Thorne had been in the middle of giving the rundown of what would happen for drinks and dinner. She noticed me right away, and I doubted she found the smile I plastered across my face convincing.

She didn't even pause and continued with the speech then dismissed us. Like the ballet we'd become over the last week or so, we went to work serving pre-dinner drinks. We glided through the clients, taking empty glasses and replacing them with the fresh. All the while, I stole glances at Michele.

He'd look in my direction, too—peer through his lashes while he attempted to remain in conversation or blatantly look at me. Each time, my heart would flutter. My opinion of him had begun to change after the previous night. I no longer saw him as *just* sexy or intimidating. He was now kindhearted as well. If anything, that only helped his initial allure.

* * * *

The night had been uneventful, seamless. Everything had gone as it was supposed to, which meant that I could devote my time to cleaning the main floor of the yacht. I had been left to myself to do so. The sheer square footage of the ship meant that we hardly saw the clients unless directly interacting with them or sought out. Being docked meant the likelihood of that had been reduced further. And yet...

I'd been in the middle of vacuuming the main living area, the one that overlooked the aft deck and shared space with the dining room, when Michele appeared in the hall. He hadn't materialized within the shadows as he tended to, which I appreciated.

Stepping on the power button, I turned the vacuum off.

"Good evening, Mr. Sacchi," I said politely. "Would you like me to leave?" He might have wanted to sit in the living room in peace.

"No." He shook his head and continued to approach.

"Is there anything I can get for you?"

He shook his head again and finally reached me in the center of the living room. His gaze danced over me for a moment.

"How are you feeling today?"

I blushed, the warmth taking my cheeks in an instant and roaming down my neck. The high collar of my shirt would prevent him from seeing my chest turning red, too.

"I'm fine," I replied. "But I don't know if I thanked you last night. I really appreciate you helping me out."

His eyes brightened with a smile that spread across his lips a second later. "You did," he said with a gentle head tilt. "And you are most welcome."

We lingered, neither offering the other anything in the way of conversation. Awkwardness seeped in, though I had no idea if he felt it, too. It could have been just me.

Then I spoke and I wished to hell I hadn't.

Just as Michele shifted to walk away, before he'd even rotated his body, I blurted out, "Do you still want to know my rules?"

The words flowed from me so quickly that they sounded like one.

When Michele turned to me once more, his eyes had darkened. He arched a brow.

My heart lodged itself within my throat. How could I have asked that? How could I have brought that up again?

It seemed that for every step forward Michele and I took toward having any kind of professional relationship, I would do something that set us a thousand steps back and closer to breaking every guideline there was to working on a yacht.

"Yes," he said, his voice having changed tone.

Well, you brought it up. Can't back out now, dumbass.

Michele waited patiently for me to overcome my internal struggle. I managed to reason with myself, though the argument had been lacking. Pretending that it was best he knew my rules so he wouldn't overstep meant nothing. In the end, it gave him the perfect blueprint of how to fuck with me if he so chose, and given our previous interactions, there had been no proof that he wouldn't choose to again.

"Okay, um, no marks I can't hide." *Might as well get right into it.* "I have to work, so I need to be able to cover up anything with clothes or makeup."

"Fair."

"If I say my safeword, you have to stop. Until that point, anything within reason is fair game."

"And what is your safe word?"

"Kumquat."

He blinked a few times and struggled to hide a grin but didn't succeed very well.

"Kumquat," he said monotone.

I nodded. "It's a funny word, and I like sour fruit."

"All right," he chuckled. "Anything else?"

"If I can't speak, you have to get my consent."

His smirk faded and a serious expression took over. "An example?"

"If we're doing something, then you gag me," I said, pausing when a shiver raced through me at the thought. "Then, if you're going to change it up, going to do something different, I just want you to make sure it's okay with me, first."

"Agreed," he said without hesitation. My relief had been immediate. For whatever reason, that seemed to be the one rule nearly every one of my partners either forgot...or *forgot*.

"Number Four is...protection is a must. No exceptions."

His wicked little smirk returned and mischief flickered in his eye. "Are you asking me to fuck you, Miss Hurst?"

Another wave of shivers tore through me so completely that I couldn't keep from visibly shuddering. To hear the words come from his mouth had been, without a doubt, one of the sexiest things I'd heard in a long time.

"And finally, Number Five." I chose to ignore his question. Somehow I knew he already had my answer. "No kissing."

His brows twitched together, and he cocked his head to the side. I couldn't tell if the rule surprised him or just confused him.

"It's too intimate," I said. "You kiss people you're in love with, not the people you play with."

Michele nodded in understanding.

I shifted in my spot, wringing my hands on the handle of the vacuum and doing my best to gain the courage to ask.

"What about you?"

Michele approached at a languid pace, casual in every sense of the word. I wondered if he'd done so to put me at ease or to fool me into thinking he had to consider his rules. If he had any, he knew them without question.

When he stood over me, he met my eye. "I haven't needed them, yet."

His answer shocked me. "Really?"

He nodded.

"So, you don't have any preferences?"

His smirk appeared once more. "I didn't say that. Tell me, *bella*. Can you be a brat?"

I arched a single brow. Everything in me tingled at the prospect. I hadn't met a good brat tamer yet, but if anyone had the makings, it would be Michele Sacchi.

"On a scale of one to ten."

He thought it over for a moment. "Perhaps, given the location, a five would be best."

Nodding, I replied, "I can be a five." Though, in reality, I could have easily been a ten, as well.

He smiled wide, either pleased with my response or already thinking of ways to test me.

"*Perfetto*," he said. "Good evening, Miss Hurst."

"Goodnight, Mr. Sacchi."

He walked away, disappearing down the hall and leaving me to do my work. Before another distraction could emerge, I turned on the vacuum and resumed my chores.

In the back of my mind, I wondered if the brat relationship would work on the ship. It might, but it might not. There were plenty of eyes on *The Silver Wind*, so I couldn't be outwardly rude to Michele. My teasing and taunting would have to be done in private, if possible.

The prospect excited me, though. Who didn't love a little bit of punishment for misbehaving?

Wait... Didn't I have rules about him? Guidelines?

Chapter Eight

Earlier that morning, Captain Gus took us from the Hvar port, and a small part of me had been grateful for it. When I woke up after the deepest sleep I'd ever managed on a ship, I found us anchored in the middle of the Adriatic Sea. Kennia told me that we weren't far from the coast of San Marino.

It'd been a normal morning until ten o'clock. A call went out over the walkie-talkies stating that we were expecting visitors. It wasn't uncommon for one yacht to hail another, but I hadn't anticipated what I saw.

Being ferried over from another ridiculous floating mansion was a small gaggle of young women and a very stern-looking older gentleman. His expression told me he'd long since reached his patience limit with them.

A couple of the deckhands met them at the sea deck and tied off the boat, helping everyone aboard. I had a sinking feeling that I couldn't quite identify, and it bothered me greatly.

The Gaggle could be heard long before they emerged. The young woman in the lead was incredible, absolutely stunning and clearly aware of the fact. Every bleached lock had been sprayed into perfect curls, her tan expertly contoured over her fit body, which she chose to show off with a bikini, and her makeup likely cost more than the whole of my on-board wardrobe.

Her friends appeared to be quite similar to her, though their hair had been less blonde so as not to detract from their leader's golden glow. To my mind, they seemed to be her background, her 'yes men'.

Why are there always three?

Michele and his group rose to meet the newcomers. Dominic seemed overjoyed, throwing his arms around Thing One's and Thing Two's necks and kissing them on each cheek. He hadn't been shy about grabbing their asses, either. Unlike the staff, they seemed to appreciate the attention.

Michele didn't share his cousin's exuberance but remained polite when the leader looped her arms around him and planted her painted lips on his. My brows rose before I could stop them, guided by the shock and agitation of seeing him kiss someone.

Stop it, stupid. He's not yours just 'cuz you've played together.

He cradled her waist as they parted after the brief kiss. She swooned against him, pressing her undoubtedly expensive breasts into his chest. I didn't like her, didn't like the kind of person I assumed her to be and her name didn't help matters.

"*Boungiorno*, Yasmin."

She beamed and giggled. "Hello, Mickey."

He winced at the nickname but forced a smile, regardless.

The elder gentleman approached the group, and the level of respect he received told me he was an important individual.

After being ignored for some time, we stewards were flagged down and drink orders were given. While the addition of four new bodies brought the total list of passengers to ten, *The Silver Wind* and her crew were more than capable of handling it. We could do our jobs.

Ten guests kept us on our toes, however, forcing us to weave in and out of one another as some brought drinks, others cleared them away and some of us brought snacks. We had become a team of dancers once again — but wearing much less impressive outfits.

Days like that would end who-knew-when, which irritated some of us, but there was nothing that could be done. We were at work, after all.

* * * *

My lunch break had been a nap, something to get me through the day because, much to my dismay, Yasmin and her flock were staying for a while. I had to prepare myself for more time around them.

I didn't outwardly hate the trio, but their personalities and mine clashed. They were bright and loud, showing off everything that they were and grabbing attention where they could. I'd always been a much more subdued person, less flashy. It wasn't their fault they irked me, so I would be polite, kind and bend over backward for them, regardless.

The three of them kept us busy. It became clear from the jump that Yasmin had been the sort of woman who had been handed everything in life. She had the attitude of a person who'd grown up not with a silver spoon in her mouth but with a platinum one. She barked orders, accepted no hesitation with delivery and seemed to delight in lording her power over the staff. I'd worked for a couple of people like that before. While most might ignore the worker bees, some enjoyed reminding them of their place on the ladder. Yasmin was one of those.

Mrs. Thorne had given me directions to make up two of the smaller cabins for Thing One and Thing Two. I'd have called them by their names, but no one seemed to know them. They were simply Yasmin's entourage.

I didn't like that I only had to make up two rooms. In the back of my mind, a voice told me that it meant Yasmin would be bunking with Michele. Given how she'd hung on him since her arrival, it seemed a fair assumption. It made me queasy, and I maintained that it had nothing to do with jealousy. It'd been because Yasmin was horrible, in spite of my lack of evidence.

Each of the rooms was given a quick turn down, the pillows fluffed and the mirrors polished. I dripped essential oil onto small pads and hid them beneath furniture in the corners of the rooms, allowing them to fill the spaces with a soft scent of roses, and I made sure the bathrooms were stocked with toiletries.

I spent an hour or better doing it, meticulous and careful because I had no doubt that they would find a staff member and yell about inadequate preparations.

Besides, I did actually enjoy my job.

When I left down the corridor, I'd nearly made it to the hidden staff stairwell that would take me to the below deck when someone grabbed me. The suddenness of it left me breathless as I was shoved against the wall and pinned in place.

Panting, I looked up into the dark eyes of Michele. He'd appeared from nowhere again, hiding in another room, waiting to grab me.

"Have you been avoiding me?" he asked in a gruff voice.

"No, sir," I replied, sure to instill the proper hesitation. I assumed he wanted to play.

He reached up and held my jaw. "I don't believe you."

I jerked out of his grasp, glaring at him when I said, "I don't care what you believe."

I'd barely had the chance to turn and take a step when he grabbed me again, much harsher than before. My heart skipped and my stomach filled with butterflies while he held my throat, pushing me into the wall like before. My pulse raced beneath his fingers.

"Did I say you could leave?" he asked through his teeth. I shook my head. "You will go when I say you can go." I nodded. "Say it."

"Yes,"

"Yes, what?"

"Yes, *Sir*."

"That's better." He cooed the words.

Still holding tight, he glided his other hand down my cheek and to my chest. He brought it up under my breast and squeezed hard. My breath caught in my throat.

He watched himself massaging me and pinching my nipple through the fabric. Running his bottom lip through his teeth, he squeezed me again.

"Your nipples are already hard," he said gruffly. Michele met my eye. "Doesn't take much, does it?"

He seemed willing to leap right into the game, and I had been just as willing to follow.

I didn't reply. As though testing his previous assumption, he reached for my other breast and gave it the same attention as the first. I gasped, and he grinned.

"I wonder, are you wet, *bella*?" he asked with a taunting tone.

Remaining as defiant as I could, I replied, "No."

I was.

Michele clicked his tongue and shook his head in disapproval. With his gaze locked to mine, he used a single hand to unbutton my shorts just like before. I remained motionless, my body vibrating with anticipation.

At an agonizing pace, he guided his hand beyond the waistband and beneath my panties. His jaw went lax, parting his lips on a breath. The instant he slid his digit across my folds and felt the dampness, Michele flinched. He curled his lips back while he fought a growl. I did my best to remain stoic, but I desperately wanted to fall apart.

"You're a *liar*," he said. "Do you know what I do to liars?" I shook my head. "I punish them."

His strong digit traced multiple circles over my clit, applying the perfect pressure, but moving at a slow, taunting pace. He continued to toy with me, to caress me without giving me the pleasure I craved. My pussy ached, my clit throbbing and begging for the relief that I hoped wouldn't come.

Michele leaned forward, his lips inches from my ear. His breath had become haggard, the heat of it rolling along my neck. My eyes drifted shut.

"But, if you are a good girl," he whispered, "then I will reward you." Michele crouched low enough that he could slide his middle and ring fingers inside me. He groaned in satisfaction. "So tight."

I shuddered when he bit my earlobe. My fists had been clenched so hard that my fingernails bit into my palms. The desire to reach out and touch him grew stronger than I could stand, but I had somehow managed to refrain.

It hadn't been that long since we had been in the same exact situation, tucked away in a hall with his hand in my shorts, yet what flickered between us in that moment was new. There was understanding to it, an agreement and knowledge. Gone was the uncertainty and the need to test the grounds. I'd told him exactly what I wanted, what I liked.

Michele thrust his fingers in and out of me at a slow pace, pressing the heel of his palm against my clit again and sending shocking jolts of pleasure through me. Seconds could have been hours for all I cared.

Anyone could have entered the corridor, could have found us with my back to the wall and Michele fingering me. It wasn't the middle of the night anymore, and there were newcomers to add to the number of possible witnesses, but that knowledge didn't instill the proper fear. Instead, it fanned my flames.

"Are you going to be my good girl, *bella*?" He'd begun to pant, each breath in time with his torturous actions.

"Yes,"

"Yes, *what*?" Unsatisfied with my answer, Michele plunged his fingers deep inside and guided me to the tips of my toes like before. The pressure of my over-sensitive clit grinding into his palm was near blinding.

My head fell back, and I struggled to breathe when I said, "Yes, Sir."

He made another sound of approval and lowered me. After I was able to stand on my own feet once more, he withdrew a bit. I opened my eyes. He stared at me with his beautiful lips parted, pink gracing his olive skin and his eyes like polished obsidian. He removed his hand from between my thighs. The pain of his absence came fast.

Michele stepped back and leaned against the adjacent wall. He grabbed his dick and squeezed it, groaning when he had. It must have hurt. My frustration did, so I hoped his did, too.

"Get on your knees," he said, still stroking himself aggressively enough to, perhaps, stave off the pain of his erection.

I leveled my stare on him, peering through my lashes when I did. It hadn't been difficult. Even slouching as he was, Michele stood taller than me.

"Why?"

His jaw tensed, the muscle rolling beneath his stubble. His breathing became harsh.

"Are you disobeying me?" he asked, arching a thick brow.

I said nothing, remaining defiant when I jutted my chin out.

A single step brought him from one side of the corridor to the other. In an instant, Michele had me by the throat again, pinning me to the wall. The tension had been perfect, just enough to remind me who was in control.

"I told you to get on your *fucking* knees."

"Why should I?" I asked again, delighting in the fact that I felt every word pass over the pressure of his fingertips.

He brought my face to his, our noses touching and his lips brushing across mine when he spoke.

"Because you're going to suck my cock here, in the hall."

I let out a trembling breath before I could bite it back.

"And, if you're a good girl and I like how your mouth feels, I'm going to take you to that room over there," he said, tilting his head to the side and motioning to the rooms I'd just cleaned. "And I'm going to fuck you so hard and so deep that they will hear you on the mainland."

I believed him. Christ, I believed him — and I wanted that.

"*Now*," he said, stepping back and shoving me against the wall for good measure. Michele regained his previous position across from me. "Get. On. Your. *Knees*."

I couldn't catch my breath, so consumed by the man that I would have done anything he asked.

Stare still locked to mine, Michele undid his belt. He slid the expensive leather out of the golden buckle and allowed the ends to fall uselessly to the side. His fingers made easy, but slow work of the button on his slacks.

My body finally remembered that I had feet and the ability to move. I took a step forward then another, closing the distance between us. The faint whir of his zipper caused my skin to prickle.

"Kneel."

I obeyed without question, lowering myself before him. My gaze never left his, locked to the intensity of it.

When my knees touched hard stone, movement drew my attention. He continued to squeeze his cock, to give it the slightest hint of contact, but ceased the moment I sat less than two feet from it. My throat had become dry, but my mouth watered, desperate to taste him. His dick fought against his clothing, and if it weren't caught behind his brilliant blue underwear, it might have managed to escape his trousers.

"Take it out." His voice no longer sounded human, tainted by something powerful.

I stared at him through my lashes, leaning close enough that his cock couldn't have been more than six inches from my lips. He clenched his jaw.

Reaching up, I touched his dick. It'd been nothing, a graze of my fingertips, yet his entire body twitched, and he sucked a sharp breath in through his teeth. He must have been in so much pain.

Harder than stone, his cock continued to twitch under my delicate touch, jumping as though desperate for more. Even through the thin cotton underwear, I could see the thick vein running up the length of his shaft, the bulbous, mushroom tip straining beneath the elastic band.

"You want me to suck your cock?" I asked, gliding my fingers up the whole of his length and delighting in how he tensed.

"Yes," he replied harshly. "Now, do it."

In spite of the inferno burning within me and the unwavering desire to do as he commanded, I was still me and needed a bit of my own fun first.

Leaning forward, I touched my lips to the straining fabric, placing a kiss to the sensitive spot just beneath the head. Michele threaded his fingers through my hair and fisted the locks at the crown of my head. I moaned and squeezed him harder. He whimpered. It was a delicious sound.

Using my hair as a guide, he brought my mouth back to his dick. I teased it, breathed hard enough that he could feel the heat through the fabric and stroked what I could in the meantime. Michele must have wanted to go through his skin, because in no time at all, his hips were moving against me.

I caressed and rubbed, massaged his balls, and traced a hard line down the vein. I would breathe against the fabric and let out small moans, all meant to tease him like he'd teased me.

A minute passed, perhaps two, before Michele hit his limit. He jerked my head back sharply and pulled me up, no longer sitting on my knees, but unable to rise from them.

"You think this is a joke?"

I took hold of his hips and pressed my breasts against him. The corner of his eye twitched and his focus shifted. When he'd yanked me up onto my knees, he'd ensured that my breasts were crushed against his cock.

"I never said that," I said in a soft voice. "Why would I think this is funny?"

I pushed his shirt up his lean torso with one hand, revealing his tanned, toned body beneath while the other glided up his back so I could hold him close.

"Do you think I'm so cruel?" I whispered.

When I put my parted lips to his toned stomach, Michele flinched when I darted my tongue forward. I placed a tender kiss to the spot a second later.

"That I'm so mean?"

Dragging my mouth to his hip, I noticed the way both of his hips moved on their own. I doubted he was aware that he'd begun grinding into my breasts, begging for the slightest contact.

I raked my teeth along his skin just above his hipbone. Michele growled and tightened his grip in my hair.

"That I am so vicious?"

I bit down hard and the sound that left him could only be described as a roar behind closed lips. It had been subdued, yet powerful and devoid of pain.

His second hand joined the first in my hair, pinning my forehead against the trembling muscles of his stomach. His breathing had become shallow, frantic. With both hands beneath his shirt, I dug my fingernails into his back and dragged them down the length. He continued to rub his cock against my chest.

I kissed his stomach, bit and nipped it. He sighed and groaned, his hips moving with long, deep thrusts, desperate for further contact. Running my tongue up his abs, I delighted in the way they quaked beneath it.

Until, without warning, Michele had gone still.

I peered up at him. He'd thrown his head back, panting and groaning. He shook and, with a deep sigh, he slumped against the wall. No words needed. It was clear what'd happened.

His grip loosened, giving me the chance to draw back farther. Michele, once the fog in his mind had cleared, looked down at me. His brows creased, his lips parted as he regained his breath. He seemed confused as to how he'd managed to come in his pants.

With a strange sort of reverence, he cradled my cheek, trailing his thumb across my lips. It was a sweet moment for reasons many probably wouldn't have understood.

When I attempted to stand, he released me and helped. Michele stared. While my pussy continued to pulse and ache, my head remained clear enough to enjoy his expression.

"Is everything okay?" I asked.

Michele, whether out of habit or desire, zipped up and buttoned his slacks to be more presentable. I did the same.

"That's never happened before," he said.

I fought the urge to laugh. That was an excuse I'd heard many times before. Most straight women probably had. Gay men, too.

"At least, not since I was very young." His smile faded in an instant, as though he didn't have the energy to keep it long. "How did you do that?"

I arched a brow at the question. As far as I was concerned, I'd done little to nothing. True, the things I'd done helped him along, but Michele's mind had done the rest. He was the one who'd worked himself into a frenzy, the one who'd clawed his way to the cliffs of an orgasm. I'd just shoved him over the edge.

Silence stretched between us for some time until I spoke again.

"Is there anything I can help you with, Mr. Sacchi?"

He chuckled, running his bottom lip through his teeth while he looked me over.

Before he could open his mouth to speak, Yasmin bounded into the hall and froze the moment she spotted us. Michele and I looked over at her. I couldn't say whether she'd tried to hide her irritation or not, but if she had, she'd failed.

Arching a perfect brow, she planted her hands on her hips and leveled her eye on Michele. She may have intended to intimidate him. If so, she had failed at that, too.

When Michele stepped away from me, he did so without the slightest hint of urgency.

"What is this?" Her voice had been stern and filled with agitation, and her accent much thicker than his.

"None of your concern," he replied. "Come along."

Michele walked by her, but Yasmin made no attempt to follow. She continued to stare at me, to glare, until Michele grabbed her arm and forced her to join him.

They were gone a moment later, but I couldn't shake Yasmin's stare. It held a special kind of anger, the kind that people who weren't used to hearing 'no' had when someone finally said it.

It probably didn't bode well for me.

Chapter Nine

It surprised no one that dinner ended up being an elaborate display. Seven courses had been set on the menu, which meant frequent drink and plate changes. Every steward was called onto shift, regardless of whether or not we were meant to be. Mrs. Thorne needed everyone.

The first three courses had been served and the fourth was on its way up. I'd glided around the twelve-person table taking everyone's plates and almost had the tenth and final plate in my hand when it happened.

The initial attempt had gone mostly ignored. Having spent years at sea, I prided myself on being able to carry expensive breakables, sometimes on trays, while the ship rocked and swayed. While far from being an expert, I could manage. What I could not survive, however, was someone angrily kicking me in the shin.

Yasmin's first try had been avoided because a toe could do little to break my concentration. Dissatisfied, she became vicious the second time around.

She had spun in her seat when my tray was full and very pointedly smashed the side of her thousand-dollar shoe into my shin while simultaneously standing. So, unprepared for it, I stumbled and never recovered.

Leftovers sprayed my face while the tray went flying. A chorus of smashing glass was followed closely by the angry clank of metal hitting the deck. I froze in place, unable to open my eyes. Horror and carnage awaited me should I dare.

Yasmin began to curse in Italian. While I didn't speak a lot of languages, angry cursing could somehow be recognizable, no matter the tongue.

Something wet trailed down my face and something savory touched my lips. After a long, deep breath, I forced myself to inspect the damage. Every glass, plate and piece of silverware rested at my feet, very little of which had survived the fall. My clothes were covered in food, some of it being the brilliant red sauce Ryan had made to adorn the salad.

"What is your problem?" Yasmin's shrill voice sliced through my growing anger.

The model-esque woman stood with her hands on her hips and, in spite of the rage in her voice, a smirk played at her painted lips. If further proof were needed that she'd planned the entire thing, it would have been that smirk.

"What do you have to say for yourself?" she asked with a spite-filled voice. "Huh?"

I took another deep breath and let it out before plastering a wide, hopefully believable smile across my face.

"I am so sorry, ma'am. I will, of course, clean this up immediately."

She scoffed at me and turned her attention back to those she'd arrived with. The string of Italian that left her lips while I picked up the multiple pieces of broken dinnerware let me know that she was mocking 'the help'. Call it a gut feeling.

I'd begun to shake, so, as fast as I could manage, I gathered up the spilled cutlery, food and dinnerware, and placed it on the tray. Chris slid into my line of sight before I stood with a rag and bottle of cleaning solution in his hands. He offered me a sad smile, which I returned.

He went about cleaning the goop off the deck, and I left. I don't know if I had ever made the trip below deck as fast as I did that moment.

"Fucking bitch," I growled through my teeth as I dumped the porcelain into the trash.

"What's up?"

Kyle and Kennia were sat at the table eating. They must have been on break.

In my anger, I hadn't noticed them, despite walking right by the pair.

"Oh, man," Kennia mumbled as she looked over my top. "Wha' happened?"

I squared myself on them and, far meaner than I should have, I told them.

"That Barbie reject whipped out of the seat, kicked me in the leg, then shot up, shoving the tray into my face."

Kennia winced and Kyle let loose a low whistle. A sarcastic nod had been the extent of my answer, afraid that I would unleash my ire if I continued to speak.

I went back to cleaning off what I could, angry that I would have to replace the broken dishes with my own paycheck. Chris bounded downstairs seconds later.

"You all right, sweetheart?" he asked.

"Yeah, fine," I grumbled. "What the hell is that chick's problem? She's been a bitch ever since she set foot on the boat."

"You serious?" he asked with a chuckle. I shrugged in response. "That Michele guy's been staring at you since he boarded. She doesn't like it. I think they've got a thing"

"Or she wants one." Kyle added with a laugh of his own.

I blushed and mumbled under my breath that he was wrong, then left before he or the others could continue teasing. I hadn't given Chris enough credit before. It seemed he was more perceptive than I thought, and the last thing I needed was to give him or, God forbid, Kennia any further evidence that many 'somethings' had already transpired between Michele and me.

* * * *

The red sauce hadn't come out of the top as much as I'd hoped, but on many levels I hadn't been surprised. It was red. My shirt was not.

I scrubbed it as well as I could within my sink, and, to be quite honest, I'd done a decent job, all things considered. I could only pray that the pink was washed out with the proper amount of bleach. Otherwise, it would leave a noticeable stain. However, that meant I had to wear my orange shirt a day early and would have to wear it again the following day just to be on the proper schedule. The staff were supplied with single uniform pieces, not doubles, should anything happen.

With a heavy sigh, I left my shirt in the sink to continue soaking and went to retrieve the traffic-cone-orange one. While I sifted through my closet, there came a knock at the door.

"Yeah?" I called out, expecting Kennia to be the one to enter.

I was wrong.

Michele seemed frozen where he stood, his gaze fixed to my chest and door half opened. My bra had been nothing special, simple white fabric meant for support, not to titillate, but he reacted as though he'd never seen so much of my skin before, which was false. And as much as I might have enjoyed the ogling any other time, I was not in the mood.

"Yes?" I asked while I went back to my closet.

"I wanted to see if you were all right."

Part of me had been curious as to how he'd managed to find my bunk, only to remember I had friends in the galley. Kennia, ever so helpful, had probably told him where I'd gone. That little tidbit allowed me to seat myself within my anger once again. The mystery was solved.

"You shouldn't be here." I retrieved my shirt and yanked it off the hanger, causing the piece of plastic to slam into the closet wall harder than I'd meant it to. "I don't want to be rude, but I am *really* pissed off, and if you stick around, I'm afraid I might take it out on you, so please just go."

Threading my arms through the shirt, I tugged it on, expecting the Italian to have gone in the meantime. Instead, Michele stepped deeper into the room and was in the process of sliding the door closed behind him.

His gaze remained fixed to me, staring through his lashes in that sexy, intimidating way. My bunk was small, but Michele made it look downright cartoonish, looming over his surroundings like some kind of dark deity.

"You wish to punish someone?"

My back straightened while I took a deep breath. Hearing those words sparked that *thing* inside me, but the problem was I didn't know if I could be respectful. In that moment, my mind had become too clouded, too rattled, for me to stay in control of my actions. I ran the risk of hurting him and I didn't want that.

"Then do it."

I clenched my jaw. "You should go."

Michele stepped closer. "I said, do it."

"You don't—"

"Do it." He snapped at me, causing my insides to jump.

"Mr. Sacchi."

"*Do it!*"

A sharp crack filled the space. Shock swelled within me in an instant, an almost overwhelming sensation that left my heart racing and me struggling to take in breath.

Michele's head rested to the side under the force of my slap, but he said nothing. Instead, as his cheek tinted pink beneath his stubble, he returned his gaze to me.

"Is that the best you've—?"

I hadn't given him the chance to finish the taunting statement, bringing my left hand across the other side of his face just as hard as the first. Michele growled. His breathing became labored while he quivered. Something had ignited inside him, something dangerous that shone through his eyes when he met my gaze again.

Encouraged and grateful for the outlet, I couldn't help myself.

Planting my hands against his chest, I shoved Michele back, hard. He hit the door with a grunt, and I was on him a second later. Threading my fingers through his hair, I tugged on his locks, jerking his head to the side. Michele again let loose a sultry, delicious groan. He reached for me, cradling my hips and digging his fingertips in while I bit into his neck.

Michele ran his hands up my back, sliding them beneath my untucked shirt, then raking his blunt fingernails down my flesh. Shivers tore through me at the sting of it.

When I withdrew, I didn't go far, still brushing my lips against his. He'd become tense and rigid, and seemed unwilling to move. That feeling, that power, remained something I had enjoyed since discovering the BDSM world. His pleasure relied fully and completely on me...again.

"Goodbye, Mr. Sacchi."

I bit his bottom lip, dragging it between my teeth when I stepped away from him.

Michele struggled to open his eyes, but when he did, they were blacker than ink. Filled with unanswered lust, they made him appear inhuman, and I loved it. My mind flashed back to a few hours prior, to the pair of us in the hall when he had been given satisfaction and I had not.

His breathing remained ragged, but he'd closed his mouth, clenching his jaw so tight that I wondered if it hurt. And while I adored every second of his torture, I wasn't in the frame of mind to fully capitalize on it.

People on the outside tended to think that anger would help in BDSM, but no. *God no.* One of the first things I had learned when exploring my kinks was to never *ever* bring anger into the bedroom. It would only hurt the partner.

A bit of lighthearted hazing could be just what the doctor ordered, however.

I turned my attention to Michele, shedding the 'level five brat' I'd been before and wrapping myself in a solid level eight, perhaps nine.

"What's the matter?" I asked. "A little *tense*?"

In a rough tone, he said, "You will not leave me this way."

His voice mirrored the look in his eyes. I had to fight a shudder.

I arched a challenging brow and kept my voice sweet. "What way?"

Instead of verbally replying, he snatched me by the wrist and planted my open hand firmly against his dick. It flinched beneath my palm, so hard that I could have sworn I'd touched warm stone instead. My pussy craved it the longer I held him, begging to have it inside. I'd been closer to allowing it than I cared to admit.

I mean, it's been a couple of hours, but holy shit. How's he this hard again?

"Like this." He forced the words through clenched teeth. "You will not leave me like this."

"Oh," I cooed and began to stroke him through his trousers.

Michele's jaw finally relaxed, and his eyes rolled back into his head. He swallowed another groan when I squeezed him. He sank into the pleasure I chose to give him, well aware of what I was capable of doing with minimal effort.

Michele fell deeper and deeper into my touch, straddling the line between submission and control. Leaning forward, I pushed myself up onto my toes so that I could whisper in his ear.

"I can leave you however I want," I said. "And you can't do shit about it."

His muddled brain offered me the chance to back away. I retreated to the bathroom to finish cleaning myself up while he came to.

Michele turned an angry, almost hateful eye to me, staring at me through the reflection of the mirror. He'd become mindful of the fact that I had no intention of finishing him off a second time.

"Is that what you think?"

And I said the brattiest thing I could think of at the time. "You're not the boss of me."

Flames flickered in his eyes, and they weren't fueled by frustration. Some thing, some wicked thing, had crossed his mind.

"You will pay for this."

My stomach fluttered, but I said nothing. I arched a brow and was sure to appear as though I'd been unaffected by the threat. Michele cast me an evil sneer before he left.

When he'd gone, I relaxed.

Everything within me screamed to call him back so we could finish what we'd started. I genuinely ached for him, but that was the point. I loved the sexual frustration. Half the time it remained better than the actual sex, and I had no intentions of giving it up just yet.

I couldn't wait to see what punishment he had in mind.

Chapter Ten

By the time midnight rolled around, I'd been on shift for fourteen hours. I was ready to take a shower and go to bed, exhausted from the day's events. I just wanted to rest!

The Barbie triplets hadn't stayed the night. They might as well have. They'd left half an hour prior, and that had been at the urging of their curmudgeonly guardian. They made it obvious that they would've preferred staying.

I rinsed my dishes, cleaning off the remnants of my dinner, the only meal I'd had since my shift began. Someone's heavy, clomping footsteps echoed to my right where the stairs sat. Chris appeared a second later.

"Headin' to bed?" he asked with a light laugh.

"Shower...then bed."

Chris smiled and nodded in agreement until something seemed to cross his mind.

"Oh! No, you can't."

I narrowed my gaze, my internal voice warning him not to give me a task.

"Mr. Sacchi wants you to bring him some more towels."

"Which Mr. Sacchi?" Being related, most of them shared a surname.

"The tall one." A smirk twisted his lips. "The one that keeps eyin' you."

My stomach curled at the mention of Michele. The excuse had been shit. He wanted me alone so he could dole out whatever punishment he'd finally decided on. He hadn't been given the chance all day. I'd gone out of my way to avoid him since he'd left my bunk.

Maybe it'd been just to piss him off a little more, but I'd never admit it to anyone.

"He say how many?" I asked, attempting to keep my voice level.

"Nah." Chris shook his head. "Night."

"Night."

He disappeared down the hall toward his bunk. My heartbeat quickened and my thoughts became frantic, but first things first. I needed towels.

* * * *

By the time I made it to his door, I'd begun to shake. No matter how I tried to steady myself, I had no doubt of what awaited me on the other side of the barrier.

After a few deep breaths, I knocked. Michele called for me to enter.

He stood in the center of the room, his arms crossed and an unreadable expression marring his perfect face. He glanced at the pair of towels I held then jerked his head toward the bed.

"Set them down there."

I did as he said and laid them on the foot of the California King, all the while wondering if and when he planned to attack. I didn't have to wait long. No sooner than I'd placed the towels on the mattress did he loom behind me.

"Give me your belt."

The strange command took a moment to sink in. "What?"

He had a hold of the back of my neck in an instant, clasping it in his strong fingers. I gasped while a bolt of pleasure shot down my spine. I became rigid.

Michele nuzzled into the crook of my neck, his mouth centimeters from my ear.

"Give me your belt."

I did as I was told and unfastened it. Still unable to look behind me, I handed it to him over my shoulder.

"*Bene*," he said.

He took the strip of leather and remained close — but removed his hand from my neck.

"Tell me, *bella*," he said. "When was the last time you were whipped?"

I turned on my heel. Michele had been in the process of folding my belt in his large hands. He peered at me through his lashes, a wicked glint shimmering in his eyes. It'd been the same fire when he was in my bunk. He must have been thinking about his plan for hours.

Seconds went by without an answer. I couldn't find the words, and the prospect of being spanked by Michele again had short-circuited my brain.

Michele snapped my belt at me, filling the room with the crack of leather against leather and causing me to jump.

"Remove your shorts and bend over the edge of the bed."

"What?" I don't know how I'd managed to speak. I'd thought the lump of excitement growing in my throat would've made it impossible.

His response had been another harsh snap of my belt.

I complied faster than I normally would have, unbuttoning my shorts and sliding them down in front of a man I barely knew, yet somehow desired more than I thought possible. And that knowledge, or lack thereof, hadn't stopped me. If anything, it made the moment more exciting.

Once past my hips, my shorts fell to the floor uninhibited. Michele said nothing while he twirled his index finger, a silent command for me to turn around. I did.

Panties would have done nothing to stop the thin leather. A thong, the garment I'd chosen to wear that day, would do even less and ensured my ass remained bare.

I bent forward. My heart racing and body tingling, I planted my hands against the mattress, resting at a perfect angle.

And there I stood for one minute, two and perhaps even three. The soft, steady tick of a clock's second hand remained the only sound, the only indicator of passing time. I'd been bent over for so long that I began to question whether or not he intended to do anything at all.

Crack!

The belt struck my ass hard, sending biting pain down the backs of my legs. It stole the air from my lungs and made drawing in a breath almost impossible. The shock of it, the pain of it, caused me to vibrate with immediate pleasure.

He'd been as methodical in his delivery as I remembered and waited long enough for a welt to form before he brought the belt down again. The muscles in my legs trembled and my arms gave out. Soon my chest was pressed against the bed, my ass left high in the air and prime for spanking.

Again and again, and again, Michele lashed me, adding layers to the pain. I'd buried my face in the blanket, refusing to cry out, to give him the satisfaction of knowing he had begun to break me. I would hold out for as long as possible.

I gasped when he ran the flat of his hand over the curve of my ass. Any other time, it might have been too delicate to notice, but with my skin inflamed and raw, it might as well have been a thousand needles.

"Are you ready to apologize?" he asked in a voice that told me he was more than prepared to keep going.

I didn't reply. Instead, I focused on steadying my breathing while he touched me.

"You're lucky you wear shorts." His hand traveled further south. Michele sucked in a sharp breath when he massaged the backs of my thighs reverently. "These would be lovely red and pink."

He continued to rub my legs, to pinch and squeeze them in his large hand. My eyes drifted shut while he traced a line up the back of my thigh at an agonizing pace.

"Spread your legs, *bella*." His voice had become rich and thick.

I complied, parting them as best I could with my shorts clinging to my ankles. Without the slightest hesitation, he slid his fingers between my thighs and groaned. I gasped as they glided across my folds, aided by the excitement he'd caused.

Michele said something I couldn't understand, a string of Italian that rolled from his tongue. With only the tone to guide me, I assumed that he was happy and turned on.

I sank into the sensation of his digits and bucked when he grazed my clit. Michele let out a sinister chuckle. Setting my belt down on the bed beside me, he held my hip in place and went to work.

Keeping his fingers in the perfect position, Michele devoted all his attention to my clit. It'd been so deprived, so neglected, that the slightest affection nearly caused my eyes to cross.

"Oh, God," I moaned, burying my face into the comforter.

Spurred on by my response, his actions increased. My world spun, and my toes curled within my shoes.

"Don't stop." My resolve was crumbling, taking with it my ability to stay silent.

"Does it feel good, *bella*?" he asked while he increased his affection.

"Yes," I whimpered. Becoming consumed in the sensation, my hips began to gyrate, meeting him in stride. "So good."

He groaned once more, another happy, approving sound that I found I needed to hear. I liked that I pleased him with my reaction. Loved it, in fact. And he reciprocated by focusing all his affection on my sensitive bud.

But as I lost myself, as I reached the crest of an orgasm, he retracted his hand.

I couldn't keep my disappointment to myself, my protest loud enough for him to hear. Michele didn't seem bothered, leaning over me to whisper into my ear.

His slacks scraped the raw flesh of my ass, sending new sparks of pain racing up my spine.

"I need both hands to punish you," he said. Taking hold of my wrist, he guided my hand between my legs, slipping my fingers beneath my panties. He let out a contented sigh while we worked in tandem. "You do not."

Michele stepped back once again, leaving me to myself. I had no intentions of stopping, more than willing to bring about my own ends, though I would have preferred he be the reason.

"*Tre* more should do it, yes?"

He gave me no chance to answer before the belt sliced across my backside again. I panted, struggling to take in one breath after another. My legs ached, desperately begging me to either sit down or stand upright, and all the while my fingers continued to stroke. The intense pain and pleasure swelled inside me.

He whipped me again. I whimpered and my hand moved faster. While I was panting and struggling to reach the end, he brought the belt down one final time across my ass. The sharp pain caused my clit to throb. I'd been so close.

"Don't stop," I muttered, my free hand clutching at the blanket.

Michele said nothing as he slapped me again. I cried out.

Fuck, so close!

"Again," I begged.

He obliged. My hand moved even faster.

"Again!"

Michele brought the belt against my skin harder than he had previously, and it'd been enough. The sound that escaped me could have only been considered a wail of pleasure, so unexpected and loud that I bit down on the comforter to silence myself.

Blinding ecstasy surged in every vein. My heart wanted to explode within my chest and breathing had become all but impossible.

I shivered and trembled, squeezing my thighs together as I rode the waves of euphoria. My legs gave out, and unable to support my weight, I crumbled to the floor, dragging the blanket down with me.

There was no way for me to know how long I sat there, left reeling with tears welling in my eyes.

At some point, strong hands lifted me to my feet, and I somehow found enough balance to stand. Michele squatted down and tugged my shorts up. He was tender as he moved, but when he reached my ass, he placed a playful bite on my right cheek. It'd been lusciously cruel and forced a hiss through my teeth.

When the shorts rested on my hips once more, I buttoned them and turned to face him. He stared down at me with an expression stuck between excited, frustrated and sympathetic. I could tell he wondered if he'd gone too far.

Eyes locked, I reached for my belt, which he freely gave, and as I threaded it on, I smirked at him. The wave of relief had been subtle but softened his entire demeanor.

After I'd buckled my belt and tucked my shirt back in, I blinked the tears out of my eyes. They'd gathered during the spanking and were finally given the chance to fall. With the back of his curled index finger, Michele swept the trails away.

"Goodnight, Mr. Sacchi."

He smiled, placing his hands into his pockets as he stepped back. *"Buona notte, tesorina mia."*

I stared at him, wondering what he'd said to me and whether or not he planned to tell me. I recognized *goodnight*. He'd said it often enough, and it resembled the same in other languages, but I didn't know what *tesorina* meant.

I should get a translation app.

When I left his suite, I couldn't keep a smile from my lips. Never had I ever experienced something like that. And unfortunately for Michele, he'd made me crave it. My demands would only grow. He had better be prepared.

Chapter Eleven

Lying on my stomach, I stared at my phone, willing the hours to roll back. I had trouble sleeping again. My habit was to sleep on my back. Hard to do after a whipping.

The memory made me tingle all over, but I still didn't have the desire to get up.

The door to my bunk slid open and Kennia emerged, coming off her nightshift and ready for bed. She spotted me, and I saw the agitation that crossed her face.

"Lazy ass," she said as she closed the door behind her. "What you doin' in bed, hmm?"

"I got shit for sleep." It wasn't a good excuse, but it'd been the truth.

"Why's that, then?" she asked, peeling off her shirt and tossing it into the hamper to be washed.

"I may or may not have been whipped last night."

I didn't think a person could turn so fast. One second, I'd been presented with Kennia's back. Before I had the chance to blink, she was facing me, her brows high and eyes wide.

"What's that, now?"

Chewing on my bottom lip, I contemplated telling Kennia everything. In truth, I'd wanted to since finding out that Michele had been the man in London. I'd just never had the chance. I'd spent a while trying to come to terms with it, then the gameplay had started right after. Toss in wonky shifts and a gaggle of blondes, and I couldn't find the right moment.

With a sigh, I got up. It didn't matter how tenderly I sat on my ass, it remained sore and raw. I'd taken a look at it before I went to bed and there were numerous, *numerous* welts. He did well.

"You start somethin' with that lad?" she asked, stepping closer. "What's his name again?"

"Michele," I said. His name felt strange on my tongue. I'd never said it out loud before.

"Holy shit, Bay. You sure you know what you're doin'?"

I took a deep breath and said, "We've met before."

I hadn't thought it possible for her eyes to get wider.

"All right, then." Kennia lunged toward me and promptly began to push me out of the way until she could join me on my bunk. Crossing her legs, she stared at me unblinking, ready for a story. "Start from the beginnin'."

So I did. I told her that I knew there'd been something about him the moment he'd stepped on the yacht. I told her about him confronting me and telling me that he'd been the one to flog me in London. I even told her that we'd already fooled around, though I saved her the details. No, I saved *myself* the act of relaying them. Kennia had done her best to pry.

"And last night, he did it again."

Kennia said nothing. She leaned against the wall at the foot of my bed, her hands resting in her lap. There'd been no indication which way she leaned, no way to tell whether she was angry with me or not.

After a while, she spoke. "Huh."

I furrowed my brow. "Huh?"

She nodded. "Yeah, huh. I don't really know what to say."

Her response surprised me. Perhaps it shouldn't have. "Oh. Um, okay."

"Well," she said, scratching a spot behind her ear. "You at least know what you're doin'?"

I slumped against the wall at the head of my bed, squaring myself on her. She met my gaze.

Yup. Sitting officially hurts.

"I mean, it's all fun and games, right?"

Kennia arched a brow.

"It's not like we plan to date or anything. We're just having fun."

She didn't seem convinced, but I suppose I didn't expect her to be. In reality, I had no idea what I was doing. I'd never done anything like it before. I just assumed that whatever Michele and I had would end when the ship docked in Venice. That would be the logical thing.

"All right," Kennia said as she slid off the bed. "I know I don't need to tell ya this, but I'm gonna, anyway. Be careful."

Smiling to myself, I replied, "I'm a grown-up. I don't fall for every guy I play with."

"Nah, not that," she said with a shake of the head. "I mean be careful so no one else finds out. I don't want people thinkin' I associate with some bloody tart."

Kennia had barely made it to the end of the sentence before she began to giggle. Reaching back, I grabbed my pillow and lobbed it at her. Laughing like a maniac, she swatted it away, stuck her tongue out at me and disappeared into the bathroom before I had the chance to throw anything else at her.

Kennia didn't care what I did with my personal life so long as I took care of myself, so it made sense her warning had been of the professional kind. She didn't want my relationship with a client to come to light, a fear I myself had harbored. It would taint my reputation and, if I chose to continue stewarding, it'd be difficult for me to get a job on another yacht. I could respect her for that.

That being said, I had no intention of letting anyone find out. Although, that meant I should probably stop dropping to my knees in the middle of a hall that anyone could walk down.

Heaving myself to my feet, I got ready for the day.

* * * *

Breakfast came, and as I had so many times before, I served the guests alongside another steward.

Most of the guests were seated at their favorite place to lounge, the aft deck. One of the older gentlemen stood off to the side in the sun, speaking quite angrily to someone on his phone.

The second older man was sat beside one of the middle-aged gentlemen, leaning forward with his elbows on his knees as he spoke. The middle-aged man, who I believed was Patritzio, listened intently. At the head of the table, the other middle-aged man, Antony, listened with much less interest.

Michele sat next, across from Patritzio and beside Dominic, who was busy with his cell phone. Michele didn't seem the slightest bit interested in what was happening around him, leaning back in his chair with an elbow resting on the arm. His gaze fell to me when I emerged from the depths of the ship, and I had trouble looking away, but I needed to work.

There was an order to things. It helped prevent people from bumping into one another and spilling anything. That order kept me from being the one to hand Michele his plate, but that hadn't stopped him from reminding me he was there. How he'd thought I'd forgotten, I don't know.

When I set the plate down in front of Antony, the seat next to Michele, he shifted to the side. I'd assumed he did it to give me more space, but no. He had done so to give him a better angle with which to grab me.

He cupped my ass with his hand and gave it a gentle squeeze before I stepped away. My breath hitched, a shock of pain causing my muscles to seize for a brief second until I regained control.

As I walked away, I peered back over my shoulder. Michele met my eye and winked. Butterflies fluttered in my stomach.

He's such a shit.

Mandy retired to the galley to retrieve the final set of plates while I slipped into the salon to make the mimosas.

I had just finished pouring the orange juice into the six flutes when he approached.

"When breakfast is done," Michele said, "come to my room."

"I can't," I said. With a rag over the top of the champagne, I did my best to remove the cork without hurting myself or anyone else. When the pop came, I jumped. No matter how many bottles I'd opened, I would always jump. "I have to work. Besides, it might get a little suspicious if I keep going to your room, wouldn't it?"

He smirked. "If you are worried about appearances, there may be some towels to launder."

His playful tone made me smile. Michele lingered, watching as I poured the champagne.

"Please?"

The *please* surprised me to the point that I had been compelled to look up. There'd be no denying the sincerity in his request. It made me curious.

"Okay," I said. "After breakfast, I'll come get the towels."

Michele smiled and walked away to join the others. I finished the drinks moments later and handed them out, then went on to clean up. In an hour, it appeared that I would be visiting Michele in his room, and I didn't know if I should've been happy or worried.

Perhaps a pleasant mixture of the two.

* * * *

Heart in my throat, I approached Michele's door and was surprised to find it open. I knocked on the threshold regardless. He appeared from the bathroom, a handful of 'used' towels in his grasp. I suspected they were the towels from the previous night, and he'd done nothing more than unfold them to give the appearance of use.

"Come in," he said, dropping them onto the bed.

"How can I help you, Mr. Sacchi?"

He met me in stride, his gaze dancing over me. With his brows together, he met my stare.

"How are you feeling?"

My heart swelled and I had to lower my chin so he couldn't see the smile that had formed. When I could control myself again, I looked up at him.

"I'm fine," I said. "A bit sore, but I'm fine."

"Show me."

His request surprised me, but perhaps it shouldn't have. It made sense that he'd want to see his handiwork.

I hesitated, my fingers tingling and heartbeat quick. Since I'd worn my shorts the day before, I stood in front of Michele in a denim skirt.

It does make things easier.

Turning my back to him, I took hold of the hem and tugged the garment up. The fabric was stiff but molded to my desires and soon came to rest in a mass above my hips.

Michele leaned to the side, tilting his head to get a better look. He held my waist in his hands, tensing and squeezing while he examined me. He didn't seem to realize it.

"You've bruised," he said with a disappointed sigh. "That wasn't my intention."

"That's probably my fault," I replied. "I think I got a little carried away."

He shook his head. "No," he said. "No, I became overzealous. It was my fault, completely."

"Well, regardless, there's nothing we can do about it now."

He had nothing to apologize for as far as I was concerned. He'd done better than I could put into words.

"I have something that may help."

Michele stepped into the bathroom. I pushed my skirt back into place and nearly had it settled when he returned. He held a small bottle, simple in design and reeking of money.

"What is that?"

"An oil," he said. "It helps with many things, one being bruising and aches."

I raised my brows. *Why would he have something like that?*

"Does it work?"

"Very well."

The thought of being able to sleep on my back in the next few days intrigued me. Sitting wasn't an issue once I found the right technique. I could control the pressure. Sleep had been a nightmare. Being unconscious and unable to adjust, the pain was enough to wake me up many times.

"Okay," I said after a moment of thought. "How do I use it?"

A smirk twisted his full lips, tugging his facial hair up in the corner. The wickedness I'd grown to enjoy flashed in his eyes once again.

"You lie across my lap, and I will apply it."

I chewed on my bottom lip and thought about his hands on my body again. My agreement must have come quicker than I expected.

Within seconds, he'd taken a seat on his bed and I, with my skirt pulled up, had lain across his lap.

Cold droplets of oil caused me to twitch. They warmed to my skin and trailed down the slope of my ass, but their path had been interrupted by Michele's delicate touch.

He proceeded to caress me, to rub the oil into my bruises and welts. Resting my head on my folded arms,

I reveled in the sensation, flinching only when he touched a particularly sensitive area.

While I was comfortable in the silence, something began to press into my stomach. I thought nothing of it at first, but the more persistent it became, the more I couldn't ignore it.

"Are you getting hard again?" I doubted I removed the smile from my words.

"Forgive me," he said. "It has a mind of its own. I have no control over it around beautiful women."

A blush came to my cheeks. I did my best to suppress it while Michele continued to smear the oil over my skin. It stung but offered a surprising level of relief as well.

"Do they still hurt?" he asked, doing his best to remain gentle while he caressed me.

"A little bit."

Sounding more worried than before, he asked, "Was it too much?"

Smiling to myself once more, I replied, "I would've said something if it was."

He chuckled. "I have no doubt."

Another silence fell and, as I lay there, relishing the sensation of his hands, I began to slip. So relaxed, I could have fallen asleep if allowed, and that was a problem.

"Are you almost done?"

"I've been finished for some time."

"What?" I shifted to look back at him.

Michele smirked down at me. "I was simply enjoying myself."

I elbowed his thigh. Michele snickered and didn't stop me when I stood.

"You're an ass," I said, a giggle lacing my words.

He shrugged a shoulder, looking anything but apologetic. Rolling my eyes, I did my best to appear presentable once again, using the giant mirror on the wall to do so. When I had, I turned to face him.

"Thank you."

He smiled and gave me a small nod. "Of course."

With little else to say, I stepped around him and began to gather the towels.

As I counted them, draping each over my arm as I did, Dominic burst into the room in boisterous fashion, smiling wide. He spotted the pair of us, and the happy expression shifted into a sneer. He said something to Michele in Italian. Michele brushed his comment away and said something else. I understood nothing but a single word, *Yasmin*.

My gut twisted, but I did my best to keep the emotion from my face. Stepping around him, I gave Michele my attention. I'd intended to wait until he'd finished his conversation with Dominic, but instead, he held up a slender finger to keep his cousin from speaking.

"Yes, Miss Hurst?" His professional tone was as lovely as his normal voice.

"I'll take these down to the laundry and bring up replacements right away."

He nodded. "Thank you."

"Of course, sir."

As I left, Dominic winked and blew kisses at me. I didn't scowl, though the desire had been there.

"Sir," I said, with no warmth in my voice.

He chuckled, seemingly amused with something to the point where a slap to my ass had been his version of an appropriate response. The pain and ache rocketed through my body, tensing the muscles that'd been given the chance to relax over the few previous moments.

I refused to turn around and acknowledge that he'd done anything at all, though my gait had changed to cope with the throbbing. Michele's angry voice followed me into the hall but faded the farther away I'd walked. He didn't sound happy with Dominic's slap.

A hidden crew stairwell nearby offered me a place to descend instead of walking the length of the vessel to go downstairs. Bounding down the narrow steps, I thought about what Dominic had said. Yes, I'd been ignorant of the language, but I wasn't an idiot. Given intonation and body language, deep down, I knew Yasmin and her crew would be stepping foot on *The Silver Wind* at some point that day.

The good feelings left over from the sweet moment I'd shared with Michele vanished. I really, *really* didn't want to spend time around The Gaggle.

Chapter Twelve

Twenty minutes after I'd left his suite, I returned with an armful of towels and found Michele pacing. It seemed as though he'd been waiting on me, which I hadn't expected.

"I have your towels," I said for no known reason other than to alert him of my arrival.

Michele nodded and thanked me under his breath, but something seemed off. I hesitated to step into his bathroom, waiting to see if he'd speak further, but when he hadn't, I did my job and put the towels in the bathroom cupboard. When I returned to the bedroom, Michele hadn't stopped pacing, apparently still deep in thought.

I'd nearly made it to the door before the urge to speak took over. "Are you okay?"

He paused, peering at me through his lashes. An awkward silence stretched between us. I'd overstepped. Prying was part of neither agreement Michele and I had. It had nothing to do with our playtime, and a stewardess was meant to be seen, not heard.

"I'm sorry," I was fast to say. "I shouldn't have asked. Excuse me."

"No, wait," he said before I stepped out of the door. I gave him my attention. "I apologize. I am a bit distracted at the moment."

"You don't have to apologize. I shouldn't have pressed. It's none of my business."

"Perhaps," he said, his hands finding their way into his pockets. He did that a lot. I wondered if it was a nervous habit, a 'comfort blanket' of sorts. "We will be hosting our guests again. In fact"—he checked his watch and sighed—"they will be here shortly."

"And you're not happy about that." I did my best to remove the deadpan tone and come across as sympathetic, but it was difficult, given my personal distaste for Yasmin.

"Not particularly, no."

"Well, the boat's big. I'm sure we could hide you in a closet somewhere."

Michele smiled a little, chuckling at my comment and aware that it'd been a joke.

"She may find me regardless, I'm afraid."

"Yasmin."

I heard the agitation in my voice the moment I spoke her name. The attempt to keep my tone light and casual had been in vain.

Michele's gaze fixed to me. He arched a brow. "You don't like her, do you?"

The words bubbled up my throat, scratching and clawing to escape, but I bit down hard on them. I refused to voice my opinion.

"I don't know her," I said. "But she seems lovely."

Michele scoffed, suddenly laughing at my remark. The reaction had been so unexpected that I jumped.

He had a beautiful laugh, richer than I'd expected it to be.

"You are a terrible liar."

My cheeks burned. "Yeah, well..." I mumbled to myself.

"Our families have been in business for a long time," he said. "I suppose I've become used to her behavior, but it does rub some the wrong way."

As much as I wanted to remind him that she'd thrown food in my face and that was far beyond *rubbing people the wrong way*, I didn't. What left my mouth instead had been much worse.

"She likes you, though."

He cocked a brow at the comment. I cringed. Whether they were meant to be or not, those few words had come across as jealousy, and I hated myself for it. There'd been no reason for the emotion and yet, there it was for him to hear.

Shit.

It would have been impossible for me to backtrack and try to act as though I'd meant nothing by it. Jealousy remained one of those things that, once entering a person's mind, no one could convince them of anything else. The more it was denied, the more the other person believed it to be true.

Knowing that, I remained silent. No need to dig that hole deeper.

"You truly dislike her."

I didn't speak.

He stepped toward me, closing half the distance. My pulse quickened.

"You haven't answered my question."

"It might be a good idea that I don't."

But that had been plenty. Michele's eyes sparkled with a smile that soon graced his lips.

"Interesting."

My embarrassment began to twist into irritation. I didn't like being put on the spot and wanted to ignore the fact that I'd fallen into a trap of my own making. I had a habit of being rude when backed into a corner.

"Is it your turn to be the brat?" I asked without a thought as to who I was speaking to.

Michele perked. "Now that's a stimulating idea. I'm not certain that would work, however. If someone punished me, I might retaliate."

"That a fact?"

"Hmm." He nodded. "Admittedly, I can lose control." His tone deepened. "I can be quite rough in response...animalistic."

A shiver tore through me, a shiver that I did my best to suppress. He was baiting me, egging me on and hinting at what might happen if I did anything to him. Then again, I could have been reading too much into it, and my interpretation might have been wishful thinking. Either way, I was intrigued.

The chirp of my walkie-talkie brought me out of the moment. I was being called to help in the galley and replied promptly.

"Excuse me, Mr. Sacchi."

Michele bowed to me like he had a dozen times before and smiled. I left, replaying the conversation over and over again in my head.

* * * *

By one in the afternoon, *The Silver Wind* had become a typical party boat, and it made my skin crawl. Horrendously loud dance music blared from the outdoor speakers, women dressed in almost nothing slithered around the deck and the alcohol flowed.

Because I was the best at mixing drinks, I'd been forced to endure the party. Kennia and Chris joined me. I couldn't put into words how much I appreciated them being there. They were my buffer, my shield.

The elders had left long ago, disappearing to another room on one of the many levels. They'd separated themselves from the 'young'uns' rather quickly, in fact. I didn't blame them. I'd have done the same, given the chance.

I lost count of the number of cocktails and shots I'd handed out, but it was enough to alter everyone's attitude. It made those with an obnoxious personality even more so, something I hadn't thought possible.

Thing One and Thing Two clung to Dominic, sandwiching him between their breasts as they danced and giggled in one end of the eight-foot-long pool. He grabbed their asses and kissed their necks. At one point, he ordered me to bring him a bottle of vodka, which he poured on their bodies and licked off. I couldn't imagine it tasted very good mixing with their tropical sun oil.

The more drinks those three had, the closer I assumed they were to stripping down and having sex on the deck. Whether or not the staff was there to witness rarely mattered to clients I'd had in the past. It came down to what sort of exhibitionist streak they possessed, and given more than once during the vodka pour Dominic had shifted a bikini top out of the way to suck on their nipples, I doubted they were too self-conscious.

Not one to judge someone for their kinks, it only annoyed me because I would've been the one they asked to clean up after the fact. Mopping up after drunken sex was something I'd done and didn't much want to do again.

Not far from them on the deck stood Yasmin and Michele. Yasmin danced and pressed her ass against him. He kept time with the beat, but she'd been far more exuberant in her movements than him…at first.

I found it difficult to look away, transfixed by the sight for half an hour or longer. Michele eventually took notice.

He stared at me, and I could have sworn he could read the thoughts running through my head. I hated it, hated the way he would chew on his bottom lip when Yasmin ground against him, hated the way he glided his hands along her waist at the same time and hated that I cared at all. One voice in my head barked at me, told me that I'd become jealous. Another voice contradicted the first and said that no, it was *who* he had dancing against him, not that it was another woman.

I ground my teeth when Yasmin guided Michele's hand to her breast and he complied. In fact, a little smirk pulled at his lips. He had the *gall* to look me in the eye while he groped *her*, of all people.

This is him being a brat, isn't it?

Of course it is. Look how happy he is. He already told me he doesn't really like her. He's doing it to get under my skin.

You should do something about it. He whipped you for being a brat.

I can't whip him. We're in public.

Maybe not, but he deserves something. Look at that smug smile.

"Y'all right there, Bay?" Kennia's concerned voice broke through my internal conversation.

"Yeah, why?" Even I could hear the rage in my words.

"'Cause you're white-knuckling the chamois."

She was right. At some point during cleaning, I'd stopped wiping down the bar and begun my staring contest with the Italian. My grip on the cloth had become so tight, so intense, that my knuckles had turned white and my fingers bright pink.

The moment I opened my hand, blood rushed back to my digits, returning feeling to them. I cleared my throat and attempted to appear more in control than I was, but Kennia and Chris saw the truth.

"Not a fan of our guests then, eh?" Chris asked with a small laugh lacing his question.

"She dumped food on me," I replied. "I should...shove her into the pool." *And he'd go in with her.*

Chris and Kennia began to stifle their laughter and failed horribly.

"That's not right," Kennia forced herself to say. "That's... That'd be unprofessional."

"But funny," Chris added.

"No, stop." Kennia slapped Chris' arm, but her heart hadn't been in her protest. "She can't do that."

I turned to the pair. "Why not?"

Their laughter died while they stared at me in confusion. They were stuck between taking me seriously and being sure that it'd been a joke.

Chris was the first to realize that I might've been serious, and his expression brightened substantially as a result.

"Hundred pounds," he said with a sharp snap. "I'll give you a hundred…dollars. Shit, I only have U.S. Still, a hundred dollars if you shove her into the pool."

"Stop encouragin' her," Kennia grumbled, but Chris clearly knew what he wanted.

"Got a deal?" He offered me his hand.

"Deal," I replied as I shook it, sealing our bargain.

"You're gonna get fired, the pair of you," Kennia said, pointing a stern, motherly finger at the two of us.

"*Pft.*" Chris rolled his eyes. "She's awful. You should've seen the havoc she caused in the galley earlier. That diva *needs* her makeup messed."

Kennia shook her head and turned her attention to me.

"Bay, be serious," she said, exuding a powerful maternal vibe. "She's a client. Just because she's on your—"

"She's a tag-a-long," I interrupted. My jealousy flashed to the surface. It'd taken root. I didn't like her. Uppity people happened in this line of work, true, but there were no words for Yasmin.

No one had *ever* purposefully thrown food in my face before then berated me for it. She deserved some kind of petty revenge. All I had to do was wait for my chance for it to reveal itself.

Ten minutes after the bargain had been struck, my 'name' was bellowed from the deck.

"Bay leaf!" Her accent twisted every syllable, turning the words ugly and blunt.

I glanced to my friends, giving them a brief and silent confirmation, then exited the salon. A fake smile spread across my face.

"Yes, ma'am?"

She glowered at me through layers of black makeup.

"Clean dis up." Yasmin waved a claw at the array of glasses and empty dishes she and her friends had left sprawled across the tables and deck.

"Of course."

With so much to clean up, I waved Chris over, who bounded out from behind the bar with a smile. Together, we began to clear away the mess, doing our best to avoid the drunken dancing.

It took a few minutes, but our arms were soon full of a variety of items. Chris was somewhere behind me, ensuring that he had the last of it, while I noticed that Yasmin had once again wrapped herself around Michele. That fiery emotion swelled within me just as intensely as it had earlier, and before I could question my decision, I planted my hand in the middle of Michele's back and shoved.

From behind came a squeak, a gruff shout and a loud splash. Kennia's jaw fell open, her eyes wide at the 'carnage' left in my wake. A vindictive smile threatened to take my lips.

Once safely inside, I dared to glance back. Yasmin stood waist deep in the pool, her hair plastered to her head and every ounce of makeup sliding down her face. She shouted about her fake tan not having set before she got wet, unaware that streaks of black decorated her cheeks.

Should have worn waterproof.

I should've felt guilty, regretted being an asshole to a stranger, but what had I really done? I'd got her wet.

I hadn't hurt her in any way. She'd be fine in the end. I hadn't cost her a couple hundred dollars in crockery like she had me. I mean, Christ. She'd cost me third of my paycheck away.

Michele, on the other hand, hadn't panicked. He stood just behind her in the waist-deep water, staring at me, his eyes stern. He knew I'd done it on purpose. There was no way to deny it, so I didn't try. I stared back while he ran his hand down his face, wiping away some of the water and smoothing his hair back.

He shook his head subtly, and in it, I knew I would pay for my actions.

Chapter Thirteen

The clock neared one in the morning when the other crew members and I were able to retire. Exhausted, I wanted nothing more than to go to sleep and get the few hours I could. The following day was the last of the charter. We would be docking in Venice by late afternoon, and our guests would disembark.

Michele would go back to his life and so would I, as though nothing had happened.

Yasmin and her clan had chosen to stay the night. Part of me was glad for it. By the time the sun set, they were too drunk to stand upright. By ten p.m. they'd begun to slur their words to the point that knowing drunk-speak hadn't helped. As much as I didn't like any of them, I would rather they stayed on the yacht than get in a small, fast-moving boat. Anything could happen in the few hundred yards between the two ships.

I hadn't been one of the stewards to show them to their rooms, however. I might've wanted them safe, but that didn't mean I planned to go out of my way to be hospitable to the lushes. Although, judging by the sounds some of the crew had heard coming from Dominic's room, Thing One and Thing Two were being well taken care of.

The ship had gone silent, the throngs of individuals slinking into the shadows, including staff. The skeleton crew had taken over, and it was easy for a couple of people to disappear and make the large vessel appear abandoned.

I rolled my neck from side to side in an attempt to relieve tension while I descended the stairs. Rounding the corner, I entered the galley and froze in place. At night, lights were dimmed, which could add a haunting aura to the space. Finding Michele sitting at the staff table, leaning forward with his elbows on his knees, fingers entwined and staring at me through his lashes sent an icy spike of fear through me.

"*Ciao, cara mia.*"

"Hello, Mr. Sacchi," I said with a level of uncertainty that I knew he heard. "Is there anything I can help you with?"

He rose to his feet and crossed the space, looming over me. The air around him vibrated with intent, but I'd been afraid to know what that intent might be.

Without warning, he snatched me by the throat, pulling me even closer. His lips brushed mine. My pulse quickened to an unbelievable degree. My body had gone from zero to sixty in milliseconds.

"You shoved me into the pool," he said, his jaw tight. "Answer me."

"Yes."

"Yes, *what*?"

Excitement flickered into existence. "Yes, Sir."

"You were defiant."

"Yes, Sir."

"You will be punished."

In little more than a whisper, I replied, "Yes, Sir."

Michele shifted his grip so that he could hold the back of my neck and proceeded to guide me out of the galley, and down the hall. Most people wouldn't suspect a yacht of possessing an elevator, but *The Silver Wind* had one. I'd never used it until that moment.

We reached the elevator at the end of the hall opposite the staff bunks. Michele pressed the call button and shoved me inside ahead of him when it arrived. We rode to his floor in silence.

Less than a minute later, he brought us into his suite. I hadn't realized that I'd expected to find Yasmin lying in his bed until I was relieved to see it empty.

Michele released me to close the door. I stood in the center of the room staring at him, my heart in my throat waiting for what would happen next. Once we were secure, cut off from the rest of the world, he turned to me. Michele approached slowly, gliding toward me with his eyes shining black.

"You were disobedient," he said. "Defiant."

I swallowed hard, tensing my jaw and steadying myself. "And?"

His voice had been tight when he asked, "What did you just say?"

The brat returned, and in it, I could release some of the frustration that had weighed me down throughout the day.

"What are you going to do, spank me again?" I asked, antagonizing him. "Is that the best you can do?"

"No, no, no, *bella*," he said. "We are beyond spankings."

"Then what are you going to do?"

He let out a breath, a small laugh that held no happiness but instead a sinister joy.

"What I've wanted to do since London. What do you have to say about that, hmm?"

I hope you can keep up.

Without a word, I lunged forward, attempting to 'run from' Michele, but he was fast. He planted his hand on my sternum and pushed me back. My feet left the floor seconds before I collapsed onto the bed. He'd shoved me so hard that I'd bounced on the pillow-top mattress.

Not given the chance to settle, he appeared on top of me, guiding me up the length of the California King and to the headboard. He stared at me, his eyes blazing while a hand disappeared beneath a pillow.

"It is time for you to pay," he said in a voice as wicked as his glare.

Michele retrieved a rope he'd hidden under the mass. A bolt of fear rippled down my spine when he took hold of my wrist. I jerked it away and began to fight, but Michele held strong. Within seconds, he had my wrist secured by a sturdy, quick-release knot.

I yanked on it, but it refused to give while he dashed to the other side of the bed and repeated the action, almost too fast for me to comprehend. In seconds at most, my arms were tied down.

"Your compatriots are quite accommodating," he said as he casually got off me and approached the foot of the bed. "Ask for a bit of rope"—another strip appeared in his hand the moment he grabbed my ankle, dwarfing it in his grasp—"and they will do anything to help."

"Let go of me!"

I kicked and fought, but he was strong. A few quick actions had one of my ankles tied as securely as my wrists.

My breathing became short, my pulse raced and every inch of my body ignited with anticipation. I wondered what he'd do, what he'd planned in the hours since I'd seen him on deck. I wondered how similar we were.

Michele never tied my other ankle down. Instead, he stood at the foot of the bed, staring at me.

He dragged his gaze over my body, and I felt it as easily as tangible hands. My breasts began to tingle, desperate to be touched, and my pussy ached for the same. My only relief came when I pulled on the ropes, twisting my wrists within them. The burn gave me a slight reprieve, a chance to ignore how much I wanted him.

He remained still as a statue, his hands once again in his pockets. Michele chewed on his bottom lip until he met my eye.

My voice trembled with excitement when I spoke. "What are you going to do to me?"

He drew in a long, deep breath and exhaled it when he responded. "Whatever I like."

I jerked at the ropes again, causing the bed's frame to creak and groan, but they continued to hold firm.

"And if I scream?"

He arched a brow. With slender fingers, he loosened his tie. "Scream?"

I nodded, but he seemed less than concerned with the threat.

As before, he climbed onto the mattress and up the length of me with surprising dexterity. A sharp jerk freed him of his tie, and he didn't hesitate to use it.

He wrapped the strip of expensive silk around my head, gagging me. I stared up at him, panting and chest heaving. Hovering inches above me, Michele gripped my jaw.

"You will scream." His voice remained deep, guttural and borderline evil, filled with unanswered desires. "You will scream, you will shake and you will beg me for more." I jerked my head away. He forced it back. "Won't you?"

I didn't reply. I writhed beneath him, pressing my breasts against his chest and grinding into his erection.

"That's what I thought," he said with a growl.

He kissed my chin, trailing along my jaw until he could dip into the crook of my neck. He bit down on my throat, sending shivers tearing through me. My eyes rolled back, leaving me to rely only on my sense of touch.

Large hands pawed at my breasts, grabbing them roughly and pinching my nipples through the fabric. I yelped from the shock of it more than once. It hadn't been long since he'd touched me last, yet my body seemed to crave him, the slightest contact causing me to react as though it'd been the first time.

I opened my eyes when he sat up and adjusted himself to sit more comfortably. With a knee on either side of my thighs, he could straddle me and have complete control. As before, he bit his bottom lip, reminding me that I had yet to properly do it myself. What I'd done in my bunk had been little more than a taste.

After staring at me for a moment or two, Michele seemed to have formed a plan. He reached for my shirt and untucked it, then shoved it up my body and over my breasts. The fabric had been gathered beneath my chin when he did the same with my bra, exposing my bare chest.

His body visibly tightened and he clenched his jaw. A shadow crept over his entire demeanor, wiping away anything human that had once remained. My clit throbbed at the intensity of him.

"*Perfezione*," he muttered.

I didn't know what it meant, but I knew what it sounded like, and he'd said it about my breasts.

Michele seemed to find life, to find the ability to move once again. He dove for my breasts and claimed one of them with his mouth. I moaned into my gag as the wet heat encompassed my nipple. He would sweep his tongue across the sensitive skin, suck and kiss it while he massaged the other aggressively. Then he'd switch and pay the twin equal attention. He pressed them together, attacked them at the same time and buried his face between them.

Catching my nipple between his teeth, he sucked hard enough that I shuddered. Wrapping my hands around the ropes, I did my best to remain steady, grounded, while he did all he could to rob me of my wits.

I wanted to grab him, to run my fingers through his hair and pull it hard, but I couldn't. The point of being bound remained the wonderful, painful torture of it.

Michele continued down my body, nipping and kissing my stomach and hip until he reached my skirt. The belt and button put up little resistance, unable to deny his dominating will.

When he had them undone, he jerked and pulled the garment down my legs, threading the one he'd left untied through the skirt until it was out of the way. He could have easily pushed the fabric up instead, but it seemed as though he wanted as little on my body as possible.

Breathing became loud, obstructed by my gag. It was all I could hear, even drowning out the sound of my erratic heart.

My panties might have kept me from being completely nude below the waist, but they were unable to withstand the slightest pressure, a theory given proof when Michele wrapped the thin fabric around his hand and yanked. My thong snapped, exposing me to him.

He groaned at the sight of me, so I closed my legs. The pleasure he let seep through his stoic exterior had been more than enough for me to be vengeful, and it worked. The instant my thighs were pressed together, he shot his gaze to mine. Fire raged within the blackness of his eyes, and while I adored the way it washed over me, I refused to give in.

He lunged forward and tried to pry my legs apart, but I held them together for as long as I could.

His brute strength won out in the end, and I was forced spread-eagled before him.

"So insolent," he said through his teeth. "You won't deny me."

The feeling of his mouth between my thighs had been almost enough to push me over the edge. After days of build-up, of teasing and games, everything had come to a head. The instant his tongue swept across my clit, I became electrified. I shuddered and shook, my muscles clenched so tight that they'd gone sore, and the ropes bit angrily into my limbs.

With the skill of a man who'd caused many women to scream his name, he sucked on my clit, flicked it with his tongue and drew hard circles around it. I bit down on the gag, my teeth grinding against the silk.

But he didn't stop. He didn't give me a chance to regain my sanity. Instead, Michele devoured me, and just before my orgasm would have washed me into a sea of oblivion, he withdrew.

I shot my eyes open, and my focus landed on him. Michele sat on his knees between my legs, wiping a hand down his face and staring back as though he didn't have a care in the world. I growled into the gag and yanked ferociously on my binds. His response was nothing more than an arched brow.

"Something wrong?" His voice dripped with derision.

"Oo muverfugger!" I said around the tie.

"That was rather rude." He unbuttoned his shirt.

When he'd finished, he stepped off the bed, removing the garment in the process and laying it over the back of a chair. Michele took a seat and began to remove his shoes and socks.

"You have left me similarly before." His casual tone raked over me like nails. "It seems only fair you feel the pain of that."

In frustration, I pulled even harder on my ropes, but the knots held. They refused to budge in the least. He'd done well, and had I not been swimming in rage, I'd have complimented him for it.

Michele went on to disrobe until he stood naked before me. My struggle ceased, and rather than continuing to attempt escape, my attention became devoted to admiring every inch of him. I'd seen most of it when he'd chosen to swim, but not everything.

His cock stood rigid, seeming harder than stone and ready. In spite of the distance, I could see the thick vein that ran the length of it and recalled thoughts of running my tongue over it, over the russet-colored head before guiding it deep down my throat. It was as impressive as the man who owned it, and I ached to have it inside me, one way or another.

He retrieved a condom from his trousers and made quick work of the wrapping. The groan he gave when he slid the piece of latex on was one I knew I would always remember.

He sauntered toward me and crawled up the length of the bed until his chest pressed firmly to mine, crushing my breasts. He rubbed his erection against my thigh, begging for entrance that I was willing to give.

"Are you ready to scream, *cara mia*?" He nipped on my bottom lip. "Tell me." Michele wrapped a hand around my breast and squeezed hard while he continued to tease a kiss I knew wouldn't come. "Tell me I can give us both release."

He drew back just far enough to see me nod emphatically.

Almost without warning, Michele thrust into me. White flashed in my eyes and every cell exploded with pleasure. I couldn't say how long he fucked me before the orgasm I'd been denied roared to life again, but it hadn't been long. The build-up had been days long. Hell, it'd been over six years in the making, and when finally given the thing I'd wanted so badly, my body had been overtaken.

I pulled against my ropes and my back arched as I drowned in the euphoria he'd created.

When my head cleared seconds later, I somehow managed to pry open my eyes. He'd propped himself above me and watched me come, but the frustration I saw told me he was far from satiated. It didn't surprise me.

He traced a line across my jaw with his rough thumb.

"*Bellissima,*" he whispered.

He lingered a moment longer, staring at me with what I could only compare to endearment before he sat up.

Reaching behind him, he slid almost entirely out of me as he went for the rope around my ankle. A sharp tug of the quick-release line caused the knot to disappear and the tension in my leg to lessen.

Michele's attention returned to me. In an almost loving way, he guided my thigh to his side, relieving the ache that had formed in the last few minutes. He took hold of my other leg and, with his grip secured, brought me hard against him, slamming his cock back into my depths.

The pleasure pulsated throughout, eliciting a moan and causing my lids to flutter, but I forced them to remain open. With our stares locked, he slid out, then aggressively brought me against him once more.

White dots flashed in my eyes each time he hit a depth no man had previously reached. The sensation of him plunging into me, of the ropes biting into my skin and the silk dampening in my mouth had created a perfect storm.

He soon developed his rhythm, his grunts falling in line with each drive. I wanted to reach out and touch him, to run my fingernails along the curve of his shoulders or down his stomach, but the binds kept me in place.

Michele fucked me harder and harder, plowing into me with dizzying intensity. The muscles in his arms bulged, his chest tense. His brows pooled in the center of his forehead while he bit down on his bottom lip. Everything about him was beautiful, enchanting.

As he lost himself in his actions, he collapsed against me. He drove his fingers through my hair, gripping my locks so tight that my head had been forced to the side. I wanted to rake my fingernails down his toned back. I wanted to bite into his thick shoulder and feel the muscle roll beneath my teeth. I wanted to make him c —

He shoved himself as deep as he could and threw his head back while he roared from his orgasm. He trembled against me, shaking under the force of it until he went still. His body engulfed mine when he relaxed, each panting breath echoing in my ear until he could move again.

His pulling out had left me with a surprising emptiness, a void that I wanted him to fill once more, but I'd somehow managed to keep the disappointed groan from my throat.

Reaching to the left, he tugged the quick-release line and freed my wrist then repeated the action with the other. The lack of tension in my arms and shoulders had been more painful than when they were tied, but it was a satisfying ache.

Propping himself on an elbow, he looked down at me. Humanity had begun to seep back into his features, the animal now satiated and sent to the dark recesses.

Hooking his finger beneath the tie, Michele shimmied it down. I shifted as best I could to help and soon my gag was gone. Still breathing heavily, he cradled my jaw and muttered something I couldn't understand.

He leaned forward, brushing his lips across mine, and for a moment I'd wondered if he planned to kiss me. The situation called for it, but our agreement did not. Seeming to remember that fact, he placed a kiss just to the left of my lips and proceeded down to my neck.

Finally able to touch him, I ran my fingers through his soft hair and held him while I sank into the bed.

I would have been content to stay in that moment, to allow the second orgasm that'd been building inside me to wither away and vanish.

He wasn't.

He danced a trail down my heated body with his fingers, between my breasts and over my stomach until he slid them between my legs. I bucked and whimpered in surprise. My clit was too sensitive, from both need and previously getting what I'd wanted.

Dipping into the crook of my neck, he placed a tender kiss on my fluttering pulse while tracing a circle over the sensitive bundle of nerves.

"One more, *bella*," he whispered and slid two thick fingers into my core. "May I give you one more?"

"Yes." The question had been answered before my mind even absorbed.

He raked his blunt teeth along my neck, down to my shoulder, which he tenderly bit while his fingers went to work. He pumped them inside me, curling the digits to hit that special spot and was sure to press the heel of his palm hard against my clit. The man knew how to coax every hint of pleasure from his partner.

I could love him for it.

The grip in his hair remained tight, eliciting a soft groan from him when I flexed it. I clutched my free hand at his biceps, desperate for something to hold while he drove me closer to the cliffs once again.

I began to writhe on the bed, my hips meeting in time with his actions, lifting and rolling to ensure I got everything I could from it.

"That's it," he whispered. "So close."

His actions increased, his triceps becoming as hard as marble beneath my fingernails.

The wet smack of his hand against me narrated his determination and soon, it, combined with him, had been enough.

Electricity pulsed through me, causing my back to arch and the sound of pure elation to leave my parted lips. I clung to him, clamping my thighs down around his hand while I came.

"Yes," he said. He ran his tongue up the side of my neck, nipping at my earlobe when given the chance. "Every drop."

No matter how hard my thighs squeezed him, he kept curling his fingers until everything had been wrung out of me.

With trembling breath, I sank into the mattress. My body had become an overheated, quivering mass while Michele, my one-time stranger and growing obsession, stayed pressed to my side.

I pried open my eyes to see him staring at me, his head resting in his propped-up hand. The one that'd been busy at work had come to lay across my lower stomach.

A strange sort of silence fell between us. It didn't harbor the same awkwardness that should have accompanied sleeping with someone for the first time. In fact, that sensation should've been unavoidable, given how our lives had become entwined, but it was lacking.

When he suddenly leaned in, my heart leaped. A part of me, no matter how small, had thought a kiss on the lips would've been his objective. It wasn't.

As before, he dipped into the crook of my neck. I rolled my head out of the way, giving him the chance to place an uninhibited kiss to my skin. His lips lingered for just a breath longer than normal and I'd been willing to sink into it.

He withdrew shortly after, getting off the bed and padding across the marble floor to the bathroom. When the door closed behind him, I sat up, shoving my clothing back into place. My torn panties rested on the edge of the bed, clinging to the comforter for dear life. Thank God they weren't expensive, and I had more.

Standing, my knees wavered, but I took my time to steady myself. It'd been longer than I'd expected since I'd had actual sex with someone and even longer since it'd been any good.

By the time I made myself presentable, Michele emerged from the bathroom wearing a pair of pajama pants. His expression seemed sad, and I didn't understand why until he spoke.

"Tomorrow is the final day of the charter, isn't it?"

My heart dropped to my feet, but I forced a smile. "Yes."

He nodded, approaching me slowly. "Do you know when we will arrive?"

"Not exactly, no. The captain thinks around five p.m."

He nodded once more, his gaze lingering on me. Then, as though he too had to force it into fruition, Michele smiled. It didn't appear natural and seemed almost pained. I hoped mine hadn't looked that unconvincing.

"Perhaps I should book the yacht for a few more weeks," he said with a light smile that seemed more genuine than the previous.

I smiled, too, brushing the comment aside for the absurdity of it. Yachts weren't cheap. Super-yachts such as *The Silver Wind* were even less so. They cost six-figures a week to rent, and the thought of him casually saying he'd do so for a few weeks was ridiculous. Sweet, but ridiculous.

"I, um." I cleared the nerves from my throat. "Goodnight, Mr. Sacchi."

"Goodnight, Miss Hurst."

It'd been the first time I could recall that he'd spoken those words to me in English.

With a gentle bow of the head, I walked by him and through the door. The moment I was free of the room, I counted my breathing to my walk, forcing an inhale to last three steps and an exhale to do the same. I had to get my body under control once more, to wash him from my system, because in less than twenty-four hours, Michele Sacchi and I would go our separate ways.

Chapter Fourteen

At six a.m., my alarm went off, rousing me from a shallow sleep. I hadn't been able to get comfortable, though not for the same reason as before. The welts had faded substantially, possibly from Michele's oil, so the unease had nothing to do with the physical.

Kennia emerged from the bathroom, running her hand along her hair to press it back into place after sleeping. I sidestepped her and got ready, too.

We moved with ease, gliding around one another and hardly speaking a word until something inside me snapped. There'd been no build-up, nothing that had led to it, but the statement flowed out of my mouth before she had the chance to reach for the doorknob.

"I had sex with Michele last night."

She froze, mid-reach. I was horrified at what'd I'd done, my eyes wide in shock.

Stupid, stupid, stupid*!*

She faced me, her head cocked to the side while a strange expression twisted her features.

"You plan on seein' him? For real, I mean."

That had been the consequence of blurting out something that should've been calmly stated.

Swallowing hard and chewing on the inside of my cheek, I shook my head.

"I..." She paused. "I'm...a little disappointed."

A phantom fist slammed into my stomach.

I trusted Kennia's opinion when it came to relationships. She possessed an incredible talent for reading people, something I hadn't come across in anyone else. It came down to how she'd been wired, and if she chose, she could've made millions as a shrink, undoubtedly being able to pinpoint and root out problems.

There'd never been judgment from Kennia. Disappointment, perhaps, but never judgment, and that disappointment hadn't been for my lifestyle. Kennia had always been vocal about my lack of personal connection. Sex could come from anywhere, anyone, but a true connection was hard to find. In a lot of ways, she was the only person I *could* talk to about sex, because it was inconsequential to her.

Until I'd met Kennia, I, to the best of my knowledge, had never met anyone who identified as asexual and didn't have any idea what it meant. I'd initially thought that asexuals were, for the most part, nun-like or priest-like individuals who considered sex an unsavory part of life, so they chose to ignore it. She set me straight by saying that, in spite of most depictions in media, asexual people weren't virginal idiots who knew nothing about sex and freaked out or vomited at the mere mention of it. They just didn't care about it. It wasn't a factor that played into their relationships. Kennia's only concern was the connection she felt toward her partner. It was deeper than sex and in a lot of ways purer, without the added complication. Whether she'd chosen to date a man or a woman at the time, her relationships came down to how their personalities and interests fit together. That wasn't to say she'd never had sex with her partners, but it remained far from her motivation or care.

So when she told me that she was disappointed I hadn't found something similar, or that she wished I'd at least tried, I knew her words came from somewhere very different from that of my mother or my sisters. Mom's concern tended to hover somewhere around marriage and kids, my sisters' about whether or not my boyfriend was hotter than theirs.

It was Kennia's opinion I trusted. I valued it above all those around me. It was her I went to for advice.

It was her who could deal the most damage with a simple phrase.

"What's wrong with this one, then?" She crossed her arms, staring at me with a level of maternal disappointment that would've given my actual mother a run for her money. "Thought he was your perfect fit?"

"It's…" My excuses fell away under the weight of her gaze. I let out a heavy sigh, my shoulders dropping. Running my fingers through my hair, I had no choice but to keep with my honesty. "That's not what this is."

"It never is, though, is it, Bay?" An edge had taken her voice. "What's wrong with this one, hmm? Too handsome? Too charming? Oh, I know, too perfectly suited."

"Kennia, I—"

"No." She stepped toward me, her delicate brows creasing. "You do this *every time*. Look… I know you've had issues in the past, but that don't mean you can keep cuttin' yourself off from people."

I shifted on my feet. "That's... That's not what this is."

"Sounds like it to me." She was becoming irritated. I didn't blame her. I'd thrown a lot at her at once.

"Look... It's just, ugh!" My own frustrations grew to the point where I'd begun to compulsively scratch the back of my head while I struggled to find the right words. "Maybe I shouldn't have said anything."

"Then why'd you even tell me in the first place?"

"Because I like him."

The tension died in an instant, swept away by a declaration that not even I had expected to come out of my mouth.

"You do?" she asked, a sympathetic tone replacing the annoyance.

The nod was slow to come, but I managed, regardless of my discomfort.

"That's great."

Shaking my head came easier.

"Well...why not?"

"He's a passenger," I replied with a shrug that I regretted the moment I'd done it. "And there's nothing in that long term. Besides, I doubt he feels the same for me."

"You don't know that."

Always the optimist.

"Does it matter? I'm only here for a couple more days, then it's right back to Arizona. Whatever might've happened between us can literally *only* be a fling."

A new sort of thickness filled our cabin.

Kennia and I had been through a lot, been friends for a long time. Before I quit the stewarding world, she and I had been closer than sisters for almost ten years. The woman knew everything about me, from what made me laugh to what made me cry. She knew about my fucked-up home life, my fucked-up relationships and my fucked-up views on dating. She knew everything, and in that moment, I wish she didn't.

Having a front row ticket to my life as much as I did hers made it all the easier for the compassionate young woman to pity my reality.

She really could read people like a book.

Stepping forward to close the distance between us, Kennia wrapped me in her arms and embraced me tight. She caressed my back, resting her cheek on my shoulder. I hugged her just as hard.

"I'm sorry, Bay," she said with a slightly muffled voice. "But hey." She pulled back and grabbed my face in her tiny yet freakishly strong hands. "You still got a couple of days on your visa, yeah? Before you have to fly back? You can make 'em count."

I snorted a laugh and rolled my eyes.

"I'm serious," she said with a light smile. "Gotta make the best of them before you go back to that desert hellscape you call home."

"Says the Australian."

"You'll notice I'm not actually there, right?"

A true, genuine smile formed on my lips. Kennia giggled and pulled me into another hug.

With a secure final squeeze, we parted.

"Come on, then. We got rich people to look after."

She headed out of the door, leaving it open for me to follow, and I did.

I hadn't known what to expect when I'd thrown my sex-life in her face like that. I wasn't even sure why I'd done it. Maybe a part of me needed a chance to admit that I'd begun to like Michele more than I should have? Maybe I didn't have nearly as much control over my statements as I'd initially thought?

Maybe I just wanted someone in the world to know that I'd found a match and in a few hours' time would have to watch him walk away forever?

Before I left the room, I put on a set of bracelets to hide the pink rope burn on my wrists and went to work.

Chapter Fifteen

While breakfast was being served, The Gaggle and Dominic barely managed to pour themselves into their seats at the tail-end of it. They looked horrible, how one might assume someone would look after downing an untold number of bottles of varying alcohols.

None of them ate, instead clinging to various hot, caffeinated beverages. But one's focus had remained on me, regardless of how little time I spent handing off plates and pouring coffee.

Yasmin's heavy-lidded gaze was on me the second that Chris and I had emerged on deck with the plates and didn't falter. Her eyes were bloodshot, the bags unable to be hidden beneath her makeup, but there was something in them that I couldn't escape. It made the hair on the back of my neck stand on end because it was different. It'd been uninterested before, annoyed. There was something evil in her gaze that morning, and it lingered.

I'd become so distracted by it, in fact, that I hadn't glanced to Michele once. He was usually my focus and would've been, especially given our night together, but Yasmin was unblinking, cold and disturbing.

In some way, perhaps it was best that I hadn't lingered on him. It was the last day of the charter, and given the crush that seemed to be building, it would've been best to move on as soon as possible.

It was a little heartbreaking, though. I couldn't deny how well we fit, how our kinks aligned in such a perfect way.

That being said, it *was* the end of the charter, therefore the end of our deal. I had to keep repeating that fact to myself, more than I'd expected.

Although, so long as The Gaggle remained, we would be unable to pull anchor.

It'd become a *damned if you do, damned if you don't* sort of situation. On the one hand, the longer The Gaggle remained, the longer it would take for us to reach shore and disembark. On the other, it also meant it would be unlikely for Michele and me to have a final game. Not impossible, but unlikely.

Chris and I headed toward the galley with the dishes from the previous course stacked along our arms.

He let out a long whistle. "Man, seems the blonde's hatin' you a bit more each day, doesn't it?"

"Looks like it," I said with a sigh. "Could've burned a hole straight through me with that kind of rage. What do you think her problem is?"

Shouldn't have asked that, stupid.

"You kidding?" he asked with a laugh. We reached the galley and went through scraping the leftover food into the trash. "Her little boyfriend's only had eyes for you."

I scoffed and did my best to instill the proper level of disbelief into the action, though might not have been entirely successful.

"Whatever," I said. "Then again, I think it's probably best I keep away from them while they're on the ship."

"Well, I got laundry duty if you wanna switch." He wagged his brows at me. "What do you say?"

The offer had been a relief, though I tried not to seem too eager for it. My main duties were always to serve the clients, and with Yasmin doing her best to kill me with a stare and my crush becoming an issue, I was all too happy to trade.

"Sure," I said, nodding.

Chris' face ignited with a smile. "Oh, thank Christ for that. I *hate* washin' all that damn bedding."

I chuckled but said nothing further.

Scraping off the rest of my plates, I set them aside so he could load them into the dishwasher, something that would've been my job five minutes before.

"You still owe me a hundred bucks," I said while I disappeared down the hall.

His 'yeah, yeah, yeah' followed me until I turned a corner and charged up the winding stairs.

* * * *

Standing at the linen closet, I thumbed through the folded sheets and made an internal count to ensure that I had enough to turn down the beds.

I didn't mind cleaning or making the beds. I found it oddly relaxing, in fact. The tasks were simple and straightforward, albeit a little time-consuming.

The soft click of heels against a hard floor trickled into my ears. A pit formed in my gut, and I was almost too afraid to see who might've been on their way, worried that Yasmin had torn herself from the others to search me out, but the truth was something else entirely.

Gathering the courage I was surprised I lacked, I peered over my shoulder to find Michele the source. My heart leaped, doing a delightful little flip in my chest before settling as much as it could when he was around.

"Is there anything I can help you with, Mr. Sacchi?" I asked while keeping my focus on the sheets, though not truly bothering to count them anymore.

He continued to close the distance between us until he stood directly behind me. The heat of him poured into my back, warming the depths I was surprised had chilled since the previous night.

Spicy, woody cologne filtered into my nose. I would never be able to smell anything similar without it sparking a memory of him.

He leaned in, engulfing me with minimal effort. "I had difficulty sleeping last night."

Heat bloomed in my cheeks, quickly spreading throughout and finding focus between my legs. There'd been no hesitation the moment his rich, sultry voice met my ears.

I swallowed the lump forming in my throat and responded. "I'm sorry to hear that. Is there anything I can do to help?"

There was no point in pretending I was doing my job anymore.

"Perhaps," he replied. "I think my mind may have been preoccupied." His hands fell to my hips while he nuzzled the hair behind my ear. "I've been thinking about disembarking later this afternoon and hoped to capitalize on my remaining time."

My breathing became shallow, and my pulse thundered. Each heartbeat caused my clit to ache with a breed of want that was specific to him.

"I understand," I said with a slight whisper. I'd begun to lean into the action, into his touch. "If there's anything I can do to help, I would be more than willing."

He dragged his lips along the curve of my ear and my eyes drifted shut on reflex.

"Do you mean that?"

"Of course."

He glided his hands up my sides and soon wrapped them around my breasts. I shivered against him, a soft whimper escaping my lips.

Michele held me tight to his chest, kneading and massaging my breasts, pinching my nipples the way I liked. We may have been together for little more than a week, but the man had learned my code, learned how to unlock my deepest desires and pleasures.

He sighed into my ear, hot breath rolling over my skin.

"I can't stop thinking of being inside you," he said. "Of how good you feel on my cock."

I shivered once again and, filled with growing confidence, I reached between us. Openly grasping his dick was something I wouldn't have dared do a week ago.

A lot had changed.

Michele groaned in response, his mouth clamping down on my neck to deliver a spine-tingling bite.

Memories flared while I trailed my fingers up and down his length. I had a reference now, knowledge of how good he felt, and it helped fuel my desires.

"Neither can I," I said.

A growl laced his words when he said, "I want to fuck you again, Basil."

I reached for the back of his head, plowing my fingers through his hair and clutching it tight.

"Then fuck me," I said without a hint of care as to how desperate I may have sounded.

He groaned in approval at my choice of words and quickly went to work undoing my shorts.

"Is that what you want?" His hand disappeared into my shorts, cupping my sex a second later. I had no doubt he could feel how excited I'd become.

My hips bucked when his strong digits began to trace circles over my clit.

"Yes."

His breathing became labored and his fingers faster.

"Give me permission, and I will take you right here, right now."

I trembled in his grasp, my mind filling with all manner of salacious thought.

"I want you to fuck every part of me." A desperate whimper saturated my words.

He sighed, raking his teeth along the side of my neck. "Starting with your beautiful throat."

The fact that we stood in the hall exposed on all sides meant nothing to me. The fact that my rules had become distant memories meant nothing. The fact that I could have and would have been fired for what I was doing meant *nothing*. My only concern had been a repeat of the previous night's exploits.

"*Sei la tortura mia.*"

A loud bang echoed to our right, drawing our attention away from one another. A door had flown open and slammed into the wall, a figure stumbling forward without complete control of their limbs until they spotted us.

There would've been no hiding or pretending we weren't groping one another.

The intruder, the one who'd broken up our moment, hadn't been a coworker or even my boss, people that I could've reasoned with. It was Yasmin, and every hint of lingering drunkenness or hangover vanished the second her gaze landed on us.

"Shit," Michele muttered.

He withdrew from me, allowing me the chance to button my shorts again.

Her eyes blazed, and for a second I could have sworn actual flames were going to burst from the soft-brown color.

A breath passed and another, lulling me into a false sense of security until she launched herself forward.

Yasmin screamed with rage, threats pouring from her lips in Italian. While I was ignorant to the meaning of every word uttered, the hatred in her face was more than enough to guide my guess.

Michele stepped into her path, catching her by the waist while she pointed an angry finger at me. Venom dripped from every word, each syllable punching me in the gut. I'd never seen anyone so furious, so livid.

I retreated, backing away from the wild animal trying to gnaw my face off. And if I were being honest, I had no doubt that Yasmin would have used that perfect manicure of hers to peel my skin away.

The staff stairwell appeared in the corner of my eye. I scrambled with the handle, my gaze still locked on the furious woman, but she'd calmed. No longer clamoring to climb over Michele to get to me, Yasmin had instead gone disturbingly still.

I yanked open the door, ready to rush off like a terrified deer when I froze. Yasmin lifted her hand and pointed a finger-gun at me. Without a word, she pulled a phantom trigger.

It was enough to send me darting into the staff halls, slamming the door shut behind me and cutting me off from the woman who I didn't doubt wanted to kill me.

Fuck, fuck, fuck, fuck...

The word ran through my head on a loop. I'd fucked up more than I had anticipated. Until that point, I hadn't viewed Yasmin as a threat in the typical sense. She clearly had a connection with Michele, a past that I never would, but his lack of interest and my assumptions about her kept me from being worried. Except, I was wrong. There was something murderous in her eyes, so deep and genuine that I was afraid.

More so than before, hiding was the better option for me.

Chapter Sixteen

I spent a few hours perfecting the illusion that I didn't exist, darting through hidden halls and peering around corners out of fear of the rich, furious woman who wanted to do me harm. I'd avoided most everyone, in fact. It was best for me to keep my head down.

If things had to go wrong, I guess I was glad it'd been the last day, but I used to be better than that.

Making my way down the corridor that led to the laundry room to check on the dryers, I passed the galley where a handful of the crew were eating their lunch. Kennia wasn't among them. I suspected she was busy with the other deckhands preparing for the later docking, but the stewards were there.

Chris stood to put his glass in the sink and offered me a head nod in greeting. I did the same, sliding by him on my trek.

"Oh, hey," he said, jogging after me. "Have, uh. Have you been hidin' out?"

A shiver rippled across the back of my neck, but I did my best to keep it hidden.

"No. Why?"

"Don't know. It just seems like you've been avoiding everyone, especially Yasmin."

There'd been a leading way he asked the question, his tone unavoidable. It forced me to pause, turning to look at him with my brows creased. An unsettling feeling had crept up my spine and it refused to leave me.

"What do you mean?" I asked, hoping I'd instilled the appropriate emotion, even though I had no idea what that might've been. I was in uncharted territory.

"She was tearing through here asking where you were," he said. "Looked like she was on a mission to beat the hell out of you. What happened?"

I shrugged, a lie quick to form. "Maybe she found out that I pushed her into the pool?"

He seemed to give my excuse a fair amount of thought but shook his head.

"Maybe, but something's different. She was furious with Mr. Sacchi, too."

My heart sank. Not only had I put my job at risk but I'd also thrown some kind of wrench into his life, too.

I should've kept my hands to myself. There was a reason I had rules.

* * * *

The day continued in a haze, my mind too busy to bother settling on anything in particular. Of the ways I'd thought the charter would go, being hunted down by a trust fund Barbie who genuinely frightened me because I'd fucked her intended boyfriend hadn't been on that list.

Thank Christ The Gaggle had left around lunch. It seemed as though Yasmin had either lost her patience with trying to find me in the floating mansion or she'd been ushered away to avoid something terrible. I didn't care either way. She was gone.

Navigating the hall with the intent of cleaning the windows that lined the second floor of the yacht, I found the man I'd been thinking of for the bulk of the day.

Michele sat in a chair with a tablet in hand, his gaze on the screen while resting his head in his propped-up palm. The desire to turn and run had been strong, a need that bubbled inside me. But the need to apologize was stronger.

Slow, measured steps brought me close enough to draw his gaze. He peered up at me, a small flinch in the corner of his eye.

"Miss Hurst, hello," he said, setting his tablet on the end table to his left. He rose to his feet with ease and turned his full attention to me.

"I wanted to apologize," I said, getting the words out before they could become lodged in my throat, blocked from escape by my growing nerves.

His brows creased and he lolled his head to the side. "For what?"

I didn't bother hiding my disbelief. "After what happened in the hallway?"

His expression fell and his head dipped. Sliding his hands into his pockets, he relaxed his stance before he met my gaze again.

"Yasmin isn't your concern," he said. "The ordeal simply forced me to put things straight that should have been settled a long time ago."

"It doesn't matter. I overstepped *way* too much, to the point where I interfered with your actual life."

"You need to stop apologizing. You've done nothing wrong."

It didn't make me feel any better, given what'd happened. It'd been clear the moment they stepped onto the ship that Yasmin's and Michele's groups had a past, a close enough connection that the old men had embraced one another. Whether through business or something else just as important, they were close, and I'd thrown all of that into chaos.

"It's still my fault," I muttered. "She was so angry."

He stepped forward, closing the distance between us. His warm, tender hand cupped my jaw, sending a tremble radiating throughout me.

"Stop," he said with a gentle tone. "Don't apologize for things you had nothing to do with."

Our gazes remained locked. It was the first time I'd peered into his eyes without another intent lingering in the background, the first time I'd seen the warm, chocolate color they were in the midday light. They were beautiful, but in a different way than I'd expected.

Until that point, Michele had dripped sex, been the tangible manifestation of my fantasies. He'd held a level of beauty greatly influenced by those factors. But standing in the parlor with the quiet rumble of the distant engine, the soft touch on my cheek, my view of him had changed.

My heart swelled and lips parted with a breath. Something was different, but I didn't know what it was.

Then it ended. As though a hypnotist had clicked his fingers, Michele blinked the fond emotion from his eyes, though a smile appeared across his lips. He lowered his hand, returning it to his pocket.

"I should let you get back to work, Miss Hurst."

My nod was slow, but I'd managed, and with a bow of his head, he regained his seat.

Not sure of what'd happened or what'd flickered between us in that moment, I separated myself from him as quickly as I could. My crush was getting out of control, twisting things in my head and causing me to read deeper into them than I should.

The sooner we got to shore the better.

* * * *

For the rest of our journey to Venice, Michele and I shared glances, glimpses of something unsaid, but his expression remained unreadable. It'd been blank, emotionless and unsettling.

I suspected news of what'd happened with Yasmin had trickled through everyone on the ship, and he'd received a fair bit of the blame. My only evidence had been how his family eyed me when I brought them something to eat or drink, or how they'd suddenly stop speaking whenever I, not anyone else, was within earshot.

There was an unsettling atmosphere that surrounded the Sacchi family now, one I had a harder time identifying than I'd expected. The only thing I knew for certain was they didn't like me.

Our families have known one another for a long time.
I set right what should have been dealt with long ago.

His words sifted through my head, hints as to how much I'd fucked up whatever their plans might have been. Maybe she and Michele were supposed to end up together? They seemed like that sort of family, the kind that would arrange attachments like the royals. Maybe they'd dated before, and she was hoping to rekindle? They were familiar enough with one another that it'd been a possibility.

Jesus Christ, what had I done?

* * * *

Around six that evening, *The Silver Wind* pulled into the dock, and the deckhands dashed around the ship, a choreographed ballet of people who brought us in and secured the monolith to the prescribed parking spot.

As we had when they'd arrived, the crew lined up along the deck to bid farewell to the passengers. We never spoke to them, but I suppose it was meant to be polite or maybe a formal remnant of the past.

One by one the Sacchi family sauntered off the ship and onto the dock while stewards who weren't with the rest of us set their luggage on the pristine wooden slat, only to have them scooped up by men in black suits. None of them glanced at me, not even Dominic.

The last to leave, Michele spoke to the others and nodded at something I couldn't hear. Thick, burly men who seemed more the bodyguard type than bellhops retrieved the luggage and waited behind the patriarchs. They set off not long after, but he remained. Rubbing his hand over his stubble-ridden chin, Michele glanced back at me. Like he had the first day and every one since, he found me without having to search the other faces, as though he knew exactly where I'd be.

A breath passed, my heart thumping away to an unsteady rhythm.

Without a word, he dipped his chin to me in a silent farewell. A sad smile flittered at the corners of my lips, and I returned the sentiment. He walked off a second later, bringing up the rear of the retreating party.

The moment the passengers were gone, the crew split apart and began the task of cleaning the ship. There was no immediate charter after the Sacchis, but protocol had to be maintained.

"Hey." Kennia's voice caused me to turn while I headed for the aft deck. She smiled at me, hooking her elbow with mine. "You all righ'?"

I nodded and cleared the lump out of my throat. "Yeah, I'm fine."

I doubted she believed me, but she didn't press. "So, you stayin' on the ship or what?"

"No. I'm going to get a hotel then fly out from there."

"Okay. Well, guess that means we should get to work so we can get outta here in the mornin'."

Flashing another dazzling smile, she set off with the rest of the deckhands while I broke apart with the stewards. With no clients, the cleaning was uninterrupted, but that also meant we were scrubbing the ship to within an inch of its life, erasing every memory of the Sacchi family.

Chapter Seventeen

After saying my farewells to the crew and thanking them for the chance to work, I took my things and headed off the ship with plans to meet Kennia later for sightseeing. I couldn't say whether or not I'd ever be asked to return, given how things had ended between the clients and me, but I would've liked the chance to work with them again. The people on *The Silver Wind* were fun and welcoming.

The walk toward shore was longer than I'd expected it to be, winding this way and that, weaving through million-dollar boats that ranged from motored to sail. Until the six-mile mark, I hadn't realized we were tied so far back.

While that was an exaggeration, it was close to a half mile from where we'd docked to the gate that cut me off from the city of Venice, but I hadn't made it quite there before being stopped in my tracks.

How does he do that?

Michele hesitated in step as well, staring at me as though he hadn't expected to stumble across me at that moment. Fair enough. I hadn't expected to see him, either.

"Miss Hurst, hello," he said when we reached one another.

"Hi," I muttered. "Um... Did..." My brain struggled. "Uh, did you forget something on the ship? Or..."

Was I supposed to offer to help him? Was I supposed to get him something to eat?

As stupid as it might've sounded, I didn't know how to interact with Michele outside of the environment of the yacht. My only other interaction had been at Labyrinth. We had assigned roles. I knew how to behave then. Standing with him on the dock? No idea.

His gaze danced over me, from my civilian clothing to the bag hanging from my shoulder, and his brows creased.

"You're leaving?"

I nodded. "Yeah." His expression dropped and it made me a little sad to see. "But everyone is. They'll only be here long enough to restock and relax for a little while, then take another charter."

"The ship isn't going anywhere."

My head cocked. "What makes you say that?"

"Because it's ours. We intended to bring it to Venice to stay."

The words were there, hanging in the air for me to hear.

I stared at him, my eyes narrowed in confusion, unable to absorb such a simple sentence. Michele seemed unaffected by it, staring back at me with his hands in his pockets, the picture of ease and relaxation.

My gaze drifted back in the direction of the boat then to him once again.

"That thing is yours?"

Michele nodded. "My family's, but yes."

"I-I thought you were just a charter."

He shook his head. "No."

"So you're telling me that you *own that*, a vessel that costs more than half a million dollars to rent *a week*. You just...own it."

"Yes. We rent it out from time to time, but it belongs to us," he said, brows furrowing while he stared at me. "Are you all right?"

I couldn't answer because I didn't know. To rent a yacht so large, Michele or his family must have had a substantial bank account. There would've been no other way for them to be the clientele without plenty of zeros.

That being said, there was a vast difference between renting something like *The Silver Wind* and owning it. The general population liked to assume that when a boat was docked, the expenses for it ended and they could save some cash while it wasn't on open water. *Wrong.* Even when not in use, a yacht, especially a super-yacht, cost the owner hundreds of thousands of dollars a year in maintenance, docking fees, licensing, inspections and crew costs.

Who had that as a disposable income?

"Who are you people?"

The question had come out more accusatory than I meant, ruder, but Michele remained his usual composed self.

"We have a very old family."

I narrowed my eyes. That must've been the vaguest reply I'd ever received from someone before. Everyone came from an old family. There was no way to exist otherwise, but he'd said it in a way that told me he thought the answer was enough to explain everything. For some, perhaps, but not me. I let him think it had been, though.

"Okay, then," I muttered, unsure of how to proceed.

"So, you see, you and the others are free to enjoy Venice. The ship won't be leaving for some time."

The prospect of staying in one of the most historically beautiful cities in the world did excite me enough that I cared less and less about Michele owning a multimillion-dollar yacht.

But as the plans formed and I thought about the gondola rides, the hikes around the city, the food and the culture, I remembered something that should have been painfully obvious. My heart sank and took with it all of my joy.

"I can't," I said. "My paperwork is only for this trip."

"What does that mean?"

"That I have to leave soon. I'm on a work visa."

I couldn't recall the official length of my stay without checking my papers, but my working visa hadn't been for much longer than the trip. That'd been why I was hired. I wasn't full-time crew, so I wasn't afforded the same privileges.

Michele's expression remained stoic. He mulled over something then retrieved his cell phone from his pocket and searched for a number.

Placing the phone to his ear, he proceeded to have a brisk but firm conversation with whoever had answered the other end of the line. He gave concise orders that I couldn't understand.

I should really learn some damn Italian.

When he'd finished the call, Michele returned his phone and hands to his pockets. He smiled at me rather smugly.

"What was that about?" I asked.

"It appears we will be requiring your service for another two weeks."

I stared at him, my eyes wide.

"You should be receiving a phone call shortly."

True to his word, my cell phone rang a moment later. When I answered it, I was surprised to hear the voice of the woman I'd spoken to from the agency, the one who'd arranged my job on *The Silver Wind*.

She told me that the charter had been extended and until Janice had fully recovered, they'd need me to continue my stay. I stared at Michele the entire conversation, watched as satisfaction crossed his features.

The agent said that she would email me the paperwork momentarily and that I was to sign it and send it back. It'd be processed, and I would be free to remain with the ship until the two weeks ended or Janice returned, whichever came first. We hung up shortly after.

"I don't know if I should be impressed you can get things done that fast or freaked out."

The smugness disappeared, melting away until only sincerity remained, and I somehow found it more uncomfortable than the arrogance. It was sweet, even.

"Why?" I asked.

He cocked his head again, his brows pooling together. "Why what?"

"Why do you want to keep me here? It doesn't make sense."

A strange sensation tickled the back of my neck, an uncertainty that I hadn't felt for a long time. It was as though a spotlight had been shone on me, shining brighter than the sun and robbing me of a chance to conceal anything.

He saw me. I wasn't a steward or some masked woman in a club. I was me, and he *saw* me.

"You don't know anything about me. You've only seen me at work. You don't know what kind of books I like to read, the kind of music I listen to or if I'm allergic to anything. All you know is how I like to play." The words tumbled forward. "Why would you go through the trouble of reserving the crew for another two weeks?"

"I'd like to get to know you."

"Why?"

My level of confusion was met, but for an entirely different reason.

"Because I'd like to," he replied.

"Trust me. It's not worth it."

His brow rose high. "You have a very low opinion of yourself."

I opened my mouth to speak but couldn't manage.
Do I?

I'd always thought that my self-deprecating behavior had been on par with a normal person's. I didn't hate myself, but I, more than anyone, was well aware that I wasn't special enough for him to have gone out of his way like that. It didn't make sense to me.

Michele stepped forward, pulling me out of my thoughts and forcing me to focus on him.

"May I walk you to the ship?"

C. Tyler

"No," I answered quicker than I'd intended. "I mean, I've already booked a hotel room, so I might as well use it."

He nodded. "May I walk you to your hotel?"

An answer hadn't immediately come to mind, caught in the web of contradicting reasons and fumbling to escape so I could speak, but I knew what I wanted.

"I'd like that, thanks."

He smiled again, and it'd been just as warm as the last.

He held out his hand, silently asking for my bag, and while part of me wanted to childishly declare that I could hold my own luggage, I wasn't so proud to refuse the kind gesture.

Sliding it off my shoulder, he took it and looped it over his much broader one, then offered me a bent arm. Much like I did with Kennia, I looped mine around it, though, unlike when I was with her, I trembled inside.

Chapter Eighteen

Michele and I walked through the cobblestoned streets of Venice, along the canals and through the buildings guided by his knowledge of the city, though the maps app had been brought up for added insurance.

We remained arm in arm, and while I'd settled with the fact as best I assumed I could, the intimate contact left me in a bit of a daze. True, we'd had sex and done things to one another that many would have considered far more so, but they would've been wrong. That'd been our arrangement, the bargain struck to satiate our particular kinks. What we were doing on that walk was something reserved for people who were either friends or in some kind of relationship.

We were neither of those things.

And, to add to the strangeness of the situation, we weren't alone.

I hadn't noticed them at first, but perhaps half the distance to the hotel, a pair of men had come to my attention. Each was large and dressed in black, much like the ones who'd retrieved the family's luggage the previous day. I'd done my best to ignore them, but the longer they followed with their heads on a swivel, the more difficult it became.

"Mr. Sacchi."

He glanced down at me. "Please, call me Michele."

I nodded but doubted I would. It felt too informal for whatever was between us.

"Uh, who are those men?"

He shifted to peer over his shoulder, spotting the pair who stood out in stark contrast to the tourists and locals who surrounded us.

For the first time since meeting him, he seemed unsure. It'd been such a strange concept that it caused me to pause.

He stopped at my side and when I turned to face him, he did the same, though hesitated to meet my eye.

"They're my security team," he said, sounding deflated with the declaration.

I creased my brows. "You have a security team."

"Mm-hmm."

I waited for him to continue, but it didn't seem he was willing to do so. Having let a few things already fall to the wayside, including his weak explanation about the ownership of a super-yacht, I couldn't help but push.

"What is it you do that requires bodyguards?"

He could've been part of a political family. He could've been a celebrity of some kind. He could've been any number of things, but something told me that no, whatever the Sacchi family was, it was different from that.

We stood in silence, Michele sweeping his hand through his hair and scratching the back of his head.

He's nervous…

His gaze drifted to mine and, with resignation in his voice, he spoke.

"My family has many businesses," he said. "Some are quite lucrative."

You own a fifty-plus-million-dollar yacht. No shit.

"But not all are the safest ventures." His shoulders dropped. "Recently, some of our business partners have expressed their dissatisfaction."

I looked at the guards. "And that merits paying people to follow you around?"

He shrugged his shoulder. "It's unlikely anything will happen, but the precaution was prudent."

I turned my eye to him, cocking my brow. There were miles beneath the surface with him, untold depths that I doubted I would ever see.

"So," he said, hooking my elbow with his once more. "Do you and your friends have plans while in Venice?"

"Not any I'm aware of right now, but we want to explore," I said. *Guess that conversation's done.* "Do you have any suggestions?"

"Many." He smiled. "Venice has a lot to offer."

We rounded a corner and were presented with a bridge that would take us across the canal. On the other side sat my hotel, the sign prominently displayed for those who needed it.

I briefly wondered which of the windows that overlooked us belonged to the room I'd reserved.

Together, we navigated the bridge, bypassing the couples who lingered at the short stone wall in tender embraces, some snapping pictures that we'd done our best to avoid so we wouldn't interfere with the images. Others enjoyed the midday traffic through the canal.

When we reached the hotel, Michele and I lingered on the front step. He turned to me, another soft, but kind smile on his lips. In the fresh day's light, his eyes appeared almost honey in color.

"I hope you enjoy your stay in Venice, Miss Hurst," he said, handing me my bag.

"Me too."

"Would…" He hesitated, slipping his hands into his pockets once more. "Would it be possible to see you while you're here?"

The question caught me by surprise. Given how he'd all but ensured that I would stay in Italy, I thought he planned to see me plenty of times.

As it was, it seemed he'd done it so I had the chance to properly explore. It seemed as though he hadn't put any expectations at all on extending my work contract.

Oh, my God. How many thousands of dollars did he just drop keeping the crew on for two more weeks?

Am…am I obligated to spend time with him?

No. That's not it.

Looking at him had cleared my concern with the moment. There had been no arrogance, no expectation. Instead, he seemed a little uncertain, the discomfort from earlier returning while he waited for my response.

"Yeah," I said with a nod. His expression relaxed. "I'd like that."

"*Perfetto*," he said. He produced a folded piece of paper from his pocket and handed it to me. "If you need any advice on where to go or suggestions, feel free to call me."

Unfolding the paper presented me with a string of numbers written beneath his name. Heart fluttering once more, I did my best to ignore the heat swelling in my cheeks.

"I appreciate it."

"And please, let me know when you're free. I would love to show you the city."

I nodded again, and, though still unsure of how to handle the moment, I was glad to find myself in it.

Michele leaned forward, pressing his lips to my cheeks in a very typical European-style kiss. The sigh left me before I'd had the chance to pull it back, my eyelids fluttering.

He whispered in my ear, "Until then, *bella*."

Drawing back, he gave me a gentle nod and proceeded back the way we'd come. I wanted to linger, to watch him walk away, but the smarter side of me won out and I entered the building to check in.

* * * *

Lying in bed, I texted Kennia to let her know where I was and in which room. She replied that everyone was still busy with resupply and the like, but she'd let me know when they were free.

I felt a touch guilty that I wasn't there to help, given I was technically still an employee, but found a bit of solace in the fact that I wouldn't have been that great of an addition. I didn't know what was needed or what to do with it beyond purchase. The others would've had to tell me what to do, guide me through the tasks because I hadn't been on *The Silver Wind* long enough. I could've been as much of an obstacle as helpful.

Staring at my text log, I considered sending Michele a message. I wasn't certain what to say, but I did want to speak to him. I wanted to see him.

Opening a blank template, I filled in the number. My poor phone, an American product, wasn't sure what to do with the strange arrangement of numbers. I could only hope it still counted. I hadn't had to send texts to international numbers in a long time.

Hi. It's Bay.

The unsettling embarrassment of constructing such a stupid message had come before I'd even finished it, but I forced myself to send it off without a second thought. If I thought about it too much, I would've crippled myself with anxiety and not texted him at all.

The reply arrived sooner than I'd expected.

Heart in my throat, I unlocked the screen and saw a blue bubble on the left of the screen.

Hello. I'm glad to hear from you.

My pulse quickened a little, thumbs hovering over the keypad. I wanted to send something, but nothing came to mind. In fact, my head had gone completely blank, which allowed another message to pop up.

Have you made plans for the evening?

A direct question gave me a path to follow, something to anchor to.

I replied.

No. Everyone's still preoccupied on the boat for now. Any suggestions?

As before, the blue bubble appeared quicker than I'd expected.

Would you be interested in having dinner with me tonight?

The desire to agree had come fast, boiling to the surface and nearly spilling out of me, but, just as I had throughout the whole of our conversation, I hesitated.

I needed to be sure that my mind had drifted to the correct place.

Are you asking me on a date?

Chewing on my bottom lip, I sat up, bringing my knees to my chest and resting my chin on them while I waited for a response.

Yes.

I twitched.

Those things didn't belong together. I didn't play with the men I dated, and I didn't date the men I played with. They were such stark contrasts that I wouldn't allow the lines to cross.

Whenever I would introduce my partner to the world I enjoyed, their judgment shortly followed and the relationship ended not long after. And the men I played with weren't the dating sort, generally wanting nothing more than release, like me. The one who had been interested didn't seem capable of separating play from life, taking his role as my Dom much further than I wanted. I'd been glad to end that particular relationship.

A long time ago, I'd learned that I could never have both, and yes, it hurt not being able to be myself with my partners, but I coped as any adult would.

The reality was that if I wanted to be in a relationship, I had to bury that side of me deep, *deep* down. It wasn't healthy in the long-run, however, which was why I'd decided dating wasn't for me. I just stopped doing it.

But what was I supposed to do when someone who knew my kinks, knew the exact things I enjoyed, asked me on a date? Should I turn him down in spite of how badly I wanted to agree? Should I agree, even though past events had proven disappointing?

Conflicting thoughts bounced around in my head long enough that another message appeared on my screen, the time-stamp telling me four minutes had passed. I hadn't realized I'd been that distracted.

Perhaps I overstepped. I apologize.

My stomach sank. I knew the embarrassment that came with shooting a shot only to miss.

You didn't, but I don't date. You surprised me.

May I ask why you don't?

With a sigh of resignation, I decided to be honest. If there were anyone beyond Kennia with whom I could tell the truth, it'd be Michele. We'd been through enough at that point.

It's never worked well in the past. The two sides of my life never blended.

Well, I can only offer you dinner and company.

That does sound nice.

Is that a yes?

I paused, staring at the brief conversation. Was my reticence coming from a reasonable place or not? I didn't know, and that bothered me. I didn't like the uncertainty and perhaps that was what guided my answer.

Yes.

I'm happy to hear it.

A smile curled the corner of my lips.

Is there a dress code?

You can wear whatever you like.

There'd been relief in the statement, but I still intended to dress nicely.

I will be outside your hotel at 8 PM.

I'll see you then.

My smile grew and didn't show any signs of faltering. Any apprehensions I'd had seconds prior seemed to have dissipated, leaving me vibrating with excitement over the prospect.

Closing the message, I opened my previous conversation with Kennia.

I have a date with Michele tonight.

Almost as soon as I'd sent the text, her reply came.

On my way.

Chapter Nineteen

At half past six that night, I stepped out of the bathroom wearing a dress Kennia and I had found during our shopping trip. The black fabric clung to my body, soft while it shifted with each step.

A collar curled around the back of my neck, though didn't connect at the front and instead plunged to the center of my chest in a sliver meant to show just a little bit of skin. There were no sleeves, leaving my arms bare, and it had been sculpted to cradle my hips before ending just above my knees.

It was simple, but beautiful with the way the lines had been arranged to accentuate the wearer's natural shape. Whoever had created it knew how to do a lot with very little effort.

Kennia let out a wolf whistle while lying on my bed, smiling at me proudly.

"Thanks," I said with an uncomfortable tremble in the back of my throat. "Maybe I should just wear my other dress, the one I brought with me?"

"Nope," she said. "This is perfect."

"This is expensive."

She giggled at the argument I'd been giving since we'd seen the garment hanging on a mannequin because it hadn't stopped me from buying the damn thing. Although, many times since, I'd thought about returning it after the fact.

"It looked lovely on the mannequin," she said, reaching behind her back to retrieve my shoes. I took them, dropping them to the stone floor to put on. "And it looks even better on you."

My thankful smile flickered in and out. In the hours since I'd spoken to Michele, my confidence in my decision had begun to waver.

While I wiggled my feet into my shoes, the same I'd brought on the trip, Kennia retrieved the other bag on the bed. Metal chains clinked and rattled inside the paper.

"So," she said leadingly, "you still hopin' to use these, eh?"

Running my fingers through my hair to guide it out of my eyes, I spotted her lifting the cuffs with a single finger, beaming with a smile so ridiculously happy that I had no doubt the crew on the boat could see it.

My stomach fluttered while I recalled spotting them in the window of a shop we passed on the way back to the hotel. It catered to people like me, something I'd been surprised by...and enjoyed.

The cuffs were leather and inches thick to minimize the burn of ropes or the indentions handcuffs could leave behind. They were meant for comfort and not unlike the kind that he'd used to suspend me from the bar back at Labyrinth.

A six-inch chain separated the cuffs. It wasn't much in the grand scheme of things, but it was plenty for me to thread through a plank or bar of a headboard.

It may have been wishful thinking to purchase them in the first place, but if needed, I could return those, too.

"Knock it off," I said. She giggled. I swept my hands down my dress over and over, unable to shake the unease. "Are you sure I look okay?"

A sweet expression took her features. Setting down the cuffs, she slid off the edge and the bed and stood, approaching me without breaking eye contact.

"You okay?"

"Nervous," I said with a laugh to match. "I haven't had a date in a while."

She narrowed her eyes. "Define a while."

"Four..."

"Months?"

"Years."

She tried to hide the surprise, but it glimmered in her eyes a split second before she'd been able to rein it back.

"Jesus, Bay. For just a date? Not even a game or anythin' like that, but it's been that long since you've gone to dinner or a movie or somethin' with somebody?"

My nod was slow to come but did.

Her brows pooled and her lips parted with a sigh. Kennia had always been vocal about her desire for me to find someone with whom I could connect, so her sadness made sense. That didn't make it easier to see, though.

"And I'm nervous because I actually have stuff in common with this guy, but I don't know how to act."

Her features relaxed. Reaching for me, she held my arms and squared herself on me.

"Jus' be yourself," she said. "You're not so bad."

I hugged her, squeezing her tight. She chuckled at my response, but I couldn't help myself.

"Now then," she said, stroking my back. "Let's do something 'bout that hair."

My laugh came quick.

* * * *

At eight o'clock on the dot, my phone chirped with an incoming message.

I'm downstairs when you're ready.

Taking a deep breath, I rolled my head from side to side to alleviate the nervous tension, but it did little to help. Being the full-grown adult that I was, I might've been smart enough to know the build-up was the worst part of any situation, yet that knowledge did *nothing* to stop me from falling victim to it.

The end of my high, tight ponytail brushed my shoulders with each turn of my head, tickling more than I'd expected. It was the style Kennia had chosen, a slicked-back, high ponytail. It worked.

I'll be right down.

I slid my phone, wallet and room key into my clutch and made my way downstairs, breathing in time with each step.

Exiting through the front door presented me with the cool night air of Venice. A soft, warm glow surrounded the buildings, illuminating the scene with a hint of romance, and within it stood Michele.

He turned to me, spinning slowly on his heel with his hands in his pockets. He was dressed in a bespoke black suit and a white shirt, which he'd unbuttoned just enough to show a dusting of dark hair.

His gaze traveled up and down the length of me, missing nothing. I'd experienced that stare before, the one I swore I felt. A smile formed.

"You look beautiful," he said on his approach.

"Thank you."

He offered his hand and helped me down the two front steps, drawing me to his chest. As he had before, he placed a kiss on each cheek, which I'd attempted to reciprocate, but had been unable to focus the moment his cologne touched my nose.

Michele had been slow to retreat, his stubble scraping my cheek and warm breath gracing my lips. Inches soon separated us, though not many.

Heat pulsed in my veins, a tingle radiating down my spine. The want that'd become common on *The Silver Wind* had sparked to life, returning with a vengeance as though we'd spent months apart versus the hours it'd been.

Swallowing the desire that continued to build, I forced myself to speak.

"Where are we going to eat?" I asked with a whisper.

The darkness that'd seeped into his eyes faded a little, but not completely.

"I have a home-cooked meal planned," he said, standing at arm's length again.

"Sounds delicious."

When he offered me his arm, I accepted and together we walked toward the docks.

Fear licked at my insides, a shallow dread of what I was afraid would happen. I didn't want to go to the ship, to eat among the people I worked with alongside one of the clients we'd spent over a week tending to. There was no doubt in my mind that rumors had likely spread to a few of the crewmembers, if not all of them, and I didn't want to confirm their suspicions.

Anxiety climbed with each yard traveled. I fought the urge to speak up, to voice my apprehension, but the need never arose. Rather than turn toward the left when we reached the docks, we turned right. Every step took us farther and farther from the yachts and with it returned my ability to breathe.

Michele led me to a speedboat that'd been tied up, and he leaped into it first then held up his arms to help me. My dress was too tight for me to try stepping down, which he seemed to sense.

With me gripping his shoulders, he tenderly held my waist and lifted me onto the boat. I clung to him for a moment, even after he'd set me down.

"We should sit," he said.

Keeping his hand on my waist, he brought me to the long bench seat that stretched across the back of the boat. We sat side by side, his arm around my back.

After a few words spoken to the captain in Italian, we exited the harbor.

The wind whipped by the moment we were free of the *no wake* area. The nose of the boat rose above the surf, allowing us to slice through the black water.

Distant lights danced across the surface, glittering stars in the starless sky. I held him tight, desperate for the heat of his body while we traversed the choppy sea.

He leaned into me, his cheek against mine and blocking the wind in the process.

"I'm happy you agreed to see me tonight," he said just loud enough for me to hear over the outside world.

I reached for him, sliding my hand beneath his open coat and around the thick muscle of his back. He sighed in response, tensing his fingers on my back.

"So am I," I replied.

He dropped his free hand to my thigh, drawing my legs closer to him.

Michele encompassed me with nothing more than his being, the powerful aura that the man emanated. It was enough to brush away the chill that the ocean struggled to force on us and to make me forget how long had passed before the boat slowed.

The wind became less aggressive and the engine quieter. No longer pushed against the back of the seat, we drew back from one another. My gaze lingered on him, his face cast almost completely in shadow.

"We're here," he said.

"Where?"

He guided my gaze to the distance.

An island sat not far from us, one of the few that dotted the coast of Italy. Some of them were privately owned and some property of the government, much like it was in the States. Given the context and what lay before me, I could only assume that whatever we were motoring toward must have been the former.

Trees and other greenery, not unlike the sort that plenty used to landscape throughout the country, lined the island's shore and through which I spotted an estate.

"Welcome to *Cancello del Paradiso*," he said as the boat pulled into a slip with expert precision. "Or, The Gateway to Heaven."

The captain leaped out to tie us off and lowered a very stiff plank with textured indentions from the dock. He held it in place with his toe while Michele did the same in the boat.

With my hand clasped tight in his, I ascended, trading off with the captain when I neared the top. I hadn't taken a breath until I stood on the dock itself, so certain that I was going to plummet into the sea the second the speedboat shifted.

He joined me a second later with much more grace than I'd managed.

After speaking to the captain, he turned his attention to me.

"Come along, *cara mia*," he said, touching the small of my back. "Dinner awaits."

He said home-cooked meal, right?

Does he own a fucking island, too?

Chapter Twenty

A large villa sat at the top of the island, overlooking the small spit of land. Every inch of the property had been landscaped, consisting of layered patios, terraces and verandas. Stone paths sliced through beds of flowers, sculpted bushes and fruit trees. Each had been lined with lit torches, the flames dancing in the soft sea breeze.

The villa itself must have been more than a century old with marble arches, open walkways and windows that would allow every hint of sun in. It stood as a large monument, a focal point amid the beauty of the greenery.

There was so much for me to see and no chance for it to happen so late at night. Hell, I wouldn't have been able to manage during the day, either. It would take days for me to discover all the secrets that surrounded me.

Michele kept me close to his side while he guided me through the walking paths, whiffs of something floral mixing with the salty air. Somewhere in the distance the water churned, crashing against the rocks as it lapped at the island.

I was surrounded by something otherworldly, a hypnotic beauty that many never would've had the chance to witness.

We descended a small set of stairs that leveled out on another veranda. Unlike the others, it'd been laid with a design not unlike the Roman mosaics I'd seen in ancient artwork, in the center of which sat a table.

Candles lined the design, flickered with life on the tabletop and ran the length of the short stone wall that separated us from the landscaping.

He brought me to the table and pulled my chair out for me in the process.

"Thank you," I said, taking my seat. He soon joined me at the table. "This is beautiful."

He smiled. "I'm happy you like it."

"You didn't have to do this, though. You didn't have to go out of the way like this."

"I assure you, I did very little," he said. "My family has homes all over the world, many of which are in Italy, including Venice."

"So, you *do* own the island."

He seemed to weigh whether or not to reply, but as he had with every previous question I'd ever had before, he nodded.

"Does that bother you?"

I searched for the words, called on my average vocabulary for the appropriate things to say to express the strangeness that came from knowing he owned an actual island.

How much money do these people have? Is it even possible to be that rich? Jesus.

The thought was more unsettling than exciting. If my assumptions were even remotely close, within the same hemisphere of the truth, the Sacchi family had their fingers in many different businesses, and there was no way they were all above board.

A shadow appeared at my side, a sudden figure that'd come from the darkness and caused me to jump. It was a middle-aged man wearing a perfectly pressed tuxedo. He clutched a bottle of wine in his hands, a white cloth wrapped around the thick body of it.

He smiled at me and spoke, but I had no idea what'd he'd said and felt foolish for it immediately.

"I'm… I'm sorry, I don't…"

I looked to Michele for help. He'd taken to leaning forward with his elbows on the table, fingers interlaced.

"He's asking if you would like a glass of wine," he said with an airy tone that I couldn't identify.

"Oh." I turned my attention to the man in the tux. "Yes, please. Um, *si*."

"Ah," he said with a smile. "*Perfetto, signora.*"

With the grace of a man who'd poured a thousand glasses, the gentleman filled my glass, then moved to Michele and did the same. He vanished a second later.

I reached for my drink and took a sip, not much of a wine person, though willing to give it a try. To my surprise, it was fruitier than I'd expected, the taste of peach the first thing to touch my tongue.

"Tell me, Basil," he said, drawing my eye. Michele held his glass near his mouth when he asked, "Are you still singing?"

"No, not as much as I'd like. I used to sing on the weekends, but it doesn't help pay the bills." I hated myself for the awkward smile I punctuated the statement with. "I actually work at my uncle's hardware store back home. That's how I was able to drop everything to steward."

Why are you spilling your guts? Stop talking so much.

When nervous, I had trouble keeping my mouth shut. It was an issue I needed to work on more.

"Where is home?"

"Arizona. You?"

"Sicily," he said, keeping his gaze locked and engaged with me, and giving the feeling that he cared about what I had to say. It was a foreign concept.

"Is...is that all?"

He shrugged. An uncertain smile touched my lips.

"Usually people have more to say."

"My life isn't that interesting," he said. "I was born, grew up, attended school and university, and now I work for my family."

"You don't read? Listen to music?"

His smile broadened until he flashed his perfect teeth, highlighting a dimple in his left cheek I hadn't known he possessed. Actually, I couldn't recall ever seeing him grin in the first place.

Leaning against the arm of his chair, hands clasped, he seemed to chuckle to himself and spoke.

"I like to listen to books when given the chance, and my music preferences are rather eclectic."

My heart sank, and, whether I'd intended to or not, I slumped in my seat. I was failing at the date. It'd been such a long time, and it was clear that I was out of my league when it came to Michele Sacchi. He shouldn't have been the pool in which I dipped my toe when I tried dating again.

It'd been a bad idea and only served to prove my crush had begun to connect dots that weren't there. I'd been foolish to assume we had enough in common for a good time beyond a game. We didn't. His lack of chemistry was clear proof.

A woman emerged from the villa with her dark hair pulled back tighter than mine and a plate in each hand. She glided toward us and, without missing a step, set my plate down first then his. Crisp greens of varying shades were gathered in the center of the white porcelain with flecks of what appeared to be shaved almonds and a glistening dressing spread over it.

She bowed to us and disappeared just as suddenly.

I shifted in my seat, trying to ignore the fact that we were being waited on by people. I did my best to reason that it would've been no different in a restaurant. But at least they would've been busy with other customers instead of focusing wholly on us.

"You're not enjoying yourself."

His voice brought me to the moment, pulling me out of my bout of anxiety.

He appeared worried, if not a bit disappointed, and guilt seeped in as a result.

"No, it's not that," I said. "I'm sorry. It's just, like I said, I haven't dated in a long time, and it looks like I've forgotten how to do it."

"If it would make you feel more comfortable, I could always grab you by the neck and tell you what to do."

A shiver ripped through me, tearing down my spine. It'd washed over me too quickly for me to stop it.

My gaze shot to Michele. He seemed unaffected, sipping on his wine with a wicked glimmer in his eyes, accentuated by the candlelight.

A familiar sense of ease soon trickled in, wrapping me in its warm embrace and giving me control of myself again.

With a playful glare and a smirk on my lips, I replied, "As much fun as that would be, it just serves to prove my point that I'm more comfortable with the sexual side of things."

He chuckled and began to pick at his salad while I did the same.

"I don't date often, either."

"I don't believe you."

He smiled in response but said nothing.

The salad was delicious, the green complemented by the citrus sauce and the crunch of the almonds. And, while delicious, it was hard for me to think of adjectives to describe such a simple plate.

"What was it like growing up in Arizona?" Michele asked after allowing us both to enjoy the meal. It was swept away an instant later by another figure in black.

"Hot and dry," I said, almost too fast. It'd been a go-to answer for as long as I could remember. "The desert is beautiful, though, plenty of mountains and oddly hypnotic expanses of incredibly flat ground. There isn't this sort of greenery, though."

"I've never seen a desert in person."

I eyed him, tilting my head to the side. "Really?"

He nodded.

"Never?" It seemed impossible. Surely the man or his family owned a chunk of the Sahara — or perhaps half of Australia.

"No," he said with a shake of his head. "I haven't ventured far from Europe."

I couldn't explain why that surprised me, but it had. He seemed the sort who would've spent his entire life living it up, traveling to every country that existed.

Movement from the corner of my eye alerted me to the approach of the woman again, but instead of a small appetizer, she seemed to bring out the main course.

A seared piece of tenderloin sat on a fanciful splash of red that had been smeared across the white plate. Placed beside it were a few sprigs of asparagus that seemed perfectly blanched.

"May I inquire about a sensitive subject?" Michele asked while he held his knife.

Shit. That could mean a lot of things.

"Sure," I tentatively replied. I cut into the tenderloin and there hadn't been a hint of resistance, like a hot knife in butter.

"Your name," he said, giving me a surprising level of relief. "It's unusual."

"Mom likes to joke that she was inspired by the spice rack. I guess since she couldn't cook, she chose to name her daughters after herbs."

"There are more of you?"

"Rosemary and Sage, but I think I got the short end of the stick, a side-effect of being the youngest. And you?"

"Only child," he said.

The small talk that followed was easier than I'd expected, and with it, I was able to banish the unease that'd surrounded my thoughts to the dark recesses of my mind.

The steak had been the most tender, juiciest thing I'd ever tasted.

Chapter Twenty-One

After dinner, Michele took me on a stroll through the gardens until coming to an area that overlooked the water with Venice in the distance. Soft music flittered through the air, emanating from speakers tucked away near the lights that highlighted the landscaping. It was clear that the space had been used for multiple get-togethers through the years.

He stood beside me with his hands in his pockets, the gentle breeze adding a nice chill to the air that somehow cooled my overheated skin.

The reality of the moment seemed beyond my grasp. I couldn't bring myself to accept the situation I found myself in. When Kennia had called, offering me the job, I hadn't thought that just two weeks later I would be standing on a private island after eating an incredible meal with a man I couldn't describe.

"I can't get over how beautiful everything is," I said, hearing the awe lingering within the words.

"Hmm," he muttered. "I have had a fortunate life, but I don't have everything."

He shifted at my side, drawing my attention. The meaning behind the statement hadn't been well hidden, and the softness to his eyes only strengthened my thoughts. Yet, as cheesy as the line was, I couldn't fight the flutter it created.

There was no denying the blush that rose in my cheeks as a result.

"Would you like to dance?"

I nodded. He took my hand and guided me to the center of the expanse.

Pulling me to his chest, we proceeded to move to the soft orchestral tune.

Minutes might have passed while I stared into his eyes, our hands clasped and feet falling in step with one another, but I didn't know or care to check. I'd become entranced by the man that had somehow become a dominant figure in my life in such a short period of time.

I felt safe on that island with him, cared for. But more than that, I felt wanted. He knew about me, knew the truth that had sent many others running, and it didn't matter. He didn't judge me or tell me I was going to hell. He accepted what I liked and who I was.

Leaning in, Michele met my advance and our foreheads connected. I closed my eyes and let the heat of his body along with the rustic scent of his cologne saturate me. Before I left Italy, I needed to discover what it was, though it could have simply been the way he smelled.

"I don't want tonight to end," I said on a breath, the words barely escaping me. It may have been a cliché thing to utter, but it was how I felt in that moment.

"It doesn't have to," he replied. "Not really."

I let out a small laugh that came across as little more than a scoff. With more difficulty than I'd anticipated, I pulled back. He pried open his eyes and stared at me with a drugged expression.

"It's getting late. I should probably get back to my hotel room."

Michele drew his bottom lip through his teeth, nodding while he cupped my face.

"As you wish," he said.

Before we parted, he pressed a kiss to my temple.

Taking my hand, we made our way toward the boat—but in no hurry to get there.

* * * *

When we returned to the hotel, Michele walked me to my door, and we stood outside.

I stared at him, mere inches separating us in the narrow corridor. The air between us pulsed with a desire that'd I'd never been able to completely shake but which had taken a backseat to the unexpectedness of the evening. That pulse was where I felt most comfortable, and glimpses of it had been my only anchor throughout the night, sparked by moments of contact or playful words he'd spoken. I'd been given hints that perhaps he'd been on his best behavior, but that *thing* we shared was never far beneath the surface.

"Would you like to come in for a drink?" I asked, deciding to take my chance and feed the thing.

Darkness swirled within the warm color of his eyes, glimmering with the prospect of what might happen should he agree.

"I feel as though I should warn you," he said. "I may not be able to keep my hands to myself if you invite me in."

His words drew my lips into a sultry smirk, and without another word, I unlocked my door.

Stepping inside, I allowed it to remain open, a silent invitation that he was free to accept or ignore. The hotel had included a small bar with my room, nothing more than a stocked mini-fridge with some glasses overturned on top, but it was enough. I retrieved two travel-sized bottles of bourbon and poured them into two glasses.

The door slid shut behind, and the lock clicked. My heart raced as the sound of his shoes against the tile floor crept closer and closer, a long, easy stride that helped him travel the distance in seconds.

With a glass in each hand, I turned to face him. Michele's demeanor had shifted, and the shadow of want had overtaken his features. The gentleman he'd been that evening was fading fast, leaving wickedness in its wake.

I handed him his glass, which he drained of its contents in one swift gulp. He set it down on the nearest surface, his gaze never leaving mine. I sipped much slower, letting the burn of the amber liquid roll down my throat while I prepared myself for what would undoubtedly be a perfect end cap to the night.

He watched, his body seemingly tight, as though waiting to spring the second I'd finished. Curious and willing to test the theory, I set my glass aside without finishing it. Michele reacted in an instant, snatching me by the waist and hauling me against his strong chest.

Burying his face in the crook of my neck, he placed hot, aggressive kisses along my exposed skin. The feeling of his eager mouth on my body again sent a wave of pleasure coursing through my veins. I held his broad shoulders, my fingers biting into the fabric while he trailed a line along my jaw and to my lips, which he teased with the prospect of more, even though we both knew it never would.

"What do you want tonight?" he asked, his voice twisted with the moment. "Tonight is your turn."

An evil chuckle rumbled in my throat.

I slithered my hands up his neck and into his hair. Gathering my grip, I pulled, snapping his head back and exposing his perfect neck to me. He groaned, squeezing my body to his.

"Are you sure?" I asked.

He swallowed hard, his Adam's apple bobbing. Forcing his head forward, which I allowed, he stared at me with eyes that'd gone black in those few seconds.

He nodded, though it wasn't enough for me.

"Say it," I said.

I wanted his verbal consent because, to my mind, we were about to change our dynamic just enough that I needed him to be sure. What he said in response was fucking perfect.

"Si, maestra."

A wave of tremors swept over me, igniting every cell that'd been teetering on the edge of consciousness. I quivered in his arms, a bright, wide smile breaking across my face. His eyes sparkled with silent pleasure at what he'd done.

As I stepped out of his arms, I slid my hands along the sharp cut of his cheeks. I brushed my thumb over his perfect lips, which he kissed before I had released him.

"Take off your clothes," I said. "All of them."

The corners of his lips twitched, but a smile never fully formed.

In the corner of the room near the large double doors that opened onto the canal rested a chair. I took a seat and crossed my legs, giving him my full attention.

As he had in his suite on the ship, Michele removed his jacket first and laid it over the dresser nearby. With his gaze locked to mine, he unbuttoned the white shirt, which soon joined the jacket.

And so it went, with him taking his time to remove each garment with care and placing them to the side until he stood in nothing but his boxer-briefs.

The outline of his cock pressed against the expensive cotton, exaggerated but nothing compared to what I'd seen previously. In the corridor of *The Silver Wind*, it'd been so hard, so ready, that it pushed the garment away from his skin, a true tent pitched. In my hotel room, it hadn't reached that point, but it was a breath away.

When he hadn't continued, I dragged my gaze up the length of his body and to his eye. Cocking a brow, I motioned toward them.

"Everything," I said.

There'd been no hesitation on his part to comply, hooking his thumbs into the elastic band and removing them.

Michele stood before me, naked, and for the first time I was able to enjoy it. While tied to his bed, emotion and want had clouded my eyes, and angle had prevented me from properly admiring the work he'd put into his form. That was no longer an issue.

I ached at the sight of him, at the result of the love and care he'd clearly given his body. If further proof were needed that he was more than a man, I had it in that moment.

Allowing my head to loll to the side, I inspected every inch of him from my seat and found focus on the obvious. His cock twitched under my gaze, growing thicker and more rigid with each passing second.

With my thumbnail clamped tight between my teeth, I rose to my feet and closed the distance between us. His breathing hitched when I placed my hands against his chest, his heart thrumming beneath my palms.

Staring into his beautiful eyes, I ran my fingers down his torso, over the dips of his abs, the crease created by the muscles over his hips and as far down his thighs as I could manage without bending to do so. His cock rose farther, pressing into my apex.

"Lie on the bed."

He did.

I turned my back to him, retrieving the cuffs that I'd placed in the top drawer of my dresser. Giving him my attention again, I spotted him lying at the head of the bed, propped on his elbows and watching me. I showed him the cuffs, a silent request that he answered by lying down and gripping the center bar of the wrought-iron frame.

God, he's perfect.

Setting them down on his clothes, I unzipped my dress and stepped out of the mass that gathered on the floor, not willing to give it the same care as Michele had his wardrobe. It wasn't my main concern. I had other plans.

With the cuffs in hand again, I approached the bed, climbing onto it and him a second later. I had to focus on the task at hand and not the warmth of his stomach burning the inside of my thighs, or that thin lace panties were the only thing that separated us.

Practiced motions made easy work of the task, of guiding the chain around the bar and securing his wrists in leather.

Sitting upright, I stared at him, my pulse thundering and finding focus on the sensitive bundle of nerves between my legs.

The muscles in his arms strained against his bronzed skin, rolling with each twitch of his hands. His eyes burned with something unspoken and his lips parted with heavy breaths.

"*Bellissimo,*" I said. He let out a huff that might've been a laugh, but it'd become too twisted to sound like much.

Bracing myself above him, I lowered my body. My breasts brushed his chest, the friction enough to make my nipples bead. I leaned into him, teasing his lips with mine.

His eyes drifted shut while he rose to meet me.

"If you want me to stop," I whispered, nipping tenderly at his bottom lip, "tell me and I will."

I flicked the tip of my tongue against his upper lip and, to my surprise, he lunged forward to catch it, giving a soft, delicate kiss that made me shiver.

Relaxing into the pillow again, he opened his heavy lids. "I'll never tell you to stop."

My breath caught in my throat. There could've been no way to miss the sincerity and sureness of the statement, not when I was so close.

A desire to accept the challenge rose within me but vanished an instant later. I wasn't a sadist. My kink wasn't to inflict pain on my willing partner until they used the safeword we'd agreed on. I tended to lean toward the bondage aspect, though admittedly hadn't gone far beyond being restrained. I also enjoyed the masochism, a bit of pain to heighten the moment.

But when given the chance to be the Dominant, I preferred to make my partner feel torturous levels of want. I wanted to make them beg me to continue, not stop. I suppose it was safe to say that I enjoyed the BDM side of BDSM.

Chapter Twenty-Two

Taking his jaw in my hand, I pushed his head back to expose his neck, biting into it just hard enough to make him hiss.

I continued down his body, trailing kisses and nips along his chest. Clamping my teeth on his nipple awarded me another groan, the sharp snap of pain I'd caused soothed away by a sweep of my tongue.

Michele writhed beneath me, twisting and shifting to meet my mouth as I worked my way down. I teased his stomach, raking my fingernails over his sides.

Each inch I descended forced his cock to drag along my body, digging into my skin and telling me how much he liked what I was doing.

Kissing his hip, I shifted out of the way, allowing his dick to bounce free. I lifted my gaze. Michele was sitting up as best he could manage, the muscles in his stomach straining to comply. His features had grown dark, rife with frustrated anticipation. It was a look I loved.

Grasping the base of his cock caused his veneer to crack, his brows twitching. The silk-covered steel in my hand pulsed with each erratic heartbeat.

Keeping my eye locked to his, I opened my mouth and ran the flat of my tongue up his shaft, following that thick vein to the top.

A strangled moan filled the room. All at once, Michele shuddered as though he'd been left in subzero temperatures through the night, every inch of him quaking while his head fell back. It was as though I'd given him release just with my tongue.

I hadn't, but I could.

The chain ground against the wrought iron, scraping and clawing.

When I reached the head, I twirled my tongue around it once, twice, then guided him into my mouth. His breathing became labored, deep huffs that sounded more than a bear's grunt than anything human. All the while, he strained against the cuffs.

After taking him as deep as I could, I retreated, sucking hard and stroking what hadn't fit. I was slow, deliberate and more than capable of prolonging the moment.

I'd always loved to suck the dick of such a responsive partner. It fed my ego to have that sort of power over someone else's pleasure.

Up and down, twisting and sucking, I even took his balls into my mouth just to hear more of his primal sounds, but it'd begun to take its toll on me, too.

Rising from the bed, I drew his eye. The color had fled completely, his pupils so dilated that they'd become blacker than pitch. He bit down hard, grinding his teeth and causing the muscle in his jaw to cord. His knuckles were white with the pressure of his clenched fists. Everything had become so rigid that if he were glass, the slightest touch would break him.

I could do that, too.

"Where is it?" I asked, a dusky tone infecting my words.

Michele jutted his chin toward his clothes. "Jacket pocket."

While barely above a whisper, he'd barked the words.

I went to his pile of clothing and dug into the breast pocket of his jacket, finding the prize in an instant. Whether he'd anticipated anything for the night or not, I was happy one of us had had the foresight to bring a condom.

Clasping it in my teeth, I gave the man my attention again. I removed my bra, letting it fall carelessly to the floor like the dress.

His gaze landed on my chest with sharp focus. He jerked on the cuffs, filling the suite with the clank of metal on metal once more. My panties soon joined the rest of it and on my trek toward the bed, I stepped out of my heels.

Straddling his thighs, I tore through the shimmering package and removed the latex disk.

He jerked on the chain again, and in the back of my head, I noted a strange sound that shouldn't have been there, but ignored it in favor of what I wanted.

Placing it on the head of his dick, I slid the condom down, staring unblinkingly into his eyes. His breathing had become shallower, filled with anticipation.

I adjusted myself above him, guiding his cock up and down the length of my slit, teasing my clit and spreading my excitement. The hard resolve that'd been plastered across his face cracked and wavered while he watched.

"It's my turn to fuck you," I said.

His gaze shot to mine. "*Assolutamente.*"

The bulbous tip did little to prepare me for the sheer size of him as I lowered myself. My head fell back, strangled gasps falling from my lips as I sank, shoving him deeper and deeper. That night in his room hadn't prepared me for the truth. I'd been so consumed and it'd happened so fast that it had left me unprepared to have him fully seated inside.

Drawing air into my lungs had become downright impossible when I settled.

Planting my hands on his stomach, I forced myself to look at him. He didn't seem to fair much better, scarlet flashes adorning his cheeks, his bottom lip clamped tight in his teeth and his arms trembling under the strength of his grip.

I wanted to keep moving, but for those few seconds, I couldn't make it happen.

Determination soon took over, and whether ready for it or not, I rose onto my knees. I felt every millimeter of his retreat, lamenting it all until I reached the tip and dropped. He grunted, the bed's springs protested, but I was only getting started.

My style was to take my time, to wring every drop of frustration and joy out of the moment that I could, and I'd been close to managing that with him, for about thirty seconds. Honestly, I was surprised I'd lasted that long.

The bed's stiff springs aided me. I timed my thrusts with them until I'd found my rhythm bouncing on his cock, allowing him to hit depths he hadn't managed on the ship. It was a task I'd once thought utterly impossible.

Sparks of pleasure pulsated each time I ground my clit against his pelvic bone, building layers to my joy. I strained to stare at him, to watch the way my actions affected him.

The sounds of sex soon saturated the room, of flesh slapping against flesh, of a bed fighting to keep up and the animalistic grunts of the man between my legs. It created a heady mix that was hard for me to brush off. It infected me — and I wasn't the only one.

More than once, Michele had attempted to meet me in stride, to participate, and that wasn't allowed. He knew it. He was meant to lie there and take it just as I had, but he struggled, and it was perfect.

Gripping the base of his throat, I forced him to look at me. He did, his lip twitching each time I threw myself down on him. His heartbeat thundered beneath my fingers, the vein on the side of his neck fluttering erratically.

Fire raged within his eyes, hungry and untamable. It demanded satiation, demanded to be set free. I would give him the release he craved, but in the meantime, I stopped.

The room went silent as though someone had pushed pause on a movie. It hurt, I couldn't lie, but the sight of his eyes flying open in shock had been a delicious thing to witness.

"W-what are you doing?"

"Whatever I want," I replied.

"No!" He jerked harder on the chain than he ever had, and it didn't sound good. "Don't stop," he said, meeting my eye. His brows pooled and desperation flashed in his eyes. "*Per favore, non fermarti.*"

I had no idea what he'd said, but context told me he'd likely begged. And to hear those words pass those luscious lips was something I'd wanted for some time.

"Are you telling me what to do?"

He shook his head, but the frustration was hard to ignore.

"Perhaps I should just..."

I pushed myself onto my knees, sliding up his length at an agonizing pace until reaching the very tip. Michele was so close to slipping out of me that a breath would've been enough and the panic it induced astounded me.

"No, no, no, no."

He'd spoken the words through clenched teeth, pulling and jerking and yanking on the cuffs in frustration until they snapped. No longer able to cope with the power of the man they bound, the thin links crumbled under the pressure.

The suddenness of it stunned us both. I'd never expected the cuffs' chain to break, which was either a statement on how weak they'd been or an indication of how strong he was.

Michele looked at his hands then to me and, without the slightest prompting, he reached above his head and gripped the bars. He relaxed against the mattress with a breath and waited.

A number of emotions swirled inside me in that moment. There would've been nothing that could have stopped him from taking what he wanted, from reclaiming the Dominant position in our little game, and, given the circumstances, I would've understood completely. Hell, *I* would have been too swept up in the chaos and desire to stop it.

But he hadn't. In that brief second of clarity, he'd chosen to continue as we were, whether bound or not. He wanted me to be the one in charge, trusted me enough with him and his pleasure that there was no need for the cuffs at all. No one had ever done that before. For all the men that I'd been with who claimed to be switches like me, not one of them had ever really embraced me being Dominant in any regard…until Michele.

As a reward, I rolled my hips. His eyelids fluttered. I did it again, lowering myself once more.

Leaning forward, I cradled his jaw, bringing my mouth to his while I continued to grind into him.

"Are you going to keep holding that bar?" I whispered against his lips.

"*Sì, dea,*" he replied.

I didn't know what *dea* meant, but in the moment, I didn't care.

My thrusts became more prominent, and he sighed in response.

"Are you going to let go before I tell you?"

He shook his head, his tongue darting out to touch my lip. "No, *dea.*"

"Good boy." I bit his bottom lip as a reward. He groaned in approval.

There was no more build-up, no teasing. I was beyond that point, and he seemed to be, too.

Sitting upright again, I proceeded to fuck him as hard as I could, throwing myself down until those familiar white dots flashed in my eyes.

I was far from a master of being on top, never able to get the hang of a dense pillow-top mattress when it came to leverage and lacking the leg strength, but with those hard springs helping me, I could do anything.

Strumming my clit in time with my actions had been the perfect storm. I was losing myself to the coming orgasm, my coordination suffering for it. I had to relent to save us both.

"Fuck me, Michele," I said through my moans. "Fuck me, now."

The statement had barely left my lips when he lunged forward like a wild animal given release.

Wrapping his thick arms around me, he rolled me onto my back. I braced myself against the headboard he'd clung to for leverage and, with him pressed to my body, Michele did as I'd commanded.

He drove into me with the same vicious, wonderful power he had on the ship, fucking me like a man possessed, and it'd been all I needed. I reached for him, digging my fingernails into his back in a desperate bid for something to steady myself, but it was too late.

My orgasm rose from the depths, washing over me and electrifying my body. I cried out, dragging my nails down his skin while he roared.

And almost as suddenly as before, the room settled.

He held himself above me, his head falling onto the pillow that was beneath mine. He trembled, huffing while he struggled to breathe.

My thighs loosened their death-grip around his waist, falling uselessly to the bed. I couldn't recall if I'd done it consciously or not. I wasn't sure I had much control of anything anymore.

Seconds may have passed, or minutes, before either of us seemed to have the ability to move.

Michele pulled back. He stared into my eyes with a strange sort of reverence I didn't recognize, cradling my face in his large hand. I wanted to kiss him, to finally taste his lips and feel his tongue on mine, but that wasn't what we had. That was too intimate, too real.

He leaned forward and placed a soft kiss on my cheek, then repeated the same to the other. He kissed the tip of my nose and my chin, avoiding my mouth completely. I sank into the affection, allowed it to brush away the chaotic lust from minutes prior.

When he withdrew, he guided my eye to his. Thumb stroking my face, he examined me, looking over a thousand things that I couldn't see. I didn't know what he was searching for.

"Where did you buy these handcuffs?" he finally asked. "They're pathetic."

I didn't fight the laughter that burst from me at the stupidity and truth of the statement. He did, too. Not a subtle chuckle or even a chortle... He laughed just as much as I had.

As the amusement dwindled and giggles began to die, I stared at him again, chewing on my bottom lip. He seemed deep in thought all of a sudden, and while I wanted to press, I didn't. Even then, I didn't think I had the right.

It hadn't mattered in the end. He spoke, anyway.

"May I stay with you tonight?" he asked. "At least for a little while."

The request surprised me, but not as much as my joy with it.

I nodded. "I'd like that."

He smiled.

"Besides, you're still inside me. I don't think you can leave right now, anyway."

Michele chuckled and nodded, and to my disappointment, he sat back on his knees, pulling out of me in the process. I hated it.

Rising to his feet, he padded across the floor and disappeared into the bathroom to clean up. I should have done the same, a thin layer of sweat having formed on my skin, but I didn't want to. Instead, I pulled down the blankets and crawled beneath them to combat the chill that caressed my damp skin.

He emerged a moment later and spotted me bundled. With an endearing smile, he stepped around to the side he'd once occupied and slid beneath the blankets, too.

Wrapping an arm around my waist, he pulled me to his side. Minimal adjusting saw us comfortable with my back to his chest and a pillow wedged beneath our heads.

His breath danced along the base of my neck when he muttered, "I'll leave when you ask me to go."

"Okay."

I had no intentions of doing so.

Closing my eyes, I let the exhaustion take me and fell asleep in his arms.

Chapter Twenty-Three

The following morning, I awoke in bed, alone.

The thick drapes had been pulled back so the only thing to diffuse the sunlight was the sheer curtains that'd been left to flutter in the open windows.

I sat up, peering around and finding evidence that I was completely on my own. Michele's clothes were gone while mine were delicately laid folded on the dresser, my bra and panties there, too, while my shoes were on the floor beside the furniture.

I wasn't sure what to think. On the one hand, I hadn't really expected him to linger after we'd had sex. On the other, after the date and with whatever I'd thought was growing between us, why not?

Or was my crush clouding my senses?

It'd happened plenty of times before. Why would it be any different now?

Left unsure with the situation I found myself in, I got out of bed and retrieved my robe. Tying it tight around my waist, I did my best to focus on the day. I needed to get dressed and get a hold of Kennia to see if she or anyone else wanted to hang out.

When I stepped to the dresser and began to search for clothes, the door opened. The rush of fear that someone was breaking in vanished the second Michele revealed himself to be the source.

"Good morning," he said with a smile.

"Um, morning."

The disappointment that he hadn't stayed the night faded, replaced with curiosity as to why he'd returned.

No one's ever accused me of being a rational person.

He'd changed since the night before, no longer wearing a suit and instead having donned a pair of jeans and a pale blue button-up shirt, looking far more approachable than I'd ever seen. Clasped in one hand was a paper bag and a pair of small paper cups were expertly cradled in the other.

"Are you hungry?" he asked.

"Sure."

Passing me, he set the purchases on the small round table on the other side of the room.

"I thought you might be."

My stomach rumbled at the mention of food and more so when he removed some pastries from the bag, setting them down only to retrieve a plastic container filled with fresh-cut fruit.

"Thank you," I mumbled as I approached. "But you didn't have to do that."

He didn't respond to my comment, seeming to brush it aside while he uncapped the drinks.

"Cappuccino."

"Oooh." I'd never had authentic cappuccino, and it appeared as though I was unable to hide my excitement for it.

With a chuckle, he handed me the cup, which I cradled worshipfully in my hands.

A small waft of steam emanated from the frothy surface, disappearing when I blew on it. My mouth watered with the prospect of caffeine, but I wasn't stupid enough to sip it just yet. I needed my taste buds.

The table was set seconds later, a pair of large pastries each sitting on its own napkin and the open container of fruit resting in the middle. Michele stood behind a chair, his gaze fixed on me. I took the offered seat, and he joined me.

"What are these?" I asked, eying the croissant-like food and knowing that couldn't have been what they were called.

"Cornetto," he replied.

Taking his cornetto in hand, Michele tore it in half. Steam billowed from the cakey interior, demonstrating just how fresh it'd been upon purchase.

"They can have creams, jellies, honey and even chocolate inside," he said. "I personally prefer them simple." He ripped a smaller piece off the mass and dipped it into the cappuccino while looking at me. "It absorbs the flavor better." Lifting it, he allowed the excess to drip off before eating it. "*Delizioso.* Try it."

Not unaccustomed to dipping things into hot drinks, I followed his lead and tore my cornetto into a bite-sized piece.

"I usually do this with cookies," I said, allowing the pastries to soak up my drink for a second. "But I'll give this a shot."

He waited patiently for me to do so.

The cappuccino had cooled a little on the trip from cup to mouth, so it hadn't burned, but remained warm. Cornettos were sweeter than I'd expected, far more than a croissant, and denser, though still fluffy. The cappuccino infected every aspect of it, mingling the sweet and coffee-like flavors in a surprising and delicious way.

"Oh, my God," I said around the food in my mouth. "That's amazing."

His face brightened with a smile. "I'm glad you like it."

"Absolutely." I was already dipping another piece into my drink.

"Would you care for some fruit?"

I froze, eying the cup. "Is there kiwi in it?"

His brows creased when he lifted it, examining the contents with a scrutinizing gaze.

"I don't believe so." He looked at me. "Don't like them?"

"Allergic," I replied.

He cocked his head. "Really?"

"Mm-hmm. Are, uh... Are you allergic to anything?"

He seemed to give the question some thought but shook his head in the end. I wasn't entirely surprised. Food allergies weren't as common as some people assumed.

We returned to our breakfast, and, while we ate, I couldn't keep my mind from wandering. He was too perfect. There had to be something wrong, something lingering beneath the surface. I refused to believe that a man like him existed without a deep, dark secret...or many.

Searching the recesses of my memory, I did my best to recall any hints that he was more than he appeared.

Two weeks ago, the Sacchis had boarded, and we'd set sail. The senior members of the family had often seemed deep in conversation with one another, sometimes arguing on the phone. They'd kept primarily to themselves, and if they spoke English, it hadn't been to me directly.

Dominic did have the leanings of a rich kid who wanted to be a bad boy and might've dabbled in drugs and alcohol only to have his family get him off any inevitable charges, but that was hardly surprising for the wealthy.

Gun.

My mind shot to the events in Hvar when I'd been running from Creeper and both young men had produced weapons. They'd held them with such familiarity that it appeared second nature to point them at another person. And why did they have them in the first place? Where were they hidden on the ship?

Yasmin's gaggle had been another strange thing. While I'd been more distracted by the young women themselves, the older man who joined them seemed to have meetings with the Sacchi family, but what kind of business was discussed on a yacht? Did they want to keep people from overhearing them?

The blonde's reaction to catching Michele and me roared to life in my memory, the rage and hatred and that she'd physically hunted for me afterward were horrifying. They alluded to her being not only unstable but confident that nothing would happen to her if she got me. People afraid of repercussions didn't do things like that.

The security team once we'd come ashore, the money they must have made to own *The Silver Wind* and an island and the multiple international homes Michele said they possessed were even more evidence that I knew *nothing* about him.

You know how he treats you.

That was true. I'd spent enough time with him at that point to have a good idea.

You know how he makes you feel.

Again, true.

The longer I dwelled on the conflict raging in my head, the more I began to wonder if it mattered. Were his secrets big enough to affect me or were they nothing more than anyone else might have?

Chapter Twenty-Four

Singing brought us out of our breakfast conversation. The sound bounced off the walls, traveling through the open balcony door. I shifted in my seat and listened. A voice had managed to pierce the noise of the canal.

Curiosity guided me to my feet and to the doors. I gathered the sheer curtain, tucking it away, and glanced down the canal. In the distance, standing in a gondola and heading for us, was a man. His enchanting voice caused goosebumps to form across my skin. I didn't recognize the operatic aria, but the somber tone unaccompanied by music touched something deep inside me.

The chatter of everyday life and the people going about their business faded under the power of the aria. It wasn't that it dwindled compared to the song, but activity genuinely ceased. From my perch, I saw that I was one of many who'd stopped what they were doing to listen.

"This is amazing." I couldn't keep the giggle from my voice while I took a seat, my back to the doorjamb.

"Do you understand what he's saying?" He joined me, taking a seat on the opposite end so that we faced each other, and he was pointed in the direction of the approaching voice.

I shook my head. As with most arias, it had been written in Italian. Michele's gaze drifted to the singer.

"He's sad about losing the woman he loves," he said. "She died unexpectedly, and he can't accept the loss."

I furrowed my brows, his explanation punctuated with the sad tune. My heart ached at the thought of this stranger, this person who'd been written about hundreds of years ago and might not have been real in the first place, being in such pain. Regardless of the language in which it'd been sung, there was hurt.

My attention fell to the man who'd finally reached us, continuing on his somber journey without a care for those who listened. Perhaps he was singing for us in the first place?

"Why are operas so sad?" I mumbled.

"Because they're Italian."

He spoke with such certainty that it caused me to eye him. I didn't understand the sentiment, and he seemed to sense it.

"Italians love beauty," he said. "And loss, for better or worse, is beautiful."

"That's the exact *opposite* of what beauty is."

A small smile curled the corner of his mouth. He tilted his head to the side, resting it against the door frame. The singer's voice began to fade the farther he sailed.

"To feel that sort of pain," he said, "he must have loved her very much." He looked at me, deep brown eyes shining. "And that is beautiful."

I guess.

My agreement had been slow to come and unsure. I could understand his point, but I'd never been one to find pain beautiful, no matter what had preceded it. Perhaps it boiled down to my American way of thinking.

Michele and I fell into silence, enveloped in the sound of the heart-wrenching song.

I stared at his profile, the side of his forehead again resting on the door frame. He was striking, a handsome man with commanding features. His strong brow, the slope of his nose, his full lips and a jaw covered with stubble. He appeared somber, thoughtful and unlike anything I'd seen from him before.

I curled my fingers around my cell phone, and a flick of my thumb brought up my camera. I leveled it on him without a thought to ask whether or not I could take his picture in the first place. It was too perfect a moment, too perfect a composition, for me to not capitalize on the potential picture.

The camera's shutter had been louder than expected. In fact, I'd had no idea the sound was on at all until it echoed around us.

Michele's head snapped to attention, a curious expression wiped away seconds later when he spotted my phone. Heat spread across my face. He smiled.

"Sorry." There'd been no strength in the apology. "It's just… I thought it'd make a good picture."

"Did it?"

My blush intensified while I brought the photo back up and showed it to him. Michele took it from me and

I'd half-expected him to ask me to delete it. Instead, he handed it back.

"Take one with me."

Heart thumping, I replied, "I don't take good pictures."

He sighed, letting loose a disbelieving sound with a light smile. "You're beautiful."

The beating grew worse...stronger. My fingers tingled and my body pulsed with the compliment. While I understood what *bella* meant, a thing he'd called me on multiple occasions, something about receiving the compliment in English affected me differently.

"T-thank you, but that's not what I meant." And it wasn't. In the millisecond a photo captured, I managed to blink or my smile would come across as wonky. I couldn't appear comfortable and instead embodied awkwardness. "Something weird always happens."

"Please."

I met his gaze. There it was again, another 'please'. *I don't think I've heard him say that to anyone else.*

The sincerity behind the request caused me to agree in a weak hope that, just once, I might manage to look like anything other than a terrified newborn being forced to sit for their first round of pictures.

"Yeah, okay." I had no confidence in my ability, however.

"Sit here, with me. I can take it."

Michele scooted to his left, deeper into the room and opening a spot on the wall near the balcony railing. I slid into the nook beside him while he brought my phone up and shifted the focus to the front-facing lens.

He wrapped his free arm around me, bringing me close to his side while he held my phone aloft, much farther than I would have been able to. He centered us and as we relaxed, him much sooner than me, Michele shifted once more. I struggled to form a smile that wouldn't make it seem as though I were being poked with a cattle prod outside the frame. His head dipped.

Through the camera, I watched as he leaned into me, his forehead brushing my hairline. He seemed to be a step away from nuzzling into the nape of my neck or whispering in my ear, an intimate and sweet action that caught me by surprise. I couldn't help but do the same, my gaze down as I turned into him.

His breath grazed my lips. The closeness of them, of him, brought my need to a new level. It'd been a tender moment, and I hadn't experienced anything like it before. It worried me. It'd been too different, and I couldn't say whether I was afraid or willing to embrace it.

He inched closer, the soft heat of his lips touching mine. I closed my eyes, disappearing into the sensation. Michele dug his fingers into my skin where he held me. My grip on his thigh increased.

The phone's shutter startled me, a loud clicking that caused me to pull back. Clearing my throat, I'd expected Michele to return to reality alongside me, the moment gone with the snap of a picture, but he hadn't. He continued to look at me, and it didn't seem as though he'd been bothered in the least by the picture taking.

Michele pressed his lips together and swallowed, his focus elsewhere on my face until he dragged his gaze up to meet mine. My heart raced once again. Something had changed. Something new was bubbling beneath the surface, infecting the air between us to the point where it could've choked me.

He pulled me back into the little bubble that we'd surrounded ourselves in seconds prior.

"Basil?"

A deep shadow encompassed my name, turning his voice into one I didn't recognize.

"Hmm?"

"I would like to kiss you."

I flinched. The hand on the small of my back pulled me closer while his free hand rose. I had no idea he'd set my phone aside until his fingertips skated along my jaw, a gentle, sweet touch that caused me to quiver. He leaned into me, his thumb dragging across my bottom lip. It drew his eye.

In an almost inaudible voice, he asked, "May I?"

It'd been a rule set in stone since the beginning. I didn't kiss anyone on the lips, and he knew that. It hadn't been a point of contention in any regard, never debated. We'd been on the same page, but the dynamic had shifted, and I had to decide if I felt the same as he appeared to.

"Yes."

Chapter Twenty-Five

Michele inched forward, taking my bottom lip between his. They were soft and his mouth hot, threatening to set me on fire with no effort. It lasted for a breath, but that'd been more than enough to ignite a new form of longing inside me.

He deepened the kiss.

I sighed when his tongue touched mine, still sweet from the fruit we'd just eaten.

He glided his hand to the back of my head, threading his fingers through my hair. Hunger built within me, and I didn't have the strength or desire to keep it at bay.

Clinging to his sleeve, I fisted the fabric, hugging his body to mine until air seemed to dwindle.

We eventually withdrew from one another, though Michele continued to place kisses along my jaw and into the nape of my neck. He let out a long breath that caused me to shiver against him.

I cradled him close. My lips tingled, electrified as though they were given life. It'd been years since I'd kissed anyone, a heartbreaking realization that struck me harder than I'd expected it to.

He brought me into his lap, helping me straddle him. Still cradling my face, Michele met my eyes, his lips parted and skin taking on a pink hue. Wrapping a tendril of my hair that'd come loose around his finger, he guided it behind my ear, holding my face when the offending lock had been set aside.

The tails of my robe were long enough to accommodate, covering our immediate area in a blanket of thin cotton and leaving me bare to his jeans. The coarse fabric was rough against my sex, adding a bite of pleasure to the situation.

He held my face in one hand, the other wrapped around my naked thigh. The air between us continued to vibrate with unsaid words and feelings unfamiliar, neither of which stopped me from untying my robe.

The garment slid open, revealing my nakedness to him, but remaining on my shoulders, it shielded me from anyone who might shoot a glance in our direction. We were both sitting in the open, exposed to the outside world in the third-floor doorway. A wayward eye was all it would have taken for us to be discovered, and that thought meant absolutely nothing to me.

Michele trailed his hands over my exposed body, along the slope of my waist, through the valley between my breasts and over them, kneading the heavy mounds with expertise. He watched his actions intently, as though memorizing every inch of me.

When his gaze met mine once more, he held the back of my neck and brought me forward. It lacked the intensity of previous times and was instead filled with a silent question. I fell happily under his guidance and claimed his lips when they rose to meet mine.

I devoured his satisfied moans, taking them into me while our tongues dueled and our grips became more desperate.

Digging his blunt fingernails into my back, he dragged them down, causing me to break our kiss, moaning while I reveled in the sensation. The action forced my chest forward and he didn't hesitate to take my nipple into his mouth, sucking the sensitive nub into a peak.

So many men I'd been with claimed to be 'boob guys', but when it came down to it, they'd hardly give the girls their due. Michele wasn't on that list. He knew how to touch and caress, how to tease and give pleasure, and move between the two so I didn't grow numb to the sensation. He acted as though he worshiped them, and I benefited.

Driving my fingers through his hair, I held him to me, grinding my hips against his lap. He made me desperate for everything at once, and I no longer needed to be coy about it.

We eventually drew apart, and he stared at me with a level of want that enticed me further.

I stood and offered my hand. He accepted, using it to help him up. The moment he had his feet under him, Michele pulled me to his chest and claimed my lips again. I could kiss him forever, disappear into the taste of him.

We made our way to the bed, and the moment the mattress hit the backs of my knees, he lifted me into his arms, climbed onto the bed and laid me onto it. The desperate passion from our previous trysts was lacking in that moment and replaced with a tenderer, more deliberate tone.

He kissed me again, lingering on my mouth before descending. He explored my body again, but it was measured and ensured that he touched me everywhere.

Scrapes and sharp pokes of his facial hair were smoothed away by the flick of his tongue. Bites were teased, only to be soothed by a tender kiss.

Lower and lower he sank until he guided my thighs over his shoulders. Michele cradled my ass at the perfect angle before running his tongue up the length of my slit and groaning deep within his throat.

"I love your taste," he whispered, not giving me the chance to take in the statement before he pierced me with his tongue.

I cried out, arching my back off the bed while he fucked me with it and somehow stroking my clit with his nose. It was an overwhelming combination that sent me reeling.

Oh my God, I love you. Even the voice in my head had become breathy and weak.

I gripped his hair tight in a desperate bid for something to steady myself, but he refused to allow me to settle. Instead, he stoked my fires, building them higher and higher until I was near bursting.

Yanking his head away, I peered into his frustrated face. He stared at me, lips glistening with my excitement and eyes black.

"I need you."

As before, he moved in an instant, complying as though he'd been waiting for permission.

Michele kissed me, and I tasted the tang of myself on his tongue. I didn't mind. I just wanted him.

Together we did our best to shed him of his clothes. I'd attempted to be careful, to keep from damaging his shirt when he took such care with his attire, but my hands wouldn't stop shaking and a button suffered for it. The tiny white disk had been launched into the ether, ne'er to return.

"I'm sorry," I somehow managed to say.

"It does not matter," he replied.

"But it's your—"

He sat back on his knees and, with a sharp tug, snapped the remaining buttons off, tearing open the garment without a care.

That was pretty hot.

He leaned into me, clasping me by the back of my head and pulling me close.

"They're just clothes," he whispered against my lips. "They mean nothing."

With another kiss, he dissipated any worry that might have lingered.

The rest of his outfit soon shared the same fate as his shirt—not ruined, but discarded alongside my robe, leaving nothing between us. A higher level of dexterity allowed him to slip on the condom I hadn't noticed him retrieve with ease while he guided me onto my back.

A growing familiarity allowed him to slide into me, though I remained unprepared. There were no words to describe how he filled me, stretched me to fit him.

Michele rolled his hips, the action stealing my breath. He found his rhythm much sooner than I had, driving into me with long, slow, deep thrusts that ensured I felt every inch of his girth. The frantic passion of times previous had vanished and left behind something different. There was no Dom or sub. Instead, we'd become two people who wanted to be together, to make our partner feel pleasure and receive our own in the process.

He stole kisses while I clung to him, sinking within the sweltering heat of his hard body pressed to mine. I was lost to him, fully and completely, falling to the sensation of his hands, his mouth and his cock.

"I've missed you," he whispered while his pace increased.

Not in the mindset to understand the statement, I didn't reply.

He grasped my jaw and brought my mouth to his again, whispering *dea mia* before kissing me as passionately as before.

The world became a swirling vortex of tactile stimulation. My brain had no control over anything my body wanted, drifting into the background where it could swim in the dopamine.

At some point, I'd rolled onto my stomach, propping myself onto my hands and knees while Michele took his stance behind me. He picked up right where we'd left off, gripping my hips hard and fucking me from behind.

Things were coming to a head, sensations and emotions roiling, infecting the room. I clung to the headboard, gripping the wrought iron in a weak attempt to steady myself. In truth, I needed it to remember the world was real.

He lifted my hair off my heated neck, wrapped it around his wrist and pulled, snapping my head back. I cried out while the ache mixed with the pleasure as he braced his other hand on my shoulder, using both for leverage.

"God, yes," I moaned, meeting his thrusts as best I could. "Don't stop."

"Never," he replied with a growl.

He thrust harder and harder, driving into me with dizzying power, and I was on the verge of succumbing to the moment.

Teetering on the edge, it took nothing more than his reaching around and gripping my breast to push me over.

The orgasm roared through my body, every nerve exploding at once, seizing my muscles while causing them to spasm at the same time. Everything had been overtaken by the pinnacle of pleasure.

Michele wrapped his arms around me and pulled me to his chest as he followed me into oblivion.

Heartbeat racing and breathing on its way to becoming normal once again, I held him, resting my forehead against his sweating cheek. His sweltering breath graced my skin and I found relief in it somehow.

The two of us lingered in our embrace, content to wait until the world came into focus again.

Chapter Twenty-Six

I was lying in bed on the phone talking to Kennia while Michele spoke to someone at the door. To my recollection, the hotel didn't offer room service, so I assumed he was speaking to someone he knew, further proof being his attire while doing so.

When he'd finished, he returned to me wearing his jeans unbuttoned, low on his hips, and the shirt we'd both had a hand in destroying hanging open. He couldn't have been doing less, yet the sight of him was enough to remind me how lucky I was to get that call about a job.

And to think I'd nearly turned it down.

He seemed pensive when he slid onto the bed behind me.

I didn't like how distressed he appeared and shifted to look at him.

"What's wrong?"

"It's nothing," he said with a heavy smile. "Just some issues with some business partners. Things seem to be getting contentious."

"I'm sorry." Even though I had no reason to apologize, it felt like the sort of situation where something like it was necessary.

It still didn't feel as though I had the right to push into his personal life, however. No matter how much I wanted to ask about the specifics, my upbringing and willful ignorance made it nearly impossible. His personal life was just that…personal.

Or was I his personal life and that was the professional?

Either way, I was uncomfortable with prying.

The clipped beep of my phone's text notification drew my eye. Kennia had texted me back. While I shifted once again to read the message, Michele leaned in, resting his forehead on the back of my shoulder. He kissed it, a tender action that gave me a shiver.

"Are you making plans with your friends?" he asked, running his lips over my skin.

"I'm trying, but Kennia keeps telling me there's no rush."

"What does that mean?"

A blush took my cheeks and embarrassment trickled in. Chewing on the inside of my cheek, I reluctantly replied.

"She knows about everything."

I peered at him over my shoulder, sure I would find him upset or annoyed that I'd divulged anything to someone else, but instead there was nothing. Michele simply waited for me to continue. Unsure of what else to do, I kept speaking.

"Kennia knows I don't connect with people very easily, so she keeps telling me that I should stay here…with you."

His eyes softened as he looked me over. "What do *you* say?"

My answer was immediate, but I held off so as not to appear too eager, giving myself two solid breaths beforehand.

"I agree with her."

His eyes sparkled with a smile much brighter than the one he allowed to show. It was a strange phenomenon but told me quite a bit.

"If that's the case," he said, snaking his hand around my waist, "perhaps I can show you the city — at least until things have been settled between you."

I rolled onto my back, tucking myself beneath him. He remained as he was until I'd relaxed, then once again placed an arm protectively around me. I was in danger of falling in love with his caring touch.

"You'd do that for me?"

He nodded. "Of course."

"But…don't you have a job or something? You said *business* associates. I don't want to keep you away from work."

He let out a breath and shook his head. "This is more pressing."

I stared at him with growing disbelief. He was perfect.

"Okay," I said with a nod. "I'd like that."

Michele smiled and placed another in a long line of kisses to my lips.

* * * *

As promised, we spent the day exploring the numerous landmarks and spots he deemed 'absolutely essential' to a visit. I stayed in a daze, my mind clouded. Nothing seemed real, yet everything was. But regardless of how fantastical it may have been, Kennia's words continued to play in the back of my mind.

Enjoy everything.

The mid-afternoon sun shone high overhead, beautiful and bright, and lacking the intense heat from back home. I didn't feel the need to run under cover when it touched my skin.

"Are you hungry?" he asked, pulling my attention away from the incredible architecture of the *Piazza San Marco*.

Until he'd asked, I hadn't realized it'd been hours since breakfast, and the meal, while delicious, had been far from filling.

"Yeah."

"Would you like to have lunch at my villa?"

"You mean the island?"

I would have liked to explore it during the day to see how beautiful it really was.

Michele shook his head. "We have a home not far from the city."

"Of course you do."

He chuckled. "Is that a yes?"

Shoving the embarrassment of the blurted statement away, I agreed.

Interlacing his fingers with mine, Michele guided me away from the hustle and bustle of the main city and toward an area where cars were allowed to travel. I'd done my best to focus on it, but the beauty of the city refused to be ignored, my head swiveling from side to side in a weak attempt to memorize it all.

While ogling and gawking at the scenery and continuing to struggle with the realization that it was my life, I spotted a pair of men standing a few yards behind us.

They were dressed in black clothing, not inconspicuous but not average, either. One had a head shaved closer than Mr. Clean and the other a mop of blond locks. They were looking around, too, but I had the impression that neither of them was interested in architecture. In fact, one looked familiar.

Hard to forget a bald head.

"Is something wrong?"

"Those men," I said, forcing him to spot the pair. "They're following us."

"Martin and Tomas," he said. I looked at him. The stern expression returned.

"They part of your security?" I asked. He nodded, lips drawn tight. "The bald one, I think I've seen him before."

"Martin," he said. "He's been my personal security for many years."

Years?

"Do they bother you?"

"N-no."

"Try to ignore them," he said with a comforting smile. "And think only of lunch."

He seemed to be doing his best to reassure me, so I forced a smile and let him think it'd worked. But it hadn't. How could it? I didn't come from a life where that sort of thing was normal.

We reached the edge of the city a little while later, and to my surprise, a pair of black Land Rovers awaited us. Not missing a step, Michele opened the rear door to the Rover in front and waited for me to enter. After I had, he slid in to join me. Through tinted glass, I watched as Martin and Tomas got into the SUV behind us.

A moment later, we set off down the road with the others close behind. I couldn't stop turning to peer back at them, so much so that it must've caught Michele's attention. I hadn't been coy about it, either.

"Is something wrong?" he asked.

"If I ask you something, will you be honest with me?" I met his gaze and held it. While seeming unsure, he nodded. "Who are you?"

"What do you mean?"

"I don't know, it's just..." I glanced at the tailing SUV again, then to him. "I know I've never been in the middle of these kinds of situations, so I don't know if it's normal for people who own giant yachts and islands, but is it the norm to have security teams following you around all the time?"

He put his elbow on the arm rest and leaned into his hand, running his fingers along his bottom lip while he thought of something to say.

"It's just, it feels like there's a *huge* piece of the puzzle missing."

"Do you trust me?" he asked, turning to meet my eye.

"I'm...sorry?" I'd been unprepared for the question.

He leaned into me, holding my hand in his. "I will always keep you safe. I want you to know that."

The warmth of the statement spread throughout me, but the strangeness of it refused to be ignored. It had somehow taken up until that minute for me to realize something that should've been clear from the beginning.

Michele spoke to me, spoke about us, as though we were already in a relationship, and not just that, he spoke as though we'd been in one for a while.

I shifted in my seat to better meet his gaze, pulling my hand from his.

"What is this?" I chose to be blunt.

"I don't know what you're asking."

"I don't understand what's happening anymore. This whole thing started out as fun, but it's becoming something else, and you've kind of been acting like it was already something else, though I don't know how that's possible and I—" I'd spoken so much so quickly that I had to force myself to take a breath or risk hyperventilating. Exhaling slowly, I calmed down enough to finish. "I just don't understand."

Michele leaned back in his seat, letting his head fall against the headrest. Like before, he seemed to dip into his thoughts, a brooding expression marring his features while he chewed on his bottom lip.

"I never stopped"—he said unsurely. He met my gaze and no doubt saw my confusion deepening—"thinking about you."

My brows lifted.

"For years, I had accepted that I would never see you again, until I walked onto that ship and found you singing."

"Really?" I asked with the same level of apprehension.

He nodded. "Something happened to me that night at Labyrinth. I've never experienced it with anyone else, before or since. Have you?"

I answered honestly. "No."

He chewed on his lip again, seeming to struggle with something unsaid until, with a heavy sigh that caused his shoulders to slump, he continued.

"I have been in love with you for nearly seven years."

My stomach sank.

"And I am not naïve enough to assume you feel the same. I'm only asking for the opportunity to change your mind."

A heavy silence filled the vehicle. *Love? Did he seriously say love?* It was a very small word for a very large thing—and not one I threw around lightly. He didn't seem the sort, either.

So was I supposed to accept that he was telling me the truth? To the best of my knowledge, he hadn't lied to me before that point.

His declaration had cleared a few things up, though. It explained why he seemed so much further in whatever our relationship was than I was. It explained his sweet and tender actions, his attentiveness and how ready he'd been to spend genuine time with me. To him, it was more than a simple game. It was real, and worse yet, it was becoming very real to me, too. My gaze drifted to the window.

The scenery had been, without description, beautiful beyond words. It had the feel of the old world, of a time centuries gone, untouched.

Incredible.

While I peered out at the water as we wound up the side of the mountain, a black SUV swept into view. It sped aggressively forward, unwilling to remain behind the short caravan we'd created. It seemed the driver had an issue with the speed limit.

I rolled my eyes, wishing it would hurry up so that I could see the ocean again and distract myself, but it kept pace. I began to glare, and as the rear window rolled down, I thought I might get a chance to see the asshole responsible.

The gun came from nowhere, emerging from the shadows and gleaming in the sunlight. I barely had a chance to register what I saw before it fired.

Arms encircled me, curling me into a ball and pushing me down toward the floorboard. Michele lay his body over mine, smothering me as something pelted the side of the car, pinging off the metal and smashing into the glass. A part of me knew what was happening but refused to accept it as the truth.

Michele barked orders at the driver. The engine accelerated, though I couldn't tell whether or not we were going faster, only that the gunfire began to recede until the blood rushing through my ears and my heavy breathing were all I could hear.

I trembled beneath him, shaking uncontrollably while I struggled to come to terms with the fact that someone had shot at us.

Chapter Twenty-Seven

Sometime later, our vehicle pulled over and stopped. The SUV lurched forward so hard that I slammed into the back of the driver's seat.

Michele rose, lifted me with him and we exited the car. He held me close to his side and argued with someone, who spoke just as angrily. It took him grabbing my face to bring me out of my thoughts.

His brows were pushed tightly together, fear saturating every feature when he asked, "Are you all right?"

I had opened my mouth to reply, but words wouldn't come.

He began speaking Italian while he searched me for injury, guiding my head from side to side, checking my arms, my front and back. Something about the jostling snapped me out of my comatose state.

"What was that?" I asked. His attention locked on me. He seemed relieved I'd spoken, and I found his relief infuriating. "What the hell was that?"

"Nothing," he said. Michele motioned to someone else and spoke to them. His blatant lie angered me further.

I shoved at his chest, forcing him back a step. He looked at me in shock.

"What the fuck was that?" I demanded. "That was not *nothing*. What the fuck was that!"

"*Calma*," he said. "*Calma*."

He set his hands on my shoulders. I shrugged them away.

"Don't tell me to calm down." Tears welled in my eyes. "Tell me what's going on."

"All right," he said with a resigned nod.

He took my arm and held it tenderly while he guided me into the villa. I caught a glimpse of the SUV out of the corner of my eye as we passed it. The side of it and the rear had been riddled with bullets. There were holes everywhere and enormous splotches of broken glass. The sheer devastation of it caused my stomach to wrench.

Inside, Michele set me down on a sofa in some random room. His bodyguards and others surrounded him, most I didn't know but a couple I recognized as his family. He spoke to them briskly, with stern words that illustrated just how angry he seemed to be.

Still trembling, I watched the display with mild attachment. I wanted to be more in the moment, but I couldn't focus on anything beyond the near-death experience.

The sound of bullets pelting the side of the SUV, of them imbedding themselves in the bulletproof glass, rattled around inside my head.

Michele returned shortly after, his agitation remaining in spite of his attempt to wipe it from his face. Running his fingers through his hair, he stood before me. I stared up at him, tears running down my cheeks while I shook.

Shock must have been knocking on the door.

"Tell me what's going on," I said in as strong a voice as I could muster.

He chewed on his bottom lip. For a moment it seemed as though he would finally answer my question. I was disappointed.

"Martin will take you back to the hotel. He will wait for you to pack your things then take you to the airport. I will arrange a flight for you to—"

"Stop talking," I said, interrupting him sharply. "I'm *not* flying home. I'm not going anywhere until you tell me *what the fuck is going on!*"

He took in a long, deep breath and let it out slowly before he spoke.

"I am not a good person," he said. "I do bad things with worse people. Sometimes, those people like to take matters into their own hands when things do not go their way."

I may have been part of the conversation, but it remained just out of reach. Nothing was landing with me. Nothing stuck. I would've had better luck trying to catch mist with a butterfly net. But I still spoke as if I had any clue as to what I was saying.

"You're a criminal." My deadpan tone surprised me. "What? Mob? Drugs? Human trafficking?" He didn't respond, though I supposed I didn't expect him to. Someone who chose to be so vague wasn't going to admit to something directly. "Of course you are."

How do these kinds of people keep finding me? Why can't I ever just meet normal people? Everyone is violent or a criminal — or a violent criminal.

Memories of every relationship I'd ever had flashed through my mind, starting from my own family and winding through multiple boyfriends and partners until the present. It was too much. I couldn't escape.

I didn't know what to think, so I chose not to think about it at all.

Pushing myself up, I did my best to keep my balance as the blood pooled in my feet, leaving me lightheaded. Shaking the spots from my eyes, I focused on Michele.

"Have your guy take me back to the hotel," I said. "But that's it. I'm *not* going to fly back home."

"Basil."

"Take me back." I refused to give him a chance to try to convince me otherwise. As far as I was concerned, he had no right to tell me where to go, let alone tell me to fly thousands of miles.

Without waiting for a reply, I walked by him and toward the front door. Michele spoke to someone and soon I was joined by Martin, the bald bodyguard.

He led me to another vehicle, given the one I'd arrived in looked as though it'd been through a warzone. He opened my door, I got in and shortly after we headed back to the hotel.

On the way back, I couldn't help but keep my eyes open. Black Land Rovers were far more common in Europe than the U.S., and now I saw them everywhere. At any given moment, I expected the windows to roll down and another automatic weapon to emerge from within. I expected the SUV I was in to be showered by a thousand bullets. I expected to die before I made it back.

"I am not a good man."

I didn't know if that was true or not. I didn't know anything about him, and that realization hit me hard.

Shock might have set in, though I couldn't be sure. I should have been more emotional, more freaked out. I just should have been *more*…but I wasn't.

What's wrong with me?

That list was long and always growing, so I didn't dwell.

Martin pulled into the parking lot and let me out of the back. I began my walk to the hotel, navigating the streets through Venice where nothing larger than a bicycle would fit. He lingered, far too close for my liking.

His presence remained an overbearing thing looming behind me and walking in time with each step I took. No matter how hard I tried to separate myself from what'd happened, a reminder stuck to my shadow.

When I reached the courtyard, just beyond which sat my hotel, I spun in place to face him.

"Go away," I said.

He shook his head. "I have orders to walk you to the hotel."

"I'm fine. Leave me alone."

"They may still be somewhere."

"So? They want him, not me."

Martin didn't reply. He stared at me in a way that made my skin crawl.

"Right?"

He breathed deep and tensed his jaw as though contemplating telling me something that he might not have been allowed to tell me.

"There have been threats."

I furrowed my brow. "The hell does that mean?"

"I am to follow you to the hotel. You will pack. I will take you to the airport."

"No, you fucking won't. I'm not going anywhere. Leave me alone."

Martin hardened his stance. He towered over me by nearly a foot and was easily a hundred pounds heavier. I doubted I could outrun him, because he knew exactly where I was going and I knew I couldn't fight him, but I wasn't without options.

Out of the corner of my eye, I noticed a random policeman making his rounds, giving gentle nods and smiles to those he passed. Given the sheer amount of tourists who meandered around the hotels and the number of landmarks within a stone's throw, it made sense that police were a bit more common. My plan formed quickly.

"Get back in your car and drive off, or I swear to God, I will scream and tell them that you're trying to kidnap me."

He flinched. Martin's gaze drifted toward the man in uniform. He was twenty or so yards away, close enough that he could reach us if he had to. Martin stared down at me, the color in his eyes darkening substantially.

"I'll do it," I told him. "I'll fucking do it if you don't leave now. And something tells me you probably have a weapon on you somewhere. Are there carry laws in Italy?"

"Mr. Sacchi won't like—"

"I don't give a *shit*." I spat the words, fueled by an anger and fear that hadn't left me. "Get your ass back in that fucking car or I yell rape."

Martin weighed his options but seemed smarter than he looked. After a short internal battle, he turned. I hadn't moved, hadn't dared walk a step toward the hotel until I'd seen him vanish into an alley we'd used minutes prior.

Once alone, my gaze danced again. The fear trickled in and whether it'd been smart or not, I rushed toward my hotel and didn't stop my brisk pace until I'd locked my room door behind me.

* * * *

The tears arrived full-force sometime later. I was in the shower and broke down crying. How cliché.

I couldn't recall how long it took for me to get control of myself, but it'd been long enough for four phone calls and numerous texts. I didn't want to speak to Michele. I didn't want to speak to anyone. Something told me that if I tried, I would break down again.

Nothing so horrible had ever happened to me before. The most frightening experience I could remember had gone down when I'd been seven. Come to think of it, there had been heavy weaponry involved in that, as well. The only difference being those guns were held by men in uniforms, and they weren't after us. I'd been on the periphery of that raid.

Alone in my room, I couldn't help but be grateful that Kennia wasn't there. I knew that if she asked me what was wrong, I'd tell her, and she would go after Michele. She would be furious, and while I loved her for the sisterly protection that she showed me daily, I wouldn't be able to handle the added stress.

Lying down, I stared at the textured ceiling and thought about what had happened. Whether he wanted to admit it outright or not, Michele was a gangster.

In movies and TV, even in books, it was considered a romantic notion. Typical 'bad boys' were things many women fantasized about, and I was no different, but I'd been given a glimpse into the reality of that world. Hell, I'd been given a glimpse early on in life, but the drive-by had been a new angle.

Tears trickled down the sides of my face while I continued to stare blankly. I would speak to Michele again, I knew I would because answers were needed, but I couldn't do it now.

My phone rang. A wave of cold swept over me. Without bothering to see who it was, I silenced the call.

There'd been signs. Christ, there had been so many fucking signs and I'd even spent the time to list them in my head, but I hadn't followed through with a single one. That level of willful ignorance was unacceptable.

And why? Why did I ignore the red flags? Because he was handsome, kind, sincere, treated me with respect and flattered me.

He treated me better than any man ever had, and for it, I'd turned a blind eye to the possible reality until that reality had tried to kill me.

This isn't my life. I'm going to close my eyes and wake up from this fever dream.

The tears returned, and I cried harder than before.

Chapter Twenty-Eight

Around four o'clock that afternoon, a couple of hours after I'd gotten back to the hotel, I called Kennia. It may have been selfish, but I couldn't be alone anymore, and regardless of how short the conversation had been, she knew something was wrong.

There was a knock on the door, prompting me to leap off the bed and cross the room within seconds. I tugged it open, revealing a surprised Kennia, her fist still raised.

"Hiya," she said.

I didn't reply, throwing my arms around her neck and squeezing her tight.

"Oof," Kennia huffed. "Righ', then."

She shuffled us into the room and closed my door behind her. Wrapping her arms around me, she held me just as securely.

After a deep breath, Kennia asked, "How're you doin', Bay?"

My eyes burned with tears. I clung to her harder, burying my face in the crook of her neck. I didn't want to speak, not entirely certain I could manage without sobbing like a fool, so I chose to say nothing at all.

"Okay," she said in a soft voice. "Okay."

* * * *

Our elbows were hooked, shoulders together while we stared up at the ceiling. Neither of us had spoken for some time. I wasn't certain what to say after I'd blurted everything out the instant I'd been able, and Kennia wasn't one to speak without meaning.

"I'm hungry." Kennia's voice broke through the silence.

I rolled my head to the side, staring at her hairline until she did the same. She blinked at me, sincerity dripping from her features. So unprepared for the statement, I couldn't help but let out a disbelieving laugh. She smiled.

"What?"

Relief washed through me while the laughter continued. Once it'd begun, I couldn't hold it back.

The tears came again, welling in my eyes, but their meaning had changed. They weren't as desperate as before, as terrified. Instead, they were my body's reaction to the torrent of emotion that hadn't let up.

I shifted and threw my arm over her, hugging myself to her side. Kennia giggled, holding my arm to her chest and resting her head on mine.

"Just a bit peckish is all," Kennia said. "No need for the tears."

"I know." I sighed, the laughter slowly dying in my throat. Adjusting, I rested my head on her shoulder. "I just appreciate the distraction."

"So…is that a *yes* on the food?"

"Absolutely."

Before we parted, she placed a kiss on the top of my head.

Separating, we crawled off the bed. I grabbed my phone and purse while she made sure she had her things as well.

"I'll give Chris and Ryan a ring, see if they wanna joins us."

"Maybe Ryan'll know about the best places to eat?" I suggested.

"Oh, Lord save us. I hope he doesn't try an' critique the chef."

I snorted a laugh. On our way out of the door, we hooked arms once more and went in search of something delicious to help wash away my worries and do something about Kennia's hunger.

I needed every distraction I could get.

* * * *

The guys met us at a bistro Ryan had picked. Their menu consisted of things purchased from local growers, whether it'd been wines from nearby vineyards, fruit from local orchards or fish caught just off the coast. Nothing they served was shipped more than one hundred miles to the restaurant.

The food had been better than I'd expected, and to see Ryan and Chris outside the work environment gave me the chance to witness how adorable they were together. The two were the sort of couple that liked to tease one another with little biting comments and jokes, more than once sending the table into a fit of laughter as a result.

All the tension, the uncertainty and fear of the day had faded during dinner, beaten into submission with each laugh that escaped me.

"I don't snore," Ryan muttered into his wineglass.

"Right," Chris said with a smile. "Well, then, Kenny, you may want to check the engines. Sounds like someone's tossed a bunch of boulders into them."

Kennia and I both giggled at the flash of red that spread across Ryan's cheeks. He cast his boyfriend a glare, to which Chris replied with a wink and a blown kiss.

I lifted my glass, ready to take a sip if not finish it off completely when something caught my attention. Out of the corner of my eye, a shadow moved. I'd thought it was nothing, just another patron moving through the outdoor area or a pigeon fluttering, but when I gave it my focus, my heart sank.

Two men in black, one with a slick bald head and the other a mop of blond hair, were sitting a few tables over trying to blend in but failing. They were familiar enough for that to be impossible.

"Hey." Kennia placed her hand on mine, pulling me into the moment. "You okay?" she asked with worry on her face. "You've gone pale."

I said nothing but jutted my chin in their direction. She understood and shifted to look. It took her no time to spot the pair.

"That them?" She looked at me again, the worry replaced with agitation. I nodded. "Right then." She tossed her napkin onto the table. "We're goin'."

"Everything okay?" Chris asked, his gaze dancing between us.

"Yeah," Kennia said unconvincingly. "Look... We'll talk later. Let me know what this cost, and I'll Cash App my half, yeah?"

The guys nodded, though it was clear neither of them knew what to think of the moment.

"C'mon." Kennia grabbed my hand and hoisted me to my feet.

We immediately set off for the hotel three blocks away, all the while checking behind us for the bodyguards.

We wove through the alleys and walkways until emerging on the other side of the narrow bridge that led to the hotel. I couldn't stop glancing over my shoulder, and while they kept their distance, the pair continued following. Kennia must have noticed, too, and she was *not* happy.

Halfway across the bridge, she stopped dead in her tracks and spun, squaring herself on the two men who stood less than ten yards away.

"Stop following us!" She bellowed the words, shouting so loud that it wouldn't have surprised me if Chris and Ryan heard her. "We don't know you! Stop stalking us! These guys are trying to kidnap us!"

The bodyguards shifted, squirming on their feet and peering around, noting the people who were now very aware that they were there. I was too stunned to react.

She proceeded to cause such a massive scene that Martin and his buddy were forced to slink back into the shadows, casting us both a glare when they had.

"C'mon." Kennia snatched my hand again and dragged me away. "We're gettin' you the hell outta here."

"Yes, ma'am."

We dashed into the hotel and to my room. I threw everything into my bag as quickly as I could, and after checking out, we were on our way to the ship.

Chapter Twenty-Nine

After a sleepless night, I sat in the sun eating a bowl of yogurt for breakfast, looking out onto the water. Being such a large vessel, *The Silver Wind* had to be backed into her slip so the only way to get aboard was via the sea deck. Unlike most ships, it allowed us a bit more of a view.

There were still a shitload of boats in the way, though.

My 'shift' would begin in about an hour, so in the meantime I chose to enjoy myself for as long as I could. It wasn't much of a work schedule without people to look after, but touchups and the like were mandatory, and it would keep me busy. I appreciated it.

I'd settled about as much as possible since the ordeal the day before, but I hadn't spoken to Michele. I wasn't sure what to say to him, and the conversation we needed to have was the sort that would benefit from a game plan. I wanted to have questions ready so nothing could slip through the cracks, and I wasn't there yet.

In the end, it didn't matter.

"You haven't returned my calls."

Hearing his voice, especially so close, sent a chill down my spine. I didn't turn around and instead chose to pick at the yogurt, eating very small bites so that I could extend the life of it.

"Nope," I replied.

I reasoned that I must have been too deep in thought to hear his shoes click against the deck because they were loud as hell as he walked around me. While I continued to scrape at my yogurt, I saw those expensive shoes appear in my line of sight.

"Why?" he asked in a solemn voice.

"Because I didn't have anything to say."

"I wanted to make sure you were all right. I was worried."

"I'm pretty sure Martin told you I made it back without a problem."

"Martin told me you threatened him."

"I did," I said freely. My yogurt supply dwindled. "Is that all you wanted to know?"

Michele didn't reply. He stepped closer and knelt. Even though I could see him just out of the corner of my eye, I refused to meet his gaze. He seemed just as unwilling to be ignored.

He clasped my breakfast and took it, setting it aside so that I had nothing else to distract myself with. He tenderly touched my chin, guiding it up so that I had no choice but to look at him. Michele peered back at me, his brows creased with uneasiness.

"I have been worried about you," he said. "I needed to hear that you were okay."

"I wasn't okay," I replied a bit meaner than I'd intended. "I was shot at by a *very* big gun."

"I know." He nodded. "And the situation is being dealt with, trust me. You won't have to be afraid anymore."

I narrowed my eyes on him. "So, they *were* after me."

Michele's expression fell and his face went blank. He clenched his jaw. Being so close, I could see him doing his best to cover the slip, but I didn't intend to let him.

"They were, weren't they?" I asked. He didn't reply. "Martin said there were threats."

He scowled. "Martin should have kept his mouth shut."

"Why? He's the only one who's being honest with me."

"Things are...complicated."

"Not really," I snapped. "One thing leads to another. Someone was clearly pissed off so they —" It hit me like a fist to the face. "It's Yasmin, isn't it?" Michele dropped his gaze and that was all the answer I needed. "It was! That bitch tried to kill me."

I didn't know why she was my first thought. The young woman had been gone for a couple of days, little more than a memory, yet I could think of no one else.

It'd been the rage in her face when she'd caught Michele and me in the hall that brought her to mind, that pure, unadulterated rage. And his reaction to the statement had been enough for me to suspect that things were worse than I could've known.

"The situation is being handled."

"Handled? The situation is being *handled*? Are you kidding me?"

Michele stood and stepped away, turning his back on me in the process. He put his hands to his hips, his head dropped and I was certain he was deep in thought, but I didn't care.

There was no more letting things slip by, no more ignoring the obvious.

I pushed myself to my feet.

"Normal people don't do that kind of shit. What is wrong with her?"

"We don't know for certain if she is involved or not," he said. "It may have been something else entirely."

"That's not better!"

"I know!" he shot back, spinning on his heel to face me. I shrank away, surprised by the outburst from the normally stoic man. He took a steadying breath and, in a much calmer tone, he repeated, "I know."

"Wh-who *are* you?" I couldn't wrap my head around anything. "I don't know anything about you."

"I've never lied to you."

"Oh my God." My shoulders slumped. "I *hate* that excuse. As if you would've said anything if I somehow thought to ask if you're in the fucking mob."

A knot formed in my chest and a lump in my throat. It itched, signaling to me that if I didn't walk away, I would begin to cry. But I couldn't leave. I wasn't that smart.

"And I liked you so much."

He glanced up at me, confused by my declaration at first, but the words seemed to slowly seep in.

"But no longer," he said with a despondent tone.

"Does it matter?" The itch became worse and my vision blurred.

"Always," he said.

My heart sank.

"No, no it doesn't."

He stepped forward and I instantly met him reverse, determined to keep the same distance between us. He noticed and remained where he was, sliding his hands into his pockets.

"People are trying to kill you — or kill me for knowing you. That's not normal. You see that, right?" I didn't expect an answer. "I… I can't." It became hard to speak around the lump. "I can't do this."

Michele flinched. He dropped his head and stared at the deck. The urge to apologize came strong, but I had to fight it. I had nothing to be sorry for. It wasn't my fault that I didn't want to die.

After a moment or two, Michele lifted his head once again, but he didn't look at me right away. Instead, he stared somewhere in the distance.

Before he did finally meet my gaze, Michele wiped his thumb across his eye. I didn't understand why, at first.

His eyes had become pink and glassy in those few minutes. It shocked me. I hadn't thought him capable of crying or coming close to it. Logically, of course he could, but I'd never witnessed it, therefore it wasn't real to my brain. But seeing it broke my heart. He seemed human, mortal, as though the Romanesque god he'd been since our meeting had melted away.

"Would you like me to leave?" Even his voice had become thick with emotion.

I couldn't speak. The words were lodged in my throat, but he seemed to know, anyway.

Nodding softly, he said, "*Sei l'amore della mia vita e lo sarai sempre.*"

"I don't…"

He nodded once more. "I know."

After taking a deep breath, he approached me, unwilling to translate what he'd said. Frozen in place, I did nothing when he tenderly grasped my jaw. Michele placed a soft kiss on my forehead. A torrent of emotion poured into me from it.

Shortly after, he let go and walked briskly away.

The tears fell, gliding down my overheated cheeks. I wanted to cry. I wanted to sob and break down. I wanted to do many things, but I'd gone numb. The best I could manage was to silently weep.

My phone's ringtone startled me. The once-dulcet tune sounded so angry all of a sudden.

Digging into my pocket, I spotted my sister's name flashing across the screen. I answered it.

"Hey, Sage. This isn't a good time. Can I call you back later?"

My question was met with a silence that lasted long enough that I had to check whether or not the call was connected.

"Sage?"

"Yeah, uh," she muttered. Her voice was thicker than mine. Something was wrong.

"What happened?"

My mother flashed in my mind, Rose and even Sage herself. Did Mom have a heart attack? Was Rose in an accident? The possibilities were endless.

"It's John. He had a stroke yesterday. He's not doing very good."

A pit formed in my gut so dense that it threatened to take me to the ocean floor.

I slowly regained my seat, staring into nothingness while I tried to absorb the statement.

"Okay," I mumbled. Propping my elbow on my knee, I buried my lips in my hand. "So, what's going to happen now? What'd the doctors say?"

Sage let out a long, heavy sigh. I couldn't tell if she was fighting tears, probably not, but it seemed the stress of the situation pulled at her.

"They don't think he has very long."

"Shit."

"Yeah," she sighed. "Look, um... Uncle Al said you were working again. Where are you?"

"Italy."

"Holy shit."

"Mm-hmm."

"Well, um... Damn." She seemed to be muttering more to herself than me for a moment or two. "You think there's any way you could get some time off? Mom wants us to see him before, y'know..."

"He dies?"

My callousness surprised me, but I didn't bother reining it in.

"Basically."

"Uh..." I tore through the internal checklist of shit going on in my life, wiggling things around to get them straight where needed. "Probably. My ticket's still open-ended, so I should be able to get the date changed to something sooner. I'm not a full-time employee and there aren't any more charters, so that should help." I paused. "Are we really going to go through with this?"

Another long silence filled my ear, no doubt Sage struggling with the same things that I couldn't shake.

"I mean, Mom thinks it'll be a good idea and Rose? Well, Rose still wants everyone to get along."

I rolled my eyes and kept my derisive comments to myself.

"Look," she said. "I know he's an asshole, okay? I mean, Jesus Christ, the guy is a certified piece of shit, no matter whose list of criteria you're going off of, but he's still our grandpa."

I scoffed, chewing on my cheek. "The local sheriff has to be glad."

"Why do you say that?"

"Well, now he doesn't have to roll out to the old man's house every week for God-knows-what."

Sage let out a breathy laugh that held no happiness whatsoever.

With a heavy sigh, I let my shoulders drop and take with them every hint of tension that'd once remained.

"I'll see what I can do, okay?" I said. "It might take a couple of days to find a flight, but I can probably make it."

"Thanks," she said. "I don't want to do this either, but I'm glad you're coming."

I smiled a little.

Sage and I spoke for a moment longer with the promise of future updates when there were some to give.

When I hung up, I set my phone aside and buried my face in my hands, running my fingers through my hair and doing my best to keep from pulling it all out.

When it rains, it pours.

No shit.

Chapter Thirty

Well, damn.

A red-eye flight had been available on short notice, allowing me to fly out of Italy at two in the morning and arrive in Phoenix around noon. There were a few stops along the way and the fucking flight would last eighteen-plus hours, but I'd found one less than three weeks away.

As I'd hoped, it was easier for me to get out of my contract than most. The agency simply needed proof of what was happening, which wasn't difficult to provide, and the crew took my word, for the most part.

There were a few who gave me the side-eye, though. Those tended to be the other crew I hadn't grown very close with since my hiring, and they no doubt thought I was getting special treatment, but I didn't much care.

"When was the last time you even spoke to the man?" Kennia asked while I double-checked my luggage.

"I don't know. Since I was fourteen?"

"Christ. More than half yer life then, isn't it?"

I nodded. A strange sentiment, given the man lived less than five miles from the house I grew up in, but the relationship between his side of the family and mine was contentious at the best of times.

"And…what about everythin' else?"

I paused in the middle of counting my toiletries, dividing them into things I could and couldn't take with me.

The ache returned, the sadness and confusion when confronted with thoughts of Michele. It rose in my throat, clawing and scratching, angry that I tried to ignore it.

Swallowing hard, I spoke. "It doesn't matter. It's over now."

"Hmm."

I turned to her. "What's that supposed to mean?"

"Nothing. Just means *hmm*."

She met my eye without reservation, staring at me with nothing to hide.

"Bullshit."

She sighed, rolling her eyes while she scratched her chin.

"Look… I'm not sayin' I'm a genius or anythin', but it just seems like the pair of you have somethin' pulling you together."

"What are you talking about?"

"Well, somethin' made your paths cross again. Maybe it'll happen a third time?"

"So what if it does? Someone shot at us. That should be more than enough reason for me to stay away."

She said nothing at first, blinking at me and seeming to wait for me to come to some kind of epiphany, but as far as I'd been concerned, there wasn't one to have.

"S'pose it should be," she said. "Question is, *will* it be?"

My heart sank. I didn't know.

"You tell 'im you're leaving yet?"

My brows creased. "You think I should?"

She shrugged. "Seems the thing to do, for some reason, but I don't know. Up to you." Kennia pushed herself off my bunk and to her feet. "I'm going to grab somethin' to eat. Need my energy for the drive."

Absently nodding, I sank into my thoughts. She wasn't wrong. It did seem like the sort of thing I should relay. He deserved to know that I was leaving, for no other reason than I was cutting my contract on his vessel short, but there was another. There were many more, in fact, and in the end, they were what guided my hand.

Alone in the room, I took a seat on my bunk and retrieved my phone. Michele's text conversation remained toward the top of the queue because he'd continued to message me. I clicked on it and ignored the previous text blocks in favor of sending a new one.

I'm leaving Italy.

It was better to be to the point.
His reply was quick to come.

When?

In a few hours. My flight leaves at two a.m.

There was a hesitation that lasted nearly two minutes. The timestamp told me so.

If this is about what happened, I promise you needn't leave. You are safe.

I believed he thought so.

It's not. My grandpa had a stroke. The doctors don't think he's going to last very long.

As I had so many times before, I chose to be honest with him.

I am so sorry.

The sentiment was sweet, but undeserved. Still, I hadn't told him that. What would've been the point?

Thank you.

Another long pause punctuated the moment.

May I ask something of you?

I stared at the message, wondering what he might want. In theory, it could've been anything.
Morbid curiosity drove my thumbs across the keypad.

What's that?

He replied.

I'd like to see you before you leave.

My heart sank and my stomach twisted. A conflict unlike anything I'd experienced before roiled inside me. Logic told me to say no, to tell him I wasn't ready to see him in person again, but I wasn't a very smart woman.

Okay.

* * * *

At eleven o'clock that night, I found myself standing on the dock, curled within a jacket waiting as a dark figure approached from a distance. The glow of multiple lights told me who it was, but I hadn't been able to settle.

Michele kept his hands in his pockets while he closed the distance between us, soon standing near enough that I could see the distress in his face. It broke my heart, but I stood firm in my decision to stay distant.

We lingered in a thick quiet for some time, the tension only broken by the soft sounds of the city and the churn of the ocean.

"I'm not certain what to say," he said after a lengthy silence.

"I don't know."

He wiped his hand down his face, scratching his chin before returning his hand to his pocket.

"When does your flight leave?"

"Two."

He nodded. "And of course you'll need to leave soon, international travel being what it is."

I said nothing, staring at him questioningly. He met my eye for the first time in a while.

"I'm not a gangster," he said. I flinched but tried to conceal it. There was no way to know if I'd been successful. "But it would be a lie to say I don't have ties to that world."

The pit in my chest grew denser.

"I would have kept you safe," he said. "No matter what it took. I want you to know that."

"I believe you," I said, regardless of how badly I'd wanted to remain silent. "But that's not the point."

"Then tell me what is," he said, taking a step forward.

The words bubbled in my throat, rising to the surface. I'd considered keeping them to myself, but it wouldn't help. If there were a time to expose some of my deepest secrets, it was now.

"I didn't have a good childhood," I said after a steadying breath. "My grandpa, the one who's sick, was in and out of jail for years. So were my uncles and my aunt. I don't even know my cousins from that side of the family. But the worst one, by far, is my dad."

His eyes narrowed and he tilted his head to the side.

"He used to run book, was a message boy, a bruiser..." The shame descended, pushing on my shoulders like it had for the bulk of my life. "And a thief. He stole from the people he worked for, and they were *very* bad men." The lump in my throat was scratching, making the words harder to say. "The point is, I've lived in that world before. Maybe that's why I'm so fucked up when it comes to relationships, I don't know. But either way, I can't do this...not again."

He nodded and his chin dropped. "I understand."

Exposed and uncomfortable, I couldn't help but wrap my arms around myself, desperate for something to hold onto.

"Maybe I should go," I said after a minute or two of nothing.

He looked at me again, staring at me through his lashes. My heart raced. Regardless of what'd happened during that drive, memories of the days leading up to it were stronger, weighed by emotion and revelation. They were what clouded my sense, what interfered with the resolution I'd tried to keep.

"Of course," he said.

Neither of us attempted to move, seemingly stuck in place by some unseen force.

I'd become cold, yet I was somehow sweating. My fingers tingled, my stomach had filled with butterflies and my heart beat so hard that it hurt. Too many things were happening at once, and there was only one way I knew to resolve it.

He met my approaching step and paused. When I stepped again, so did he until the space between us had closed.

Michele swept me into his arms, encircling me in his strong limbs and pinning me to his chest like a drowning man clinging to a life raft. I gripped his shirt hard, twisting the fabric beneath my clenched fists and burying my face in his shoulders.

His trembling breath glided along my neck, punctuated by the subdued shaking that'd overtaken him. I slammed my eyes shut harder, squeezing out some of the tears that'd gathered behind my lids. I didn't want to let him go and he seemed to feel the same.

We lingered on the dock, embracing one another far longer than most might have, but I couldn't make myself let him go. I knew I had to, but I just couldn't.

After minutes glued to one another, he loosened his arms. The lack of tension brought me out of my bubble, and I followed suit. We drew back.

His forehead rested on mine, a hand on my cheek. I couldn't open my eyes, almost afraid of what I'd see. A large part of me wanted him to ask me to stay because I would have, in a heartbeat.

"*Dea mia*," he whispered, brushing my lips with each word.

"I don't know what that means," I said, forcing the words over the painful lump in my throat.

"It means you are my goddess."

Rather than being the sweet endearment they should've been, his words hit me hard in the gut. I nearly broke down in that moment.

Seeming to be on his way to losing himself as well, Michele leaned in and tenderly placed his lips to my cheek then repeated the same to the other, moving so slow that it felt deliberate.

"*Addio per ora*," he muttered. I could only assume he was saying goodbye and that simple word sparked an intense fear inside me.

Before he had the chance to withdraw, I jutted my chin forward, capturing his bottom lip. He gasped in surprise, but the shock hadn't stopped him from returning the sentiment.

Opening his mouth to mine, Michele kissed me deeply. Our tongues danced, his lips massaged mine and he held me tight. I could've lived in that moment for eternity, spent the rest of existence locked in that tender, loving embrace.

But the real world lingered just beyond our bubble, a constant pressure pushing at the walls and desperate to break in.

We forced ourselves to part. With far more effort than I could've imagined, I met his gaze. His eyes had become glassy, glittering in the dim light of nearby boats, and a damp line had trailed down his cheek, the end of which disappeared into his stubble. But despite the evidence of his emotional shift, Michele kept his voice calm when he spoke.

"Don't forget me," he whispered.

I couldn't verbally respond but shook my head.

He pulled a deep, shaky breath into his lungs and nodded.

The cold that overtook me when I no longer held him was one I had never experienced, so deep and resounding that it threatened to kill me.

My stranger, my Michele, walked back the way he'd come, soon disappearing into the night.

I'd gone numb, too overloaded with emotion to land on one.

But maybe we would see one another again. If Kennia was right and some unknown force was pushing us together, then it wasn't really goodbye.

Perhaps that small hope was what kept me from breaking.

"Hey."

The soft, delicate voice of my best friend caused me to turn. Kennia stared at me with her brows creased tight. She forced a smile that flickered in the corners of her lips but didn't linger.

"Come on," she said in that same comforting tone. "We need to head out."

I nodded. It was time to go home.

* * * *

The late hour, the lack of sleep and a thousand things in between vied for the top spot in 'the most exhausting nonsense' contest. I wanted to crash, to pass out and not wake up until I landed in Arizona and, given the length of the flight, that might've been possible.

Kennia and I stood outside the airport, my bags at my feet, hugging one another tight. The taxi waited patiently, and I appreciated him for it.

"Call me when you land," she said. "Let me know what's happenin'."

"I will."

We gave one another a final tight squeeze and parted. She smiled at me and winked.

"Love you," she said.

"Love you, too."

Taking my bag, I headed inside.

It hadn't taken long to find a teller and even less time to weave through the nearly abandoned line to reach her.

"Good evening," she said with a thick accent touching every word.

"Good evening." I dug into my purse and removed all my information for my ticket.

We went through the simple pleasantries while she typed in my name. I was still out of it, my mind still racing, so I hadn't noticed the strange expression at first.

"Something wrong?" I asked.

"No." She met my eye and flashed a smile. "There was a change to your ticket. I was confirming it."

My heart sank. "What change?"

"You've been upgraded to first class."

The words hung in the air, lingering just beyond me. I wanted to ask why, to ask how the hell it could've happened, but a larger part chose to accept the strange turn of events. With a flight so long, the extra space was welcomed, and again, I was fucking exhausted.

She finished making the arrangements and handed me my boarding pass with a dazzling smile.

"Enjoy your flight, Miss Hurst."

"Thank you."

Retrieving my things, I headed through security then to my gate and took a seat with a few other beleaguered passengers. My mind wouldn't stop racing, flashing between major life-altering situations, all of which seemed to deserve the proper amount of attention that I couldn't give them.

For better or worse, I kept thinking of Michele. To me, he was the more important concern. I didn't care that John was ill. He wasn't a good man, and I had no relationship with him, but I had something with Michele.

Tears prickled in my eyes. With a sigh, I leaned forward, propping my elbows on my knees and burying my face in my hands. The longer I thought about him, the less I cared about the shooting. *Stupid? More than likely.* But that didn't make it any easier.

While I contemplated walking away from the only person who'd come to mean anything to me, the leather seat beside me groaned as someone sat. They were a little close for my tastes, especially when the gate was near abandoned in the late hour, but I chose to ignore them. They, however, didn't choose to ignore me.

"Hello, again."

I shot my head up, my gaze landing on the very source of my distress.

It took a little while to pierce my confusion, but it was the man himself sat beside me wearing the same thing I'd seen him in on the docks not an hour prior.

He met my eyes, his expression soft and reserved.

"W-what are you doing here?"

A soft smile touched the corners of his lips but faded almost immediately, and seriousness replaced it.

"I..." His head dipped and he soon mimicked my position, sitting forward with his elbows on his knees. My heart was in my throat as I waited impatiently for him to speak. "I couldn't let you walk away again." He met my gaze, brows creased. "I do love you, Basil, and I understand that you may not feel the same, but I—"

"I love you, too."

The words had fallen from my lips, flowing out of me without my knowledge. I hadn't even known where they'd come from, but once uttered, I didn't want to take them back. They were true.

He stared at me, his eyes a little wider than usual. His confusion and surprise was cute. Something so simple from a generally composed man could have been little else.

Then his forehead creased. "Are you certain?"

I let out a breath that might've been a laugh, so unprepared for the question that I could do little else. And while I knew he was giving me an out, a way to take back what I'd said, I wouldn't.

It might've seemed fast to most, and maybe it was, but it was how I felt. Removing the intense interaction from the equation, Michele had shown me nothing but kindness. He was tender, attentive and made me feel safe.

Was there anything more important?

He reached for my hand, which I freely gave. Threading his fingers through mine, he pulled me close. I leaned into him, finally able to relax when the scent of his cologne touched my nose. Our foreheads touched, my eyes drifting shut with a sigh.

"Say it again, *per favore*."

A little giggle tickled the back of my throat, but I kept it at bay.

"I love you, too," I replied, more confidently than before.

He sighed, leaning back to place a kiss on my forehead.

When we parted, I met his gaze. "How'd you find me, anyway?"

"Your friend, Kennia."

I rolled my eyes and laughed. Of course it was her.

"And the ticket?"

A soft blush flickered to life in his cheeks. Michele shrugged.

"It seemed the right thing to do."

Shaking my head in mild disbelief, I leaned into him once more. As he already had, he kissed my forehead, then brought me as close to his side as our seats would allow.

"Does this mean you're coming with me to Arizona?" I asked after a silence.

"If you'd like," he whispered against my hairline.

My heart thrummed excitedly. I nodded.

"Looks like you're finally going to be able to see a desert."

He chuckled, and with his hand in mine, we waited for the boarding call.

Perhaps returning home wasn't going to be as bad as I'd initially thought.

Infernals: Rabid
C. Tyler

Coming June 2023

Excerpt

Raquel

My mind continued to swirl with the errands I had to run before work — groceries, gas, clean the car, pick up my prescription…yadda, yadda, yadda. It was one of those days that seemed to be filled with shit I didn't want to deal with, all those 'grownup' things that had a way of sucking out little pieces of my soul each time I had to do them.

"Fuck," I moaned when I parked in my apartment parking spot. With a heavy sigh, I dropped my head back against the seat, allowing me to notice a spot of something on the ceiling of my car. "Lawyer's office…"

I had one more errand that I didn't want to deal with, but it was the big one, the mother of all errands.

"Shit."

My lawyer, Mr. Millane, had sent me an email asking that I stop by to pick up some paperwork. I'd completely forgotten about it, somehow letting one of the most important things slip my mind.

Getting a divorce is so fucking tedious.

If I'd known it would take so long, I never would have gotten married in the first place. Hell, I barely remembered doing it.

Getting out of the car, I began the first of the two trips it'd take to get my purchases into my apartment, all the while unable to stop thinking about Alek dragging his fucking feet.

In the state of Colorado, both parties didn't have to agree on the divorce to make it happen—and thank Christ for that. The problem was, the parties could contest the shit out of the division of property, just to draw it out as long as possible, and Alek was nothing if not creative. At one point, there had been a request that I hand over the towels I'd taken when I'd moved out. His reason had been, and I quote, "*I bought them, so I should keep them.*" None of that statement was accurate. The asshole would've been fine to dry off with dirty clothes. But what did I do? I gave them back to him just to shut him up.

That'd been the theme of the divorce. He would want something, and to speed up the process, I wouldn't bother contesting, handing every single item over, just to get his signature. Maybe one day it would work.

After setting my stuff on the counter, I headed out of my place, down the exterior stairs and wove through the convoluted building layout toward the parking lot again. When I rounded the corner, placing my thumb over the trunk-popping button on my clicker, I paused. It wasn't that I didn't want to move. I did…very much. It was that I couldn't. Every muscle had seized, and I was left exposed and vulnerable.

A man sat on a black Harley in the spot beside mine. He hadn't been there a few minutes ago, and motorcycles were so common in Pleasant Pointe that I didn't even notice the sound anymore, making it absolutely possible for him to sneak up on me.

The reason for the commonality of them was the laughing devil painted on his gas tank.

The smiling devil with a cigar clasped in his sharp teeth was the sign of an Infernal, a member of the local motorcycle club. They'd been around longer than I had and probably would remain long after I died. They were so ingrained in Pleasant Pointe that nothing save an act of God could uproot them.

Long legs in tattered jeans straddled the beast, and his arms were crossed over the handlebars. Leaning forward, he rested his beard-covered chin on the inked skin of his forearms. His rust-colored hair had been shorn close to his scalp and his skin sun-kissed, but on the pink side.

Thick muscle created dips along his arms and rounded off his broad shoulders. The black tee he wore stretched across his defined back and did nothing to hide the fact that he was a large, very strong man.

His lips quirked at the corner and slender fingers hooked his sunglasses, pulling them down a broad nose. Hazel eyes glittered with sinister intent.

Ray 'Rabid' Corbin.

"Hey, babe."

His deep, rough voice rolled over me like a thousand hands — grabbing, squeezing and caressing every inch of my skin. I shivered at the sound of it and the memories it brought up. Without my permission, my body ignited with want, desire and rage.

"Fuck off," I said after ripping myself out of the stupor.

Ray chuckled, seemingly happy with my outburst. I pushed beyond how much I'd missed the sound and headed for my trunk.

"Oh, come on, baby," he crooned. I ignored him while looping the heavy fabric grocery bags over my arms. The scrape of boots on concrete drew near. Then, in my ear, he muttered, "I've missed you."

The terror had been instantaneous, causing me to shriek and shoot back. Apparently prepared for the outburst, Ray glided out of the way of my swinging elbow.

Damn. Didn't even clip his jaw.

He grinned, flashing those perfect teeth and chuckled again.

"Kinda high-strung, huh?"

I mustered all the strength I could and glared. There was no doubt in my mind that it held shit for power. My face was still burning with a blush I wouldn't shake so long as he was nearby.

"The hell are you doing here?" I slammed my trunk shut. "Figured you would've been shivved by now."

Still amused by something that escaped me, Ray fell in step behind me while I returned to my apartment, locking my car with the clicker before I was out of range.

"Not for a lack of trying," he said.

Shocker.

"What's wrong, Rocky? You not happy to see me?"

"Should I be?" I didn't let it show how much I hated him using my nickname. It would've ensured he used it as much as possible, just to poke. "Thought you had a ten-year stretch?"

He stayed close, climbing the stairs right behind me. It did little to inhibit his taunting. The man's voice remained close, which wasn't hard since the bastard was almost six-foot-five. Being one or two steps higher only put me at his level.

"Good behavior."

The scoff left me almost immediately.

"Right," I replied.

Stepping through my door, I tried to kick it shut on his face but wasn't surprised when he pushed beyond it. If my hands weren't full, I could've thrown him out properly.

Setting my groceries down on the table, I gave the man my attention and hated myself for it.

Ray had removed his sunglasses, which hung from his collar while he gently closed the door behind him. All taunting had left his features, leaving them darkened by something else. It didn't take a genius to know what. I'd seen that look a thousand times before.

My fingers tingled and stomach fluttered. No matter how hard I tried, every inch of my body continued to betray me.

Each click of his heel against my floor made my clit throb and my pussy dampen. My breasts grew heavy, and my nipples beaded, scraping against my lace bralette. I hated myself for wearing it, but my thicker ones had been dirty.

Ray dropped his gaze to my chest, no doubt spotting my nipples pressing against the cotton tee. It was hot as hell outside. It wasn't as though I could hide under layers.

While he advanced, I retreated until I had nowhere to go. My ass hit the edge of my kitchen counter, preventing me from running away. I'd literally backed myself into a corner.

Ray continued his advance until he stood over me, a powerful, looming figure of danger and sex.

"What are you doing?" My voice held no strength whatsoever.

Ray finally reached me, planting a hand against the cabinet above my head, the other on the countertop to my side. He closed in and instinct drove me to turn away. I couldn't keep staring into his eyes, peering into the chaotic swirl of brown and green that made up the color. Ray didn't seem dissuaded and dipped into the crook of my neck.

He dragged his lips across me. The soft touch of them, the heat of his breath and prickle of his beard was enough to send me through my skin, but I held strong, gripping the countertop even harder. I refused to give in.

"I missed you, Rocky." The words were little more than a growl. With a groan, he sank against me, pressing his hard chest into mine. "I know you missed me, too."

Swallowing the lump forming in my throat, I shook my head.

"No, I didn't." Each word trembled, regardless of my efforts.

He scoffed, still brushing his lips across my thundering pulse. I'd lost feeling in my fingertips, but I refused to let go, to reach out and touch him, no matter how badly I wanted to.

He traveled his mouth up to my ear while he encompassed my waist with a large hand and massaged it gently.

"Bullshit," he said with a gruff edge. "I know you."

"No, y-you don't. Not anymore."

He bit my earlobe. I gasped as the pain rocketed through my veins, electrifying my clit. In response, my pussy clenched, and I struggled to ebb the growing pain by pressing my thighs together as tight as I could manage. It did fuck-all.

The hand on my waist began a torturous journey south, the splay of his fingers so wide that I could've sworn they ran over all over my body.

Breathing became difficult, and I drifted my eyes shut with a sigh. I no longer had control, a sentiment given credence when he didn't hesitate to dip into my pants, and I parted my legs to help. I hated myself for it, more than words could express, but I couldn't fucking stop!

Ray groaned into my ear while he ran his digits the length of my slit, parting my lips so he could flick his fingers over my clit to tease me. There was no denying how excited I'd become in the few minutes he'd been around. The asshole would always bring it out in me.

He sighed into my ear, a groan laced in the back of his throat. "You're dripping." His touch became more determined. "How many times did you think about me when I was gone? While you were alone in your room or with some jag-off, how many times did you think about me instead?"

The pressure on my clit increased to a dizzying degree, and my sanity continued to dwindle, but so long as I kept a thread of it, I refused to give in.

"I-I didn't," I murmured.

Ray growled a vicious sound. "Don't lie to me."

He bit into my shoulder, apparent punishment for the lie. The pain of it radiated throughout my being, and I couldn't fight the cry of pleasure it brought out.

I suddenly clung to him, digging my fingernails into his broad back while he engulfed me.

"Don't lie, Rocky." He slid two thick fingers into me. My core clamped down on them hard, desperate.

"How many times did you wish it was my cock inside you?"

The damp heat of his tongue trailed up the side of my neck. I shivered, my grip tightening on his back.

Ray kissed my chin, hovering his lips just beyond mine. He knew what to do to get me going, knew the combination for me to lose my mind and he was clearly willing to do it.

He continued to pump his fingers in and out, curling them to hit me just right and build the enjoyment I had in the moment.

"I wanna fuck you, baby," he whispered against my mouth. His efforts between my legs increased, grinding the heel of his palm into my clit in the process and sending even more pleasure rocketing through me. "I wanna bury this cock deep."

As though giving me a preview, he shoved his fingers into me up to the hilt, forcing me up onto my toes. I whimpered and dropped my head back. The danger of giving in was no longer lingering in the background. Instead, it was licking at the surface, milliseconds from coming to fruition, and I didn't want to give him the satisfaction.

"S-stop," I somehow managed to say.

Like a hypnotist clicking his fingers, the spell dropped. The air shifted and Ray went still.

In the few seconds it'd taken for my brain to come to terms with the startling change, Ray had already separated from me, taking wide steps to put space between us.

I pried open my heavy eyelids to look at him. His face was saturated with the pain of sex denied. Every muscle bulged, trembling with the frustration that punctuated the air.

I did everything within my waning strength to pull the air into my lungs and failing. Ray's body, his words and mere presence had robbed me of it.

"You don't get to come back here and act like nothing ever happened," I said. The tremble in the back of my throat was hard to ignore, but I pushed through it. "Get out."

He flinched. The whole of it rolled over him.

"I don't want you anymore," I said.

Whatever spell had kept him still, snapped. Ray ran his hand down his face and tugged on his short beard. He licked his lips and nodded.

"Okay," he said in a voice that didn't sound human. He headed for the door and opened it. "I'll see you later, Rocky." He closed it behind him and was gone.

The moment I was alone, I let out a heavy breath I didn't know I was holding. My knees gave and I was forced to catch myself on the countertop.

Ray was a forever-weakness. I had been so over-the-moon in love with him back in the day that I would've done anything for him, but he hadn't felt the same and had made it *emphatically* clear. He didn't deserve my devotion anymore. He didn't deserve me. I just had to hold out and avoid him.

Who the fuck was the pencil-pusher who let him out?

About the Author

A fan of any genre, C. Tyler enjoys writing a wide array of stories, from fantasy and paranormal, to contemporary. Whether it's a bad boy biker, or a burly shifter, there's a little something for almost everyone.

C. Tyler loves to hear from readers. You can find her/his/their contact information, website details and author profile page at https://www.totallybound.com

Home of Erotic Romance

Sign up for our newsletter and find out about all our romance book releases, eBook sales and promotions, sneak peeks and FREE romance books!

www.ingramcontent.com/pod-product-compliance
Lightning Source LLC
Chambersburg PA
CBHW020557260626
47157CB00003B/742